Welcome Home

Her Mother's Keeper

and

Island of Flowers

ALSO BY NORA ROBERTS

Hot Ice • Sacred Sins • Brazen Virtue • Sweet Revenge • Public Secrets • Genuine Lies • Carnal Innocence • Divine Evil • Honest Illusions • Private Scandals • Hidden Riches • True Betrayals • Montana Sky • Sanctuary • Homeport • The Reef • River's End • Carolina Moon • The Villa • Midnight Bayou • Three Fates • Birthright • Northern Lights • Blue Smoke • Angels Fall • High Noon • Tribute • Black Hills • The Search • Chasing Fire • The Witness • Whiskey Beach • The Collector • Tonight and Always • The Liar • The Obsession • Come Sundown • Shelter in Place • Under Currents • Hideaway

Irish Born Trilogy
Born in Fire • Born in Ice • Born in Shame

Dream Trilogy
Daring to Dream • Holding the Dream • Finding the Dream

Chesapeake Bay Saga
Sea Swept • Rising Tides • Inner Harbor • Chesapeake Blue

Gallaghers of Ardmore Trilogy
Jewels of the Sun • Tears of the Moon • Heart of the Sea

Three Sisters Island Trilogy
Dance Upon the Air • Heaven and Earth • Face the Fire

Key Trilogy
Key of Light • Key of Knowledge • Key of Valor

In the Garden Trilogy
Blue Dahlia • Black Rose • Red Lily

Circle Trilogy
Morrigan's Cross • Dance of the Gods • Valley of Silence

Sign of Seven Trilogy
Blood Brothers • The Hollow • The Pagan Stone

Bride Quartet
Vision in White • Bed of Roses • Savor the Moment • Happy Ever After

The Inn Boonsboro Trilogy
The Next Always • The Last Boyfriend • The Perfect Hope

The Cousins O'Dwyer Trilogy
Dark Witch • Shadow Spell • Blood Magick

The Guardians Trilogy
Stars of Fortune • Bay of Sighs • Island of Glass

Chronicles of The One
Year One • Of Blood and Bone • The Rise of Magicks

The Dragon Heart Legacy
The Awakening

EBOOKS BY NORA ROBERTS

Cordina's Royal Family
Affaire Royale • Command Performance • The Playboy Prince • Cordina's Crown Jewel

The Donovan Legacy
Captivated • Entranced • Charmed • Enchanted

The O'Hurleys
The Last Honest Woman • Dance to the Piper • Skin Deep • Without a Trace

Night Tales
Night Shift • Night Shadow • Nightshade • Night Smoke • Night Shield

The MacGregors

The Winning Hand • The Perfect Neighbor • All the Possibilities • One Man's Art • Tempting Fate • Playing the Odds • The MacGregor Brides • The MacGregor Grooms • Rebellion/In from the Cold • For Now, Forever

The Calhouns

Suzanna's Surrender • Megan's Mate • Courting Catherine • A Man for Amanda • For the Love of Lilah

Irish Legacy

Irish Rose • Irish Rebel • Irish Thoroughbred

Jack's Stories

Best Laid Plans • Loving Jack • Lawless

Summer Love • Boundary Lines • Dual Image • First Impressions • The Law Is a Lady • Local Hero • This Magic Moment • The Name of the Game • Partners • Temptation • The Welcoming • Opposites Attract • Time Was • Times Change • Gabriel's Angel • Holiday Wishes • The Heart's Victory • The Right Path • Rules of the Game • Search for Love • Blithe Images • From This Day • Song of the West • Island of Flowers • Her Mother's Keeper • Untamed • Sullivan's Woman • Less of a Stranger • Reflections • Dance of Dreams • Storm Warning • Once More with Feeling • Endings and Beginnings • A Matter of Choice

NORA ROBERTS & J. D. ROBB

Remember When

J. D. ROBB

Naked in Death • Glory in Death • Immortal in Death • Rapture in Death • Ceremony in Death • Vengeance in Death • Holiday in Death • Conspiracy in Death • Loyalty in Death • Witness in Death • Judgment in Death • Betrayal in Death • Seduction in Death • Reunion in Death • Purity in Death

• Portrait in Death • Imitation in Death • Divided in Death • Visions in Death • Survivor in Death • Origin in Death • Memory in Death • Born in Death • Innocent in Death • Creation in Death • Strangers in Death • Salvation in Death • Promises in Death • Kindred in Death • Fantasy in Death • Indulgence in Death • Treachery in Death • New York to Dallas • Celebrity in Death • Delusion in Death • Calculated in Death • Thankless in Death • Concealed in Death • Festive in Death • Obsession in Death • Devoted in Death • Brotherhood in Death • Apprentice in Death • Echoes in Death • Secrets in Death • Dark in Death • Leverage in Death • Connections in Death • Vendetta in Death • Golden in Death • Shadows in Death

ANTHOLOGIES

From the Heart • A Little Magic • A Little Fate

Moon Shadows
(with Jill Gregory, Ruth Ryan Langan, and Marianne Willman)

The Once Upon Series
(with Jill Gregory, Ruth Ryan Langan, and Marianne Willman)
Once Upon a Castle • Once Upon a Star • Once Upon a Dream • Once Upon a Rose • Once Upon a Kiss • Once Upon a Midnight

Silent Night
(with Susan Plunkett, Dee Holmes, and Claire Cross)

Out of This World
(with Laurell K. Hamilton, Susan Krinard, and Maggie Shayne)

Bump in the Night
(with Mary Blayney, Ruth Ryan Langan, and Mary Kay McComas)

Dead of Night
(with Mary Blayney, Ruth Ryan Langan, and Mary Kay McComas)

Three in Death

Suite 606
(with Mary Blayney, Ruth Ryan Langan, and Mary Kay McComas)

In Death

The Lost
(with Patricia Gaffney, Ruth Ryan Langan, and Mary Blayney)

The Other Side
(with Mary Blayney, Patricia Gaffney, Ruth Ryan Langan, and Mary Kay McComas)

Time of Death

The Unquiet
(with Mary Blayney, Patricia Gaffney, Ruth Ryan Langan, and Mary Kay McComas)

Mirror, Mirror
(with Mary Blayney, Elaine Fox, Mary Kay McComas, and R. C. Ryan)

Down the Rabbit Hole
(with Mary Blayney, Elaine Fox, Mary Kay McComas, and R. C. Ryan)

ALSO AVAILABLE . . .

The Official Nora Roberts Companion
(edited by Denise Little and Laura Hayden)

Welcome Home

Her Mother's Keeper

and

Island of Flowers

TWO NOVELS IN ONE

NORA ROBERTS

St. Martin's Paperbacks

This is a work of fiction. All of the characters, organizations, and events portrayed in this novel are either products of the author's imagination or are used fictitiously.

First published in the United States by St. Martin's Paperbacks, an imprint of St. Martin's Publishing Group.

For information, address St. Martin's Publishing Group, 120 Broadway, New York, NY 10271.

www.stmartins.com

ISBN: 978-1-250-78102-4

Our books may be purchased in bulk for promotional, educational, or business use. Please contact your local bookseller or the Macmillan Corporate and Premium Sales Department at 1-800-221-7945, ext. 5442, or by email at MacmillanSpecialMarkets@macmillan.com.

Printed in the United States of America

St. Martin's Paperbacks edition 2020

10 9 8 7 6 5 4 3 2 1

Her Mother's Keeper

CHAPTER 1

The taxi zipped through the airport traffic. Gwen let out a long sigh as the Louisiana heat throbbed around her. She shifted as the thin material of her ivory lawn blouse dampened against her back. The relief was brief. Squinting out of the window, she decided the July sun hadn't changed in the two years she had been away. The cab veered away from downtown New Orleans and cruised south. Gwen reflected that very little else here had changed in the past two years but herself. Spanish moss still draped the roadside trees, giving even the sun-drenched afternoon a dreamlike effect. The warm, thick scent of flowers still wafted through the air. The atmosphere was touched with an easygoing indolence she nearly had forgotten during the two years she'd spent in Manhattan. Yes, she mused, craning her neck to catch a glimpse of a sheltered bayou, I'm the one who's changed. I've grown up.

When she had left Louisiana, she'd been twenty-one and a starry-eyed innocent. Now, at twenty-three, she felt mature and experienced. As an assistant to the fashion editor of *Style* magazine, Gwen had learned how to cope with deadlines, soothe ruffled models, and squeeze in a personal life around her professional one. More, she had learned how to cope alone, without the comfort of familiar people and places. The gnawing ache of homesickness she had experienced during her first months in New York was forgotten, the torture of insecurity and outright fear of being alone were banished from her memory. Gwen Lacrosse had not merely survived the transplant from magnolias to concrete, she felt she had triumphed. This is one small-town Southern girl who can take care of herself, she reflected with a flash of defiance. Gwen had come home not merely for a visit, a summer sabbatical. She had come on a mission. She folded her arms across her chest in an unconscious gesture of determination.

In the rearview mirror, the taxi driver caught a glimpse of a long, oval face surrounded by a shoulder-length mass of caramel curls. The bone structure of his passenger's face was elegant, but the rather sharp features were set in grim lines. Her huge brown eyes were focused on some middle distance, and her full, wide mouth was unsmiling. In spite of her severe expression, the cabbie decided, the face was a winner. Unaware of the scrutiny, Gwen continued to frown, absorbed by her thoughts. The landscape blurred, then disappeared from her vision.

How, she wondered, could a forty-seven-year-old

woman be so utterly naive? What a fool she must be making of herself. Mama's always been dreamy and impractical, but this! It's all *his* fault, she thought resentfully. Her eyes narrowed as she felt a fresh surge of temper, and color rose to warm the ivory tone of her skin. *Luke Powers*—Gwen gritted her teeth on the name—successful novelist and screenwriter, sought-after bachelor and globe-trotter. *And rat,* Gwen added, unconsciously twisting her leather clutch bag in a movement suspiciously akin to that of wringing a neck. A thirty-five-year-old rat. Well, Mr. Powers, Gwen's thoughts continued, your little romance with my mother is through. I've come all these miles to send you packing. And by hook or crook, fair means or foul, that's what I'm going to do.

Gwen sat back, blew the fringe of curls from her eyes and contemplated the pleasure of ousting Luke Powers from her mother's life. Researching a new book, she sniffed. He'll have to research his book without researching my mother. She frowned, remembering the correspondence from her mother over the past three months. Luke Powers had been mentioned on almost every page of the violet-scented paper; helping her mother garden, taking her to the theater, hammering nails, making himself generally indispensable.

At first Gwen had paid little attention to the constant references to Luke. She was accustomed to her mother's enthusiasm for people, her flowery, sentimental outlook. And, to be honest, Gwen reflected with a sigh, I've been preoccupied with my own life, my own problems. Her thoughts flitted back to Michael

Palmer—practical, brilliant, selfish, dependable Michael. A small cloud of depression threatened to descend on her as she remembered how miserably she had failed in their relationship. He deserved more than I could give him, she reflected sadly. Her eyes became troubled as she thought of her inability to share herself as Michael had wanted. Body and mind, she had held back both, unwilling or unable to make the commitment. Quickly shaking off the encroaching mood, Gwen reminded herself that while she had failed with Michael, she was succeeding in her career.

In the eyes of most people, the fashion world was glamorous, elegant, full of beautiful people moving gaily from one party to the next. Gwen almost laughed out loud at the absurdity of the illusion. What it really was, as she had since learned, was crazy, frantic, grueling work filled with temperamental artists, high-strung models and impossible deadlines. And I'm good at handling all of them, she mused, automatically straightening her shoulders. Gwen Lacrosse was not afraid of hard work any more than she was afraid of a challenge.

Her thoughts made a quick U-turn back to Luke Powers. There was too much affection in her mother's words when she wrote of him, and his name cropped up too often for comfort. Over the past three months, Gwen's concern had deepened to worry, until she felt she had to do something about the situation and had arranged for a leave of absence. It was, she had decided, up to her to protect her mother from a womanizer like Luke Powers.

She was not intimidated by his reputation with words or his reputation with women. He might be said to be an expert with both, she mused, but I know how to take care of myself and my mother. Mama's trouble is that she's too trusting. She sees only what she wants to see. She doesn't like to see faults. Gwen's mouth softened into a smile, and her face was suddenly, unexpectedly breathtaking. I'll take care of her, she thought confidently, I always have.

The lane leading to Gwen's childhood home was lined with fragile magnolia trees. As the taxi turned in and drove through patches of fragrant shade, Gwen felt the first stirrings of genuine pleasure. The scent of wisteria reached her before her first glimpse of the house. It had three graceful stories and was made of white-washed brick with high French windows and iron balconies like lace-work. A veranda flowed across the entire front of the house, where the wisteria was free to climb on trellises at each end. It was not as old or as elaborate as many other antebellum houses in Louisiana, but it had the charm and grace so typical of that period. Gwen felt that the house suited her mother to perfection. They were both fragile, impractical and appealing.

She glanced up at the third story as the taxi neared the end of the drive. The top floor contained four small suites that had been remodeled for "visitors," as her mother called them, or as Gwen more accurately termed them, boarders. The visitors, with their monetary contributions, made it possible to keep the house in the family and in repair. Gwen had grown up with these visitors, accepting them as one accepts a small itch. Now, however, she scowled up at the third-floor windows. One of the suites housed Luke Powers. Not for long, she vowed, as she slipped out of the cab with her chin thrust forward.

As she paid her fare, Gwen glanced absently toward the sound of a low, monotonous thudding. In the side yard, just past a flourishing camellia, a man was in the process of chopping down a long-dead oak. He was stripped to the waist, and his jeans were snug over narrow hips and worn low enough to show a hint of tan line. His back and arms were bronzed and muscled and gleaming with sweat. His hair was a rich brown, touched with lighter streaks that showed a preference for sun. It curled damply at his neck and over his brow.

There was something confident and efficient in his stance. His legs were planted firmly, his swing effortless. Though she could not see his face, she knew he was enjoying his task: the heat, the sweat, the challenge. She stood in the drive as the cab drove off and admired his raw, basic masculinity, the arrogant efficiency of his movements. The ax swung into the heart of the tree with a violent grace. It occurred to her suddenly that for months she had not seen a man do anything more physical than jog in Central Park. Her lips curved in approval and admiration as she watched the rise and fall of the ax, the tensing and flow of muscle. The ax, tree and man were a perfect whole, elemental and beautiful. Gwen had forgotten how beautiful simplicity could be.

The tree shuddered and moaned, then hesitated

briefly before it swayed and toppled to the ground. There was a quick whoosh and thump. Gwen felt a ridiculous urge to applaud.

"You didn't say timber," she called out.

He had lifted a forearm to wipe the sweat from his brow, and at her call, he turned. The sun streamed behind his back. Squinting against it, Gwen could not see his face clearly. There was an aura of light around him, etching the tall, lean body and thickly curling hair. He looks like a god, she thought, like some primitive god of virility. As she watched, he leaned the ax against the stump of the tree and walked toward her. He moved like a man more used to walking on sand or grass than on concrete. Ridiculously, Gwen felt as though she were being stalked. She attributed the strange thrill she felt to the fact that she could not yet make out his features. He was a faceless man, therefore somehow the embodiment of man, exciting and strong. In defense against the glare of the sun, she shaded her eyes with her hand.

"You did that very well." Gwen smiled, attracted by his uncomplicated masculinity. She had not realized how bored she had become with three-piece suits and smooth hands. "I hope you don't mind an audience."

"No. Not everyone appreciates a well-cut tree." His voice was not indolent with vowels. There was nothing of Louisiana in his tone. As his face at last came into focus, Gwen was struck with its power. It was narrow and chiseled, long-boned and with the faintest of clefts in the chin. He had not shaved, but the shadow of beard intensified the masculinity of the face. His eyes were a clear blue-gray. They were calm, almost startlingly intelligent under rough brows. It was a calm that suggested power, a calm that captivated the onlooker. Immediately, Gwen knew he was a man who understood himself. Though intrigued, she felt discomfort under the directness of his gaze. She was almost sure he could see beyond her words and into her thoughts.

"I'd say you have definite talent," she told him. There was an aloofness about him, she decided, but it was not the cold aloofness of disinterest. He has warmth, she thought, but he's careful about who receives it. "I'm sure I've never seen a tree toppled with such finesse." She gave him a generous smile. "It's a hot day for ax swinging."

"You've got too many clothes on," he returned simply. His eyes swept down her blouse and skirt and trim, stockinged legs, then up again to her face. It was neither an insolent assessment nor an admiring one; it was simply a statement. Gwen kept her eyes level with his and prayed she would not do anything as foolish as blushing.

"More suitable for plane travelling than tree chopping I suppose," she replied. The annoyance in her voice brought a smile to the corners of his mouth. Gwen reached for her bags, but her hand met his on the handle. She jerked away and stepped back as a new source of heat shot through her. It seemed to dart up her fingers, then explode. Stunned by her own reaction, she stared into his calm eyes. Confusion flitted across her face and creased her brow before she smoothed it away. Silly, she told herself as she struggled to steady her pulse. Absolutely silly. He watched the shock, confusion and annoyance move across her face. Like a mirror, her eyes reflected each emotion.

"Thank you," Gwen said, regaining her poise. "I don't want to take you away from your work."

"No hurry." He hoisted her heavy bags easily. As he moved up the flagstone walk, she fell into step beside him. Even in heels, she barely reached his shoulder. Gwen glanced up to see the sun play on the blond highlights in his hair.

"Have you been here long?" she asked as they mounted the steps to the veranda.

"Few months." He set down her bags and placed his hand on the knob. Pausing, he studied her face with exacting care. Gwen felt her lips curve for no reason at all. "You're much lovelier than your picture, Gwenivere," he said unexpectedly. "Much warmer, much more vulnerable." With a quick twist, he opened the door, then again picked up her bags.

Breaking out of her trance, Gwen followed him inside, reaching for his arm. "How do you know my name?" she demanded. His words left her puzzled and defenseless. He saw too much too quickly.

"Your mother talks of you constantly," he explained as he set her bags down in the cool, white-walled hallway. "She's very proud of you." When he lifted her chin with his fingers, Gwen was too surprised to protest. "Your beauty is very different from hers. Hers is softer, less demanding, more comfortable. I doubt very much that you inspire comfort in a man." His eyes were on her face again, and fascinated, Gwen stood still. She could nearly feel the heat flowing from his body into hers. "She worries about you being alone in New York."

"One can't be alone in New York, it's a contradiction in terms." A frown shadowed her eyes and touched her mouth with a pout. "She's never told me she worried."

"Of course not, then you'd worry about her worrying." He grinned.

Resolutely Gwen ignored the tingle of pleasure his touch gave her. "You seem to know my mother quite well." Her frown deepened and spread. The grin reminded her of someone. It was charming and almost irresistible. Recognition struck like a thunderbolt. *"You're Luke Powers,"* she accused.

"Yes." His brows lifted at the tone of her voice, and his head tilted slightly, as if to gain a new perspective. "Didn't you like my last book?"

"It's your current one I object to," Gwen snapped. She jerked her chin from his hold.

"Oh?" There was both amusement and curiosity in the word.

"To the fact that you're writing it here, in this house," Gwen elaborated.

"Have you a moral objection to my book, Gwenivere?"

"I doubt you know anything about morals," Gwen tossed back as her eyes grew stormy. "And don't call me that. No one but my mother calls me that."

"Pity, such a romantic name," he said casually. "Or do you object to romance, as well?"

"When it's between my mother and a Hollywood Casanova a dozen years younger than she, I have a different name for it." Gwen's face flushed with the passion of her words. She stood rigid. The humor faded from Luke's face. Slowly, he tucked his hands in his pockets.

"I see. Would you care to tell me what you'd call it?"

"I won't glorify your conduct with a title," Gwen retorted. "It should be sufficient that you understand I won't tolerate it any longer." She turned, intending to walk away from him.

"Won't you?" There was something dangerously cold in his tone. "And your mother has no voice in the matter?"

"My mother," Gwen countered furiously, "is too gentle, too trusting and too naive." Whirling, she faced him again. "I won't let you make a fool of her."

"My dear Gwenivere," he said smoothly. "You do so well making one of yourself."

Before Gwen could retort, there was the sharp click of heels on wood. Struggling to steady her breathing, Gwen moved down the hall to greet her mother.

"Mama." She embraced a soft bundle of curves smelling of lilac.

"Gwenivere!" Her mother's voice was low and as sweet as the scent she habitually wore. "Why, darling, what are you doing here?"

"Mama," Gwen repeated and pulled away far enough to study the rosy loveliness of her mother's face. Her mother's skin was creamy and almost perfectly smooth, her eyes round and china blue, her nose tilted, her mouth pink and soft. There were two tiny dimples in her cheeks. Looking at her sweet prettiness, Gwen felt their roles should have been reversed. "Didn't you get my letter?" She tucked a stray wisp of pale blond hair behind her mother's ear.

"Of course, you said you'd be here Friday."

Gwen smiled and kissed a dimpled cheek. "This is Friday, Mama."

"Well, yes, it's *this* Friday, but I assumed you meant *next* Friday, and . . . Oh, dear, what does it matter?" Anabelle brushed away confusion with the back of her hand. "Let me look at you," she requested and, stepping back, subjected Gwen to a critical study. She saw a tall, striking beauty who brought misty memories of her young husband. Widowed for more than two decades, Anabelle rarely thought of her late husband unless reminded by her daughter. "So thin," she clucked, and sighed. "Don't you eat up there?"

"Now and again." Pausing, Gwen made her own survey of her mother's soft, round curves. How could this woman be approaching fifty? she wondered with a surge of pride and awe. "You look wonderful," Gwen murmured, "but then, you always look wonderful."

Anabelle laughed her young, gay laugh. "It's the climate," she claimed as she patted Gwen's cheek. "None of that dreadful smog or awful snow you have up there." New York, Gwen noted, would always be "up there." "Oh, Luke!" Anabelle caught sight of him as he stood watching the reunion. A smile lit up her face. "Have you met my Gwenivere?"

Luke shifted his gaze until his eyes met Gwen's.

His brow tilted slightly in acknowledgement. "Yes." Gwen thought his smile was as much a challenge as a glove slapped across her cheek. "Gwen and I are practically old friends."

"That's right." Gwen let her smile answer his. "Already we know each other quite well."

"Marvelous." Anabelle beamed. "I do want you two to get along." She gave Gwen's hand a happy squeeze. "Would you like to freshen up, darling, or would you like a cup of coffee first?"

Gwen struggled to keep her voice from trembling with rage as Luke continued to smile at her. "Coffee sounds perfect," she answered.

"I'll take your bags up," Luke offered as he lifted them again.

"Thank you, dear." Anabelle spoke before Gwen could refuse. "Try to avoid Miss Wilkins until you have a shirt on. The sight of all those muscles will certainly give her the vapors. Miss Wilkins is one of my visitors," Anabelle explained as she led Gwen down the hall. "A sweet, timid little soul who paints in watercolors."

"Hmm," Gwen answered noncommittally as she glanced back over her shoulder. Luke stood watching them with sunlight tumbling over his hair and bronzed skin. "Hmm," Gwen said again, and turned away.

The kitchen was exactly as Gwen remembered: big, sunny and spotlessly clean. Tillie, the tall, waspishly thin cook stood by the stove. "Hello, Miss Gwen," she said without turning around. "Coffee's on."

"Hello, Tillie." Gwen walked over to the stove and sniffed at the fragrant steam. "Smells good."

"Cajun jambalaya."

"My favorite," Gwen murmured, glancing up at the appealingly ugly face. "I thought I wasn't expected until next Friday."

"You weren't," Tillie agreed, with a sniff. Lowering her thick brows, she continued to stir the roux.

Gwen smiled and leaned over to peck Tillie's tough cheek. "How are things, Tillie?"

"Comme ci, comme ça," she muttered, but pleasure touched her cheeks with color. Turning, she gave Gwen a quick study. "Skinny" was her quick, uncomplimentary conclusion.

"So I'm told." Gwen shrugged. Tillie never flattered anyone. "You have a month to fatten me up."

"Isn't that marvellous, Tillie?" Anabelle carefully put a blue delft sugar and creamer set on the kitchen table. "Gwen is staying for an entire month. Perhaps we should have a party! We have three visitors at the moment. Luke, of course, and Miss Wilkins and Mr. Stapleton. He's an artist, too, but he works in oils. Quite a talented young man."

Gwen seized the small opening. "Luke Powers is considered a gifted young man, too." She sat across from her mother as Anabelle poured the coffee.

"Luke *is* frightfully talented," Anabelle agreed with a proud sigh. "Surely you've read some of his books, seen some of his movies? Overwhelming. His characters are so real, so vital. His romantic scenes have a beauty and intensity that just leave me weak."

"He had a naked woman in one of his movies," Tillie stated in an indignant mutter. "Stark naked."

Anabelle laughed. Her eyes smiled at Gwen's over the rim of her cup. "Tillie feels Luke is single-handedly responsible for the moral decline in the theater," Anabelle continued.

"Not a stitch on," Tillie added, setting her chin.

Though Gwen was certain Luke Powers had no morals whatsoever, she made no reference to them. Her voice remained casual as instead she commented, "He certainly has accomplished quite a bit for a man of his age. A string of best-sellers, a clutch of popular movies . . . and he's only thirty-five."

"I suppose that shows how unimportant age really is," Anabelle said serenely. Gwen barely suppressed a wince. "And success hasn't spoiled him one little bit," she went on. "He's the kindest, sweetest man I've ever known. He's so generous with his time, with himself." Her eyes shone with emotion. "I can't tell you how good he's been for me. I feel like a new woman." Gwen choked on her coffee. Anabelle clucked in sympathy as Tillie gave Gwen a sturdy thump on the back. "Are you all right, honey?"

"Yes, yes, I'm fine." Gwen took three deep breaths to steady her voice. Looking into her mother's guileless blue eyes, she opted for a temporary retreat. "I think I'll go upstairs and unpack."

"I'll help you," Anabelle volunteered, and started to rise.

"No, no, don't bother." Gwen placed a gentle hand on her shoulder. "It won't take long. I'll shower and change and be down in an hour." In an hour, Gwen hoped to have her thoughts more in order. She looked down at her mother's smooth, lovely face and felt a hundred years old. "I love you, Mama," she sighed, and kissed Anabelle's brow before she left her.

As Gwen moved down the hall, she realigned her strategy. Obviously, there was little she could say to her mother that would discourage her relationship with Luke Powers. It was going to be necessary, she decided, to go straight to the source. While climbing the stairs, she searched her imagination for an appropriate name for him. She could find nothing vile enough.

CHAPTER 2

A shaft of sunlight poured over the floor in Gwen's room. The walls were covered in delicate floral paper. Eggshell-tinted sheer curtains were draped at the windows, matching the coverlet on the four-poster bed. As she always did when she entered the room, Gwen crossed to the French windows and threw them open. Scents from Anabelle's flower garden swam up to meet her. Across the lawn was a spreading cypress, older than the house it guarded, festooned with gray-green moss. The sun filtered through it, making spider-web patterns on the ground. Birdsong melded with the drone of bees. She could barely glimpse the mystery of the bayou through a thick curtain of oaks. New York's busy streets seemed nonexistent. Gwen had chosen that world for its challenges, but she discovered that coming home was like a sweet dessert after a full meal. She had missed its taste. Feeling unaccountably more lighthearted, she turned back into her room. She plucked up her white terry-cloth robe and headed for the shower.

Mama's romanticizing again, Gwen mused as the water washed away her travel weariness. She simply doesn't understand men at all. *And you do?* her conscience asked as she thought uncomfortably of Michael. Yes, I do understand them, she answered defiantly as she held her face up to the spray. I understand them perfectly. I won't let Luke hurt my mother, she vowed. I won't let him make a fool of her. I suppose he's used to getting his own way because he's successful and attractive. Well, I deal with successful, attractive people every day, and I know precisely how to handle them. Refreshed and ready for battle, Gwen stepped from the shower. With her confidence restored, she hummed lightly as she towel-dried her hair. Curls sprang to life on her forehead. Slipping on her robe, she tied the belt at her waist and strolled back into the bedroom.

"You!" Gwen jerked the knot tight as she spied Luke Powers standing beside her dresser. "What are you doing in my room?"

Calmly, his eyes traveled over her. The frayed robe was short, well above the knee, revealing slender legs. Its simplicity outlined her nearly boyish slenderness. Without makeup, her eyes were huge and dark and curiously sweet. Luke watched her damp curls bounce with the outraged toss of her head.

"Anabelle thought you'd like these," he said as he indicated a vase of fresh yellow roses on the dresser.

His hand made the gesture, but his eyes remained on Gwen. Gwen frowned.

"You should have knocked," she said ungraciously.

"I did," he said easily. "You didn't answer." To her amazement, he crossed the distance between them and lifted a hand to her cheek. "You have incredibly beautiful skin. Like rose petals washed in rainwater."

"Don't!" Knocking his hand away, Gwen stepped back. "Don't touch me." She pushed her hair away from her face.

Luke's eyes narrowed fractionally at her tone, but his voice was calm. "I always touch what I admire."

"I don't want you to admire me."

Humor lit his face and added to its appeal. "I didn't say I admired you, Gwen. I said I admired your skin."

"Just keep your hands off my skin," she snapped, wishing the warmth of his fingers would evaporate and leave her cheek as it had been before his touch. "And keep your hands off my mother."

"What gives you the notion I've had my hands on your mother?" Luke inquired, lifting a bottle of Gwen's scent and examining it.

"Her letters were clear enough." Gwen snatched the bottle from him and slammed it back on the dresser. "They've been full of nothing but you for months. How you went to the theater or shopping, how you fixed her car or sprayed the peach trees. Especially how you've given her life fresh meaning." Agitated, Gwen picked up her comb, then put it down again. His direct, unruffled stare tripped her nerves.

"And from that," Luke said into the silence, "you've concluded that Anabelle and I are having an affair."

"Well, of course." His tone confused her for a moment. Was he amused? she wondered. His mouth was beautiful, a smile lurking on it. Furious with herself, Gwen tilted her chin. "Do you deny it?"

Luke slipped his hands into his pockets and wandered about the room. Pausing, he studied the view from the open French windows. "No, I don't believe I will. I believe I'll simply tell you it's none of your business."

"None of my . . ." Gwen sputtered, then swallowed in a torrent of fury. "None of my business? She's my mother!"

"She's also a person," Luke cut in. When he turned back to face her, there was curiosity on his face. "Or don't you ever see her that way?"

"I don't feel it's—"

"No, you probably don't," he interrupted. "It's certainly time you did, though. I doubt you feel Anabelle should approve of every man you have a relationship with."

Color flared in Gwen's cheeks. "That's entirely different," she fumed, then stalked over to stand in front of him. "I don't need you to tell me about my mother. You can flaunt your affairs with actresses and socialites all you want, but—"

"Thank you," Luke replied evenly. "It's nice to have your approval."

"I won't have you flaunting your affair with my mother," Gwen finished between her teeth. "You should be ashamed," she added with a toss of her head, "seducing a woman a dozen years older than you."

"Of course, it would be perfectly acceptable if I were a dozen years older than she," he countered smoothly.

"I didn't *say* that," Gwen began. Her brow creased with annoyance.

"You look too intelligent to hold such views, Gwen. You surprise me." His mild voice was infuriating.

"I don't!" she denied hotly. Because the thought made her uncomfortable, her mouth moved into a pout. Luke's eyes dropped to her lips and lingered.

"A very provocative expression," he said softly. "I thought so the first time I saw it, and it continues to intrigue me." In one swift motion, he gathered her into his arms. At her gasp of surprised protest, he merely smiled. "I told you I always touch what I admire." Gwen squirmed, but she was pinned tight against him, helpless as his face lowered toward her.

His lips feathered lightly along her jawline. Gwen was caught off guard by the gentleness. Though his chest was solid and strong against her yielding breasts, his mouth was soft and sweet. Disarmed, she stood still in the circle of his arms as his mouth roamed her face. Through the slight barrier of the robe, she could feel every line of his body. They merged together as if destined to do so. Heat began to rise in her, a sudden, unexpected heat as irresistible as his mouth. Her lips throbbed for the touch of his. She moaned softly as he continued to trace light, teasing kisses over her skin. Her hands slipped up from his chest to find their way into his hair, urging him to fulfill a silent promise. At last his lips brushed hers. They touched, then clung, then devoured.

Lost in pleasure, riding on sensations delirious and new, Gwen answered his demands with fervor. She rose on her toes to meet them. The kiss grew deeper. The roughness of his beard scratched her skin and tripled her heartbeat. A tenuous breeze fanned the curtains at the open windows, but Gwen felt no lessening of heat. Luke moved his hands down her spine, firmly caressing her curves before he took her hips and drew her away.

Gwen stared up at him with dark, cloudy eyes. Never had a kiss moved her more, never had she been so filled with fire and need. Her soft mouth trembled with desire for his. The knowledge of what could be hers lay just beyond her comprehension. Luke lifted his hand to her damp curls, tilting back her head for one last, brief kiss. "You taste every bit as good as you look."

Abruptly Gwen remembered who and where she was. The fires of passion were extinguished by fury. "Oh!" She gave Luke's chest a fierce push and succeeded in putting an entire inch between them. "How could you?"

"It wasn't hard," he assured her.

Gwen shook her head. Tiny droplets of water danced in the sunlight. "You're despicable!"

"Why?" Luke's smile broadened. "Because I made you forget yourself for a moment? You made me forget myself for a moment too." He seemed to enjoy the confession. "Does that make you despicable?"

"I didn't . . . It was you . . . I just . . ." Her words

stumbled to a halt, and she made ineffectual noises in her throat.

"At least try to be coherent," Luke said.

"Just let me go," Gwen demanded. She began a violent and fruitless struggle. "Just let me go!"

"Certainly," Luke said obligingly. He brushed back her disheveled hair with a friendly hand. "You know, one day you might just be the woman your mother is."

"Oh!" Gwen paled in fury. "You're disgusting."

Luke laughed with pure masculine enjoyment. "Gwenivere, I wasn't speaking of your rather exceptional physical virtues." He sobered, then shook his head. "Anabelle is the only person I know who looks for the good in everyone and finds it. It's her most attractive asset." His eyes were calm again and thoughtful. "Perhaps you should take time to get to know your mother while you're here. You might be surprised."

Gwen retreated behind a film of ice. "I told you, I don't need you to tell me about my mother."

"No?" Luke smiled, shrugged, and moved to the door. "Perhaps I'll spend my time teaching you about yourself, then. See you at dinner." He closed the door on her furious retort.

The front parlor had both the color and the scent of roses. It was furnished in Anabelle's delicate and feminine style. The chairs were small and elegant, with dusky pink cushions; the lamps, china and terrifyingly fragile; the rugs, faded and French. Even when she was not there, Anabelle's presence could be felt.

Gwen pushed aside a pale pink curtain and watched the sun go down while Anabelle chattered happily. The sky gradually took on the hues of sunset, until it glowed with defiant gold and fiery reds. Its passion suited Gwen much more than the soft comfort of the room at her back. She lifted her palm to the glass of the window, as if to touch that explosion of nature. She still felt the aftershocks of the explosion that had burst inside her only a few hours before in the arms of a stranger.

It meant nothing, she assured herself for the hundredth time. I was off guard, tired, confused. I'm sure most of what I felt was pure imagination. I'm on edge, that's all, everything's exaggerated. She ran the tip of her tongue experimentally along her lips, but found no remnants of the heady flavor she remembered. Exaggerated, she told herself again.

"A month's quite a long time for you to be away from your job," Anabelle said conversationally as she sorted through a basket of embroidery thread.

Gwen shrugged and made a small sound of agreement. "I haven't taken more than a long weekend in nearly two years."

"Yes, darling, I know. You work too hard."

The cerulean blue dress suited Gwen well, but as Anabelle glanced up at her, she again thought how thin her daughter looked. She was slim and straight as a wand. Gwen's hair caught some of the last flames of the sun, and the mass of curls became a flood of rose-gold light. *How did she get to be twenty-three?* Anabelle wondered. She went back to sorting her thread. "You always were an overachiever. You must get that from your father's side. His mother had two sets of twins, you know. That's overachievement."

With a laugh, Gwen rested her forehead against the glass of the window. It was as refreshing as her mother. "Oh, Mama, I do love you."

"I love you, too, dear," she answered absently as she scrutinized two tones of green. "You haven't mentioned that young man you were seeing, the attorney. Michael, wasn't it?"

"It was," Gwen returned dryly. Dusk began to fall as she watched. With the mellowing of light came an odd, almost reverent hush. She sighed. Dusk, she thought, was the most precious time, and the most fleeting. The sound of the first cricket brought her out of her reverie. "I'm not seeing Michael anymore."

"Oh, dear." Anabelle looked up, distressed. "Did you have a disagreement?"

"A series of them. I'm afraid I don't make the ideal companion for a corporate attorney." Gwen made a face in the glass and watched it reflect. "I have too many deep-rooted plebeian values. Mostly, I like to see the little guy get a break."

"Well, I hope you parted friends."

Gwen closed her eyes and stifled a sardonic laugh as she recalled the volatile parting scene. "I'm sure we'll exchange Christmas cards for years to come."

"That's nice," Anabelle murmured comfortably as she threaded her needle. "Old friends are the most precious."

With a brilliant smile, Gwen turned toward her

mother. The smile faded instantly as she spotted Luke in the doorway. As her eyes locked with his, she felt herself trembling. He had changed into tan slacks and a rust-colored shirt. The effect was casual and expensive. But somehow there seemed little difference between the clean-shaven, conventionally clad man Gwen now saw and the rugged woodsman she had met that morning. Clothes and a razor could not alter the essence of his virility.

"It's a fortunate man who has two exquisite women to himself."

"Luke!" Anabelle's head lifted. Instantly, her face was touched with pleasure. "How lovely it is to be flattered! Don't you agree, Gwen?"

"Lovely," Gwen assented, as she sent him her most frigid smile.

With easy assurance, Luke crossed the room. From Gwen's grandmother's Hepplewhite server, he lifted a crystal decanter. "Sherry?"

"Thank you, darling." Anabelle turned her smile from him to Gwen. "Luke bought the most delightful sherry. I'm afraid he's been spoiling me."

"I'll just bet he has," Gwen muttered silently. Temper flared in her eyes. Had she seen it, Anabelle would have recognized the look. Luke both saw it and recognized it. To Gwen's further fury, he grinned.

"We shouldn't dawdle long," Anabelle said, unconscious of the war being waged over her head. "Tillie has a special supper planned for Gwen. She dotes on her, you know, though she wouldn't admit it for the world. I believe she's missed Gwen every bit as much as I have these past two years."

"She's missed having someone to scold," Gwen smiled ruefully. "I still carry the stigma of being skinny and unladylike that I acquired when I was ten."

"You'll always be ten to Tillie, darling." Anabelle sighed and shook her head. "I have a difficult time realizing you're more than twice that myself."

Gwen turned toward Luke as he offered her a glass of sherry. "Thank you," she said in her most graciously insulting voice. She sipped, faintly disappointed to find that it was excellent. "And will you be spoiling me, as well, Mr. Powers?"

"Oh, I doubt that, Gwenivere." He took her hand, although she stiffened and tried to pull it away. His eyes laughed over their joined fingers. "I doubt that very much."

CHAPTER 3

Over dinner Gwen met Anabelle's two other visitors. Though both were artists, they could not have been more different from each other. Monica Wilkins was a small, pale woman with indifferent brown hair. She spoke in a quiet, breathy voice and avoided eye contact at all costs. She had a supply of large, shapeless smocks, which she wore invariably and without flair. Her art was, for the most part, confined to illustrating textbooks on botany. With a touch of pity, Gwen noticed that her tiny, birdlike eyes often darted glances at Luke, then shifted away quickly and self-consciously.

Bradley Stapleton was tall and lanky, casually dressed in an ill-fitting sweater, baggy slacks and battered sneakers. He had a cheerful, easily forgettable face and a surprisingly beautiful voice. He studied his fellow humans with unquenchable curiosity and painted for the love of it. He yearned to be famous but had settled for regular meals.

Gwen thoroughly enjoyed dinner, not only because of Tillie's excellent jambalaya but for the oddly interesting company of the two artists. Separately, she thought each might be a bore, but somehow together, the faults of one enhanced the virtues of the other.

"So, you work for *Style,*" Bradley stated as he scooped up a second, generous helping of Tillie's jambalaya. "Why don't you model?"

Gwen thought of the frantic, nervous models, with their fabulous faces. She shook her head. "No, I'm not at all suitable. I'm much better at stroking."

"Stroking?" Bradley repeated, intrigued.

"That's what I do, basically." Gwen smiled at him. It was better, she decided, that her mother had seated her next to Luke rather than across from him. She would have found it uncomfortable to face him throughout an entire meal. "Soothe, stroke, bully. Someone has to keep the models from using their elegant nails on each other and remind them of the practical side of life."

"Gwen's so good at being practical," Anabelle interjected. "I'm sure I don't understand why. I've never been. Strange," she said, and smiled at her daughter. "She grew up long before I did."

"Practicality wouldn't suit you, Anabelle," Luke told her with an affectionate smile.

Anabelle dimpled with pleasure. "I told you he was spoiling me," she said to Gwen.

"So you did." Gwen lifted her water glass and sipped carefully.

"You must sit for me, Gwen," Bradley said, as he buttered a biscuit.

"Must I?" Knowing the only way she could get through a civilized meal was to ignore Luke, Gwen gave Bradley all her attention.

"Absolutely." Bradley held both the biscuit and knife suspended while he narrowed his eyes and stared at her. "Fabulous, don't you agree, Monica? A marvelous subject," he went on without waiting for her answer. "In some lights the hair would be the color Titian immortalized, in others, it would be quieter, more subtle. But it's the eyes, isn't it, Monica? It's definitely the eyes. So large, so meltingly brown. Of course, the bone structure's perfect, and the skin's wonderful, but I'm taken with the eyes. The lashes are real, too, aren't they, Monica?"

"Yes, quite real," she answered as her gaze flew swiftly to Gwen's face and then back to her plate. "Quite real."

"She gets them from her father," Anabelle explained as she added a sprinkle of salt to her jambalaya. "Such a handsome boy. Gwen favors him remarkably. His eyes were exactly the same. I believe they're why I first fell in love with him."

"They're very alluring," Bradley commented with a nod to Anabelle. "The size, the color, the shape. Very alluring." He faced Gwen again. "You will sit for me, won't you, Gwen?"

Gwen gave Bradley a guileless smile. "Perhaps."

The meal drifted to a close, and the evening waned. The artists retreated to their rooms, and

Luke wandered off to his. At Gwen's casual question, Anabelle told her that Luke "worked all the time." It was odd, Gwen mused to herself, that a woman as romantic as her mother wasn't concerned that the man in her life was not spending his evening with her.

Anabelle chattered absently while working tiny decorative stitches into a pillowcase. Watching her, Gwen was struck with a sudden thought. Did Anabelle seem happier? Did she seem more vital? If Luke Powers was responsible, should she, Gwen, curse him or thank him? She watched Anabelle delicately stifle a yawn and was swept by a fierce protective surge. She needs me to look out for her, she decided, and that's what I plan to do.

Once in her bedroom, however, Gwen could not get to sleep. The book she had brought with her to pass the time did not hold her attention. It grew late, but her mind would not allow her body to rest. A breeze blew softly in through the windows, lifting the curtains. It beckoned. Rising, Gwen threw on a thin robe and went outside to meet it.

The night was warm and lit by a large summer moon. The air was filled with the scent of wisteria and roses. She could hear the continual hum of the crickets. Now and then, there was the lonely, eerie call of an owl. Leaves rustled with the movements of night birds and small animals. Fireflies blinked and soared.

As Gwen breathed in the moist, fragrant air, an unexpected peace settled over her. Tranquility was something just remembered, like a childhood friend. Tentatively Gwen reached out for it. For two years, her career had been her highest priority. Independence and success were the goals she had sought. She had worked hard for them. And I've got them, she thought as she plucked a baby coral rose from its bush. Why aren't I happy? I am happy, she corrected as she lifted the bloom and inhaled its fragile scent, but I'm not as happy as I should be. Frowning, she twisted the stem between her fingers. *Complete.* The word came from nowhere. I don't feel complete. With a sigh, she tilted her head and studied the star-studded sky. Laughter bubbled up in her throat suddenly and sounded sweet in the silence.

"Catch!" she cried as she tossed the bloom in the air. She gasped in surprise as a hand plucked the rose on its downward journey. Luke had appeared as if from nowhere and was standing a few feet away from her twirling the flower under his nose. "Thanks," he said softly. "No one has ever tossed me a rose."

"I wasn't tossing it to you." Automatically, Gwen clutched her robe together where it crossed her breasts.

"No?" Luke smiled at her and at the gesture. "Who then?"

Feeling foolish, Gwen shrugged and turned away. "I thought you were working."

"I was. The muse took a break so I called it a night.

Gardens are at their best in the moonlight." He paused, and there was an intimacy in his voice. Stepping closer, he added, "I've always thought the same held true for women."

Gwen felt her skin grow warm. She struggled to keep her tone casual as she turned to face him.

Luke tucked the small flower into her curls and lifted her chin. "They are fabulous eyes, you know. Bradley's quite right."

Her skin began to tingle where his fingers touched it. Defensively, she stepped back. "I wish you wouldn't keep doing that." Her voice trembled, and she despised herself for it.

Luke gave her an odd, amused smile. "You're a strange one, Gwenivere. I haven't got you labeled quite yet. I'm intrigued by the innocence."

Gwen stiffened and tossed back her hair. "I don't know what you're talking about."

Luke's smile broadened. The moonlight seemed trapped in his eyes. "Your New York veneer doesn't cover it. It's in the eyes. Bradley doesn't know why they're appealing, and I won't tell him. It's the innocence and the promise." Gwen frowned, but her shoulders relaxed. Luke went on, "There's an unspoiled innocence in that marvelous face, and a warmth that promises passion. It's a tenuous balance."

His words made Gwen uncomfortable. A warmth was spreading through her that she seemed powerless to control. Tranquility had vanished. An excitement, volatile and hot, throbbed through the air. Suddenly she was afraid. "I don't want you to say these things to me," she whispered, and took another step in retreat.

"No?" The amusement in his voice told her that a full retreat would be impossible. "Didn't Michael ever use words to seduce you? Perhaps that's why he failed."

"Michael? What do you know about . . . ?" Abruptly she recalled the conversation with her mother before dinner. "You were listening!" she began, outraged. "You had no right to listen to a private conversation! No gentleman listens to a private conversation!"

"Nonsense," Luke said calmly. "Everyone does, if he has the chance."

"Do you enjoy intruding on other people's privacy?"

"People interest me, emotions interest me. I don't apologize for my interests."

Gwen was torn between fury at his arrogance and admiration for his confidence. "What *do* you apologize for, Luke Powers?"

"Very little."

Unable to do otherwise, Gwen smiled. Really, she thought, he's outrageous.

"Now that was worth waiting for," Luke murmured, as his eyes roamed her face. "I wonder if Bradley can do it justice? Be careful," he warned, "you'll have him falling in love with you."

"Is that how you won Monica?"

"She's terrified of me," Luke corrected as he reached up to better secure the rose in her hair.

"Some terrific observer of humanity you are." Gwen sniffed, fiddling with the rose herself and managing to dislodge it. As it tumbled to the ground, both she and Luke stooped to retrieve it. Her hair brushed his cheek before she lifted her eyes to his. As if singed, she jolted back, but before she could escape, he took her arm. Slowly, he rose, bringing her with him. Involuntarily, she shivered as he brought her closer until their bodies touched. Just a look from him, just the touch of him, incited her to a passion that she had not known she possessed. His hands slid up her arms and under the full sleeves of her robe to caress her shoulders. She felt her mantle of control slip away as she swayed forward and touched her lips to his.

His mouth was avid so quickly, her breath caught in her throat. Then all was lost in pleasure. Lights fractured and exploded behind her closed lids as her lips sought to give and to take with an instinct as old as time. Beneath her palms she felt the hard, taut muscles of his back. She shuddered with the knowledge of his strength and the sudden realization of her own frailty. But even her weakness had a power she had never tapped, never experienced.

His hands roamed over her, lighting fires, learning secrets, teaching and taking. Gwen was pliant and willing. He was like a drug flowing into her system, clouding her brain. Only the smallest grain of denial struggled for survival, fighting against the growing need to surrender. Reason surfaced slowly, almost reluctantly. Suddenly, appalled by her own behavior, she began to struggle. But when she broke away, she felt a quick stab of loneliness.

"No." Gwen lifted her hands to her burning cheeks. "No," she faltered.

Luke watched in silence as she turned and fled to the house.

CHAPTER 4

The morning was hazy and heavy. So were Gwen's thoughts. As dawn broke with a gray, uncertain light, she stood by her window.

How could I? she demanded of herself yet again. Closing her eyes and groaning, Gwen sank down onto the window seat. I kissed him. *I* kissed *him.* Inherent honesty kept her from shifting what she considered blame. I can't say I was caught off guard this time. I knew what was going to happen, and worse yet, I *enjoyed* it. She brought her knees up to her chin. I enjoyed the first time he kissed me too. The silent admission caused her to shut her eyes again. *How could I?* As she wrestled with this question, she rose and paced the room. I came thousands of miles to get Luke Powers out of Mama's life, and I end up kissing him in the garden in the middle of the night. And liking it, she added wretchedly. What kind of a person am

I? What kind of a daughter am I? I never thought of Mama once in that garden last night. Well, I'll think of her today, she asserted, and pulled a pair of olive-drab shorts from her drawer. I've got a month to move Luke Powers out, and that's just what I'm going to do.

As she buttoned up a short-sleeved khaki blouse, Gwen nodded confidently at herself in the mirror. No more moonlit gardens. I won't take the chance of having midsummer madness creep over me again. That's what it was, wasn't it? she asked the slender woman in the glass. She ran a nervous hand through her hair. Another answer seemed just beyond her reach. Refusing any attempt to pursue it, Gwen finished dressing and left the room.

Not even Tillie was in the kitchen at such an early hour. There was a certain enjoyment in being up alone in the softly lit room. She made the first pot of coffee in the gray dawn. She sipped at a cupful while watching dark clouds gather. Rain, she thought, not displeased. The sky promised it, the air smelled of it. It gave an excitement to the quiet, yawning morning. There would be thunder and lightning and cooling wind. The thought inexplicably lifted Gwen's spirits. Humming a cheerful tune, she began searching the cupboards. The restless night was forgotten.

"What are you up to?" Tillie demanded, sweeping into the room. Hands on her bony hips, she watched Gwen.

"Good morning, Tillie." Used to the cook's abrasiveness, Gwen answered good-naturedly.

"What do you want in my kitchen?" she asked suspiciously. "You made coffee."

"Yes, it's not too bad." Gwen's tone was apologetic, but her eyes danced with mischief.

"I make the coffee," Tillie reminded her. "I always make the coffee."

"I've certainly missed it over the past couple of years. No matter how I try, mine never tastes quite like yours." Gwen poured a fresh cup. "Have some," she offered. "Maybe you can tell me what I do wrong."

Tillie accepted the cup and scowled. "You let it brew too long," she complained. Lifting her hand, she brushed curls back from Gwen's forehead. "Will you never keep your hair out of your eyes? Do you want to wear glasses?"

"No, Tillie," Gwen answered humbly. It was an old gesture and an old question. She recognized the tenderness behind the brisk words and quick fingers. Her lips curved into a smile. "I made Mama's breakfast." Turning, Gwen began to arrange cups and plates on a tray. "I'm going to take it up to her, she always liked it when I surprised her that way."

"You shouldn't bother your *maman* so early in the morning," Tillie began.

"Oh, it's not so early," Gwen said airily as she lifted the tray. "I didn't leave much of a mess," she added with the carelessness of youth. "I'll clean it up when I come back." She whisked through the door before Tillie could comment.

Gwen moved quickly up the stairs and down the

corridor. Balancing the tray in one hand, she twisted the knob on her mother's door with the other. She was totally stunned to find it locked. Automatically, she jiggled the knob in disbelief. Never, as far back as her childhood memories stretched, did Gwen remember the door of Anabelle's room being locked.

"Mama?" There was a question in her voice as she knocked. "Mama, are you up?"

"What?" Anabelle's voice was clear but distracted. "Oh, Gwen, just a minute, darling."

Gwen stood outside the door listening to small, shuffling sounds she could not identify. "Mama," she said again, "are you all right?"

"Yes, yes, dear, one moment." The creaks and shuffles stopped just before the door opened. "Good morning, Gwen." Anabelle smiled. Though she wore a gown and robe and her hair was mussed by sleep, her eyes were awake and alert. "What have you got there?"

Blankly, Gwen looked down at the tray she carried. "Oh, chocolate and *beignets.* I know how you like them. Mama, what were you . . . ?"

"Darling, how sweet!" Anabelle interrupted, and drew Gwen into the room. "Did you really make them yourself? What a treat. Come, let's sit on the balcony. I hope you slept well."

Gwen evaded a lie. "I woke early and decided to test my memory with the *beignet* recipe. Mama, I don't remember you ever locking your door."

"No?" Anabelle smiled as she settled herself in a white, wrought-iron chair. "It must be a new habit, then. Oh, dear, it looks like rain. Well, my roses will be thankful."

The locked door left Gwen feeling slighted. It reminded her forcibly that Anabelle Lacrosse was a person, as well as her mother. Perhaps she would do well to remember it, Gwen silently resolved. She set the tray on a round, glass-topped table and bent to kiss Anabelle's cheek. "I've really missed you. I don't think I've told you that yet."

"Gwenivere." Anabelle smiled and patted her daughter's fine-boned hand. "It's so good to have you home. You've always been such a pleasure to me."

"Even when I'd track mud on the carpet or lose frogs in the parlor?" Grinning, Gwen sat and poured the chocolate.

"Darling." Anabelle sighed and shook her head. "Some things are best forgotten. I never understood how I could have raised such a hooligan. But even as I despaired of you ever being a lady, I couldn't help admiring your freedom of spirit. Hot-tempered you might have been," Anabelle added as she tasted her chocolate, "but never malicious and never dishonest. No matter what dreadful thing you did, you never did it out of spite, and you always confessed."

Gwen laughed. Her curls danced as she tossed back her head. "Poor Mama, I must have done so many dreadful things."

"Well, perhaps a bit more than your share," Anabelle suggested kindly. "But now you're all grown up, so difficult for a mother to accept. Your job, Gwen, you do enjoy it?"

Gwen's automatic agreement faltered on her lips. Enjoy, she thought. I wonder if I do. "Strange," she said aloud, "I'm not at all certain." She gave her mother a puzzled smile. "But I need it, not just for the money, I need the responsibility it imposes, I need to be involved."

"Yes, you always did . . . My, the *beignets* look marvelous."

"They are," Gwen assured her mother as she rested her elbows on the table and her chin on her open palms. "I felt obligated to try one before I offered them to you."

"See, I've always told you you were sensible," Anabelle said with a smile before she tasted one of the oddly shaped doughnuts. "Delicious," she proclaimed. "Tillie doesn't make them any better, though that had best be our secret."

Gwen allowed time to pass with easy conversation until she poured the second cup of chocolate. "Mama," she began cautiously, "how long does Luke Powers plan to stay here?"

The lifting of Anabelle's delicate brows indicated her surprise. "Stay?" she repeated as she dusted powdered sugar from her fingers. "Why, I don't know precisely, Gwen. It depends, I should say, on the stage of his book. I know he plans to finish the first draft before he goes back to California."

"I suppose," Gwen said casually as she stirred her chocolate, "he'll have no reason to come back here after that."

"Oh, I imagine he'll be back." Anabelle smiled into her daughter's eyes. "Luke is very fond of this part of the country. I wish I could tell you what his coming here has meant to me." Dreamily, she stared out into the hazy sky. Gwen felt a stab of alarm. "He's given me so much. I'd like you to spend some time with him, dear, and get to know him."

Gwen's teeth dug into the tender inside of her lip. For the moment, she felt completely at a loss. She raged in silence while Anabelle smiled secretly at rain clouds. Despicable man. How can he do this to her? Gwen glanced down into the dregs of her cup and felt a weight descend on her heart. And what is he doing to me? No matter how she tried to ignore it, Gwen could still feel the warmth of his lips on hers. The feeling clung, taunting and enticing. She was teased by a feeling totally foreign to her, a longing she could neither identify nor understand. Briskly, she shook her head to clear her thoughts. Luke Powers was only a problem while he was in Louisiana. The aim was to get him back to the West Coast and to discourage him from coming back.

"Gwen?"

"Hmm? Oh, yes, Mama." Blinking away the confused images and thoughts of Luke, Gwen met Anabelle's curious look.

"I said blueberry pie would be nice with supper. Luke's very fond of it. I thought perhaps you'd like to pick some berries for Tillie."

Gwen pondered briefly on the attractive prospect

of sprinkling arsenic over Luke's portion, then rejected the idea. "I'd love to," she murmured.

The air was thick with moisture when, armed with a large bucket, Gwen went in search of blueberries. With a quick glance and shrug at the cloudy sky, she opted to risk the chance of rain. She would use her berry-picking time to devise a plan to send Luke Powers westward. Swinging the bucket, she moved across the trim lawn and into the dim, sheltering trees that formed a border between her home and the bayou. Here was a different world from her mother's gentle, tidy, well-kept home. This was a primitive world with ageless secrets and endless demands. It had been Gwen's refuge as a child, her personal island. Although she remembered each detail perfectly, she stood and drank in its beauty anew.

There was a mist over the sluggish stream. Dull and brown, cattails peeked through the surface in search of the hidden sun. Here and there, cypress stumps rose above the surface. The stream itself moved in a narrow path, then curved out of sight. Gwen remembered how it twisted and snaked and widened. Over the straight, slender path, trees arched tunnellike, garnished with moss. The water was silent, but Gwen could hear the birds and an occasional plop of a frog. She knew the serenity was a surface thing. Beneath the calm was a passion and violence and wild, surging life. It called to her as it always had.

With confidence, she moved along the riverbank and searched out the plump wild berries. Silence and the simplicity of her task were soothing. Years slipped away, and she was a teenager again, a girl whose most precious fantasy was to be a part of a big city. She had dreamed in the sheltered bayou of the excitement, the mysteries of city life, the challenges of carving out her own path. Hard work, determination and a quick mind had hurried her along that path. She had earned a responsible job, established an interesting circle of friends and acquired just lately a nagging sense of dissatisfaction.

Overwork, Gwen self-diagnosed, and popped a berry into her mouth. Its juice was sweet and full of memories. And, of course, there's Michael. With a frown, Gwen dropped a handful of berries into the bucket. Even though it was my idea to end things between us, I could be suffering from the backlash of a terminated romance. And those things he said . . . Her frown deepened, and unconsciously she began to nibble on berries. That I was cold and unresponsive and immature . . . I must not have loved him. Sighing, Gwen picked more berries and ate them, one by one. If I had loved him, I'd have wanted him to make love to me.

I'm not cold, she thought. I'm not unresponsive. Look at the way I responded to Luke! She froze with a berry halfway to her mouth. Her cheeks filled with color. That was different, she assured herself quickly. Entirely different. She popped the berry into her mouth. That was simply physical, it had nothing to do with emotion. Chemistry, that's all. Why, it's practically scientific.

She speculated on the possibility of seducing Luke. She could flirt and tease and drive him to the point of distraction, make him fall in love with her and then cast him off when all danger to Anabelle was past. It can't be too difficult, she decided. I've seen lots of the models twist men around their fingers. She looked down at her own and noted they were stained with berry juice.

"Looks as though you've just been booked by the FBI."

Whirling, Gwen stared at Luke as he leaned back comfortably against a thick cypress. Again he wore jeans and a T-shirt, both faded and well worn. His eyes seemed to take their color from the sky and were more gray now than blue. Gwen's heart hammered at the base of her throat.

"Must you continually sneak up on me?" she snapped. Annoyed with the immediate response of her body to his presence, she spoke heatedly. "You have the most annoying habit of being where you're not wanted."

"Did you know you become more the Southern belle when you're in a temper?" Luke asked with an easy, unperturbed smile. "Your vowels flow quite beautifully."

Gwen's breath came out in a frustrated huff. "What do you want?" she demanded.

"To help you pick berries. Though it seems you're doing more eating than picking."

It trembled on her tongue to tell him that she didn't need or want his help. Abruptly, she remembered her resolve to wind him around her berry-stained finger. Carefully she smoothed the frown from between her brows and coaxed her mouth into a charming smile. "How sweet of you."

Luke raised a quizzical eyebrow at her change of tone. "I'm notoriously sweet," he said dryly. "Didn't you know?"

"We don't know each other well, do we?" Gwen smiled and held out the bucket. "At least, not yet."

Slowly, Luke straightened from his stance and moved to join her. He accepted the bucket while keeping his eyes fastened on hers. Determinedly, Gwen kept her own level and unconcerned. She found it difficult to breathe with him so close. "How is your book going?" she asked, hoping to divert him while she regained control of her respiratory system.

"Well enough." He watched as she began to tug berries off the bush again.

"I'm sure it must be fascinating." Gwen slid her eyes up to his in a manner she hoped was provocative and exciting. "I hope you won't think me a bore if I confess I'm quite a fan of yours. I have all your books." This part was easier because it was true.

"It's never a bore to know one's work is appreciated."

Emboldened, Gwen laid her hand on his on the

handle of the bucket. Something flashed in his eyes, and her courage fled. Quickly slipping the bucket from his hold, she began to pick berries with renewed interest while cursing her lack of bravery.

"How do you like living in New York?" Luke asked as he began to add to the gradually filling bucket.

"New York?" Gwen cleared her head with a quick mental shake. Resolutely, she picked up the strings of her plan again. "It's very exciting—such a sensual city, don't you think?" Gwen lifted a berry to Luke's lips. She hoped her smile was invitingly alluring, and wished she had thought to practice in a mirror.

Luke opened his mouth to accept her offering. His tongue whispered along the tips of her fingers. Gwen felt them tremble. It took every ounce of willpower not to snatch her hand away. "Do you—do you like New York?" Her voice was curiously husky as she began to pull berries again. The tone was uncontrived and by far the most enticing of her tactics.

"Sometimes," Luke answered, then brushed the hair away from her neck.

Moistening her lips, Gwen inched away. "I suppose you live in Louisiana."

"No, I have a place near Carmel, at the beach. What marvellously soft hair you have," he murmured, running his hand through it.

"The beach," Gwen repeated, swallowing. "It must be wonderful. I've—I've never seen the Pacific."

"It can be very wild, very dangerous," Luke said softly before his lips brushed the curve of Gwen's neck.

There was a small, strangled sound from Gwen's throat. She moved farther away and fought to keep up a casual front. "I've seen pictures, of course, and movies, but I expect it's quite different to actually see it. I'm sure it's a wonderful place to write."

"Among other things." From behind, Luke dropped his hands to her hips as he caught the lobe of her ear between his teeth. For a moment, Gwen could only lean back against him. Abruptly she stiffened, straightened, and put a few precious inches between them.

"You know," she began, completely abandoning her plans to seduce him, "I believe we have enough." As she turned around, her breasts brushed against his chest. She began to back up, stammering. "Tillie won't want to make more than two—two pies, and there's plenty here for that." Her eyes were wide and terrified.

Luke moved forward. "Then we won't have to waste any more time picking berries, will we?" The insinuation was clear.

"No, well . . ." Her eyes clung helplessly to his as she continued to back up. "Well, I'll just take these in to Tillie. She'll be waiting."

He was still advancing, slowly. Just as Gwen decided to abandon her dignity and run, she stepped backward into empty space. With a sharp cry, she made a desperate grab for Luke's hand. He plucked the bucket from her as she tumbled into the stream.

"Wouldn't want to lose the berries," he explained as Gwen surfaced, coughing and sputtering. "How's the water?"

"Oh!" After beating the surface of the water violently with her fists, Gwen struggled to her feet. "You did that on purpose!" Her hair was plastered to her face, and impatiently she pushed it out of her eyes.

"Did what?" Luke grinned, appreciating the way her clothes clung to her curves.

"Pushed me in." She took two sloshing steps toward the bank.

"My dear Gwenivere," Luke said in a reasonable tone. "I never laid a hand on you."

"Exactly." She kicked at the water in fury. "It's precisely the same thing."

"I suppose it might be from your point of view," he agreed. "But then, you were getting in over your head in any case. Consider the dunking the lesser of two evils. By the way, you have a lily pad on your . . ." His pause for the sake of delicacy was belied by the gleam in his eyes.

Flushing with embarrassment and fury, Gwen swiped a hand across her bottom. "As I said before, you are no gentleman."

Luke roared with laughter. "Why, Miss Gwenivere, ma'am, your opinion devastates me." His drawl was mocking, his bow low.

"At least," she began with a regal sniff, "you could help me out of this mess."

"Of course." With a show of gallantry, Luke set down the bucket and reached for Gwen's hand. Her wet shoes slid on the slippery bank. To help balance her, he offered his other hand. Just as she reached the top edge, Gwen threw all her weight backward, tumbling them both into the water. This time, Gwen surfaced and convulsed with laughter.

As she stood, she watched him rise from the water and free his eyes of wet hair with a jerk of his head. Laughter blocked her speech. In silence, Luke watched as the sounds of her uninhibited mirth filled the air.

"How's the water?" she managed to get out before dissolving into fresh peals of laughter. Though she covered her mouth with both hands, it continued to escape and dance on the air. A quick hoot of laughter emerged as she saw his eyes narrow. He took a step toward her, and she began a strategic retreat. She moved with more speed than grace through the water, kicking it high. Giggles caused her to stumble twice. She scrambled up the slope but before she could rise to her feet, Luke caught her ankle. Pulling himself up onto the grass, he pinned Gwen beneath him.

Breathless, Gwen could still not stop laughing. Water dripped from Luke's hair onto her face, and she shook her head as it tickled her skin. A smile lurked in Luke's eyes as he looked down on her.

"I should have known better, I suppose," he commented. "But you have such an innocent face."

"You don't." Gwen took deep gulps of air in a fruitless effort to control her giggles. "Yours isn't innocent at all."

"Thank you."

Abruptly, the heavens opened and rain fell, warm and wild. "Oh!" Gwen began to push against him. "It's raining."

"So it is," Luke agreed, ignoring her squirms. "We might get wet."

The absurdity of his statement struck her suddenly. After staring up at him a moment, Gwen began to laugh again. It was a young sound, appealing and free. Gradually, Luke's expression sobered. In his eyes appeared a desire so clear, so unmistakable, that Gwen's breath caught in her throat. She opened her mouth to speak, but no words came.

"My God," he murmured. "You are exquisite."

His mouth took hers with a raw, desperate hunger. Her mouth was as avid as his, her blood as urgent. Their wet clothing proved no barrier as their bodies fused together in ageless intimacy. His caress was rough, and she reveled in the exquisite pain. The soft moan might have come from either of them. He savaged the vulnerable curve of her neck, tasting, arousing, demanding. His quick, desperate loving took her beyond the edge of reason and into ecstasy.

She felt no fear, only excitement. Here was a passion that sought and found her hidden fires and set them leaping. Rain poured over them unfelt, thunder bellowed unheard. His hands were possessive as they moved over her. Through the clinging dampness of her blouse, his mouth found the tip of her breast. She trembled, murmuring his name as he explored the slender smoothness of her thigh. She wanted him as she had never wanted anyone before.

"Luke?" His name was half question, half invitation.

Lightning flashed and illuminated the bayou. Just as swiftly they were plunged again into gloom.

"We'd better get back," Luke said abruptly, rising. "Your mother will be worried."

Gwen shut her eyes on a sudden stab of hurt. Hurriedly, she scrambled to her feet, avoiding Luke's outstretched hand. She swayed under a dizzying onslaught of emotions. "Gwen," Luke said, and took a step toward her.

"No." Her voice shook with the remnants of passion and the beginning of tears. Her eyes as they clung to his were young and devastated. "I must be losing my mind. You had no right," she told him shakily, "you had no right."

"To what?" he demanded roughly and grasped her shoulders. "To begin to make love with you or to stop?" Anger crackled in his voice.

"I wish I'd never seen you! I wish you'd never touched me."

"Oh, yes." Temper whipped through Luke's voice as he pulled her close to him again. "I can only say I wish precisely the same, but it's too late now, isn't it?" She had never seen his eyes so lit with fury. "Neither of us seems pleased with what's been started, but perhaps we should finish it." Rain swept around them, slicing through the trees and battering the ground. For a moment, Gwen knew terror. He could take her, she knew, even if she fought him. But worse, she knew he would need no force, no superior strength, after the first touch. Abruptly, he released her and stepped away. "Unless that's what you want," he said softly, "you'd best get out of here."

This time Gwen took his advice. Sobbing convulsively, she darted away among the moss-draped trees. Her one thought . . . to reach the safety of home.

CHAPTER 5

The rain had awakened the garden. Twenty-four hours later it was still vibrant. Rose petals dried lazily in the sun while dew clung tenaciously to the undersides of leaves. Without enthusiasm, Gwen moved from bush to bush, selecting firm young blooms. Since the day before, she had avoided Luke Powers. With a determination born of desperation, she had clung to her mother's company, using Anabelle as both a defense and an offense. If, she had decided, *she* was always with Anabelle, Luke could not be. Nor could he take another opportunity to confuse and humiliate Gwen herself.

The basket on her arm was half filled with flowers, but she felt no pleasure in their colors and scents. Something was happening to her—she knew it, felt it, but could not define it. More and more often, she caught her thoughts drifting away from whatever task she was performing. It is, she reflected as she snipped a slender, thorny rose stem with Anabelle's garden shears, as if even my thoughts aren't wholly mine any longer.

When she considered her behavior over the past two days, Gwen was astounded. She had come to warn her mother about her relationship with Luke Powers and instead had found herself responding to him as she had never responded to Michael or any other man. But then, she admitted ruefully, she had never come into contact with a man like Luke Powers. There was a basically sensual aura about him despite his outward calm. She felt that he, like the bayou, hid much below the surface. Gwen was forced to admit that she had no guidelines for dealing with such a man. Worse, he had kindled in her a hitherto-buried part of her nature.

She had always thought her life and her needs simple. But suddenly, the quiet dreams inside her had risen to the surface. She was no longer the uncomplicated, controlled woman she had thought herself to be. The somewhat volatile temper she possessed had always been manageable, but in just two days the reins of restraint had slipped through her fingers.

His fault, Gwen grumbled to herself as she glared at a pale pink peony. He shouldn't be here—he should be in his beach house in California. If he were in California, perhaps battling an earthquake or hurricane, I'd be having a nice, uncomplicated visit with Mama. Instead he's here, insinuating himself into my life and making me feel . . . Gwen paused a moment and bit her lip. How does he make me feel? she thought.

With a sigh, she let her gaze wander over the variety of colors and hues in the garden. *I'm not sure how he makes me feel. He frightens me.* The knowledge came to her swiftly, and her eyes reflected her surprise. *Yes, he frightens me, though I'm not altogether sure why. It's not as if I thought he'd hurt me physically, he's not that sort of man, but still . . .* Shaking her head, Gwen moved slowly down the walkway, digesting the new thought. *He's a man who controls people and situations so naturally you're hardly aware you've been controlled.*

Unconsciously, Gwen lifted her finger and ran it along her bottom lip. Vividly she remembered the feel of his mouth on hers. Its touch had ranged from gentle and coaxing to urgent and demanding, but the power over her had been the same. It was true—there was something exhilarating about fencing with him, like standing on the bow of a ship in a storm. But no matter how adventurous she might be, Gwen was forced to concede that there was one level on which she could not win. When she was in his arms, it was not surrender she felt, but passion for passion, need for need. Discovering this new facet of herself was perhaps the most disturbing knowledge of all.

I won't give up. Gwen lifted her chin and straightened her shoulders. *I won't let him intimidate me or dominate my thoughts any longer.* Her eyes glittered with challenge. *Luke Powers won't control me. He'll find out that Gwen Lacrosse is perfectly capable of taking care of herself* and *her mother.*

"Just a minute longer." Bradley Stapleton held up

a pencil briefly, then continued to scrawl with it on an artist's pad. He sat crosslegged in the middle of the walkway, his feet sandaled, wearing paint-spattered carpenter's pants, a checked sport shirt unbuttoned over his thin chest and a beige fisherman's cap on his head. Surprised and intrigued, Gwen stopped in her tracks.

"Wonderful!" With surprising agility, Bradley unfolded himself and rose. His eyes smiled with genuine pleasure as he strolled over to Gwen. "I knew you'd be a good subject, but I didn't dare hope you'd be spectacular. Just look at this range of emotions!" he commanded as he flipped back several pages in his pad.

Gwen's initial amusement altered to astonishment. That the pencil sketches were exceptionally good was obvious, but it was not his talent as much as the content of the sketches that surprised her. She saw a woman with loose, curling hair and a coltish slenderness. There was a vulnerability she had never perceived in herself. As Gwen turned the pages, she saw herself dreaming, pouting, thinking and glaring. There was something disturbing about seeing her feelings of the past half hour so clearly defined. She lifted her eyes to the artist.

"They're fabulous," she told him. Bradley's face crinkled into a grin. "Bradley," she searched for the right words. "Am I really . . . so, well . . . artless as it seems here?" She looked back down at the sketches with a mixture of conflicting emotions. "What I mean is, are my thoughts, my feelings, so blatantly obvious? Am I so transparent?"

"That's precisely what makes you such a good model," Bradley said. "Your face is so expressive."

"But—" With a gesture of frustration, Gwen ran a hand through her hair. "Do they always show? Are they always there for people to examine? I feel defenseless and, well, naked somehow."

Bradley gave her a sympathetic smile and patted her cheek with his long, bony fingers. "You have an honest face, Gwen, but if it worries you, remember that most people don't see past the shape of a nose or the color of eyes. People are usually too busy with their own thoughts to notice someone else's."

"Yet you certainly did," Gwen replied, but she felt more comfortable.

"It's my business."

"Yes." With a smile, Gwen began flipping through the pages again. "You're very good . . ." She stopped, speechless as the pad fell open to a sketch of Luke.

It was a simple sketch of him sitting on the rail of the veranda. He was dressed casually, and his hair was tousled, as though he had been working. Bradley had captured the strength and intelligence in his face, as well as the sensual quality she had not expected another man to notice. But it was Luke's eyes, which seemed to lock on to hers, that impressed her. The artist had caught the strange melding of serenity and power that she had felt in them. Gwen was conscious of an odd quickening of her breath. Irresistibly, she was drawn to the picture just as she was drawn to the man.

"I'm rather pleased with it." Gwen heard Bradley's

voice and realized with a jolt that he had been speaking for several seconds.

"It's very good," she murmured. "You understand him." She was unaware of the wistfulness and touch of envy in her voice.

After a brief, speculative glance at her lowered head, Bradley nodded. "To an extent, I suppose. I understand he's a complicated man. In some ways, he's much like you."

"Me?" Genuinely shocked, Gwen lifted her eyes.

"You're both capable of a wide range of emotions. Not everyone is, you know. The main difference is, he channels his, while yours are fully expressed. Will you sit for me?"

"What?" Gwen tried to focus on him again. The question was out of context with the rest of his statement. She shook her head to clear it of the disturbing thoughts his words had aroused in her.

"Will you sit for me?" Bradley repeated patiently. "I very much want to do you in oils."

"Yes, of course." She shrugged and conjured up a smile to dispel her own mood. "It sounds like fun."

"You won't think so after a couple of hours of holding a pose," Bradley promised good-naturedly. "Come on, we'll get started now, before you change your mind." Taking her hand, he pulled her up the walkway.

Several hours later, Gwen clearly understood the truth of Bradley's statement. Posing for a temperamental artist, she discovered, was both exhausting and demanding. Her face had been sketched from a dozen angles while she stood or sat or twisted in accordance with his commands. She began to feel more sympathy for the models at *Style*.

She had been amused at first when Bradley rooted through her wardrobe in search of attire suitable to sitting for the portrait. When he selected a thin white silk robe, she had taken what she considered a firm stand against his choice. He ignored her objections and, to her amazement, Gwen found herself doing exactly as he instructed.

Now, tired and alone, Gwen stretched out on her bed and relaxed her muscles. A smile lurked at the corners of her mouth as she recalled how Bradley had gently steamrolled her. Any embarrassment she had felt about wearing only the robe while he studied her or moved her this way and that had been swiftly eradicated. She might as easily have been an interesting tree or a fruit bowl. He had not been interested in the body beneath the robe but in the way the material draped.

I don't have to worry about fending off a passionate attack, Gwen reflected as she shut her eyes, only about stiffening joints. With a deep sigh, she snuggled into the pillow.

Her dreams were confused. She dreamed she was roaming through the bayou picking roses and blueberries. As she passed through a clearing, she saw Luke chopping down a thick, heavy tree. The sound of the ax was like thunder. The tree fell soundlessly at her feet. As Luke watched, she walked to him and melted into his arms. For an instant she felt violent joy, then, just as suddenly, she found herself hurled into the cool stream.

From behind a curtain of water, Gwen saw Anabelle, a gentle smile on her lips as she offered her hand to Luke. Gwen struggled for the surface but found it just beyond her reach. Abruptly she was standing on the bank with Bradley sitting at her feet sketching. Ax in hand, Luke approached her, but Gwen found her arms and legs had turned to stone. As he walked, he began to change, his features dissolving, his clothing altering.

It was Michael who came to her now, a practical briefcase taking the place of the ax. He shook his head at her stone limbs and reminded her in his precise voice that he had told her she was cold. Gwen tried to shake her head in denial, but her neck had turned to stone, as well. When Michael took her by the shoulders and prepared to carry her away, she could only make a small sound of protest. From a distance, she heard Luke call her name. Michael dropped her, and as her stone limbs shattered, she awoke. Dazed, Gwen stared into blue-gray eyes. "Luke," she murmured, "I'm not cold."

"No." He brushed the hair from her cheek, then let his palm linger. "You're certainly not."

"Kiss me again, I don't want to turn to stone." She made the request petulantly. Amusement touched Luke's mouth as he lowered it to hers.

"Of course not, who could blame you?"

Sighing, Gwen locked her arms around his neck and enjoyed the warm gentleness of the kiss. Her limbs grew warm and fluid, her lips parted and begged for more. The kiss deepened until dream and reality mixed. A sharp stab of desire brought Gwen crashing through the barriers of lingering sleep. She managed a muffled protest against his mouth as she struggled for release. Luke did not immediately set her free but allowed his lips to linger on hers until he had had his fill. Even then, his face remained dangerously close. His mouth was only a sigh away.

"That must've been some dream," he murmured. With easy intimacy, he rubbed his nose against hers. "Women are so irresistibly soft and warm when they've been sleeping."

Cheeks flaming, Gwen managed to struggle up to a sitting position. "You have a nerve," she flared. "What do you mean by coming into my bedroom and molesting me?"

"Take a guess," he invited with a wolfish grin. Her color grew yet deeper as she gripped the V of her robe. "Relax," Luke continued. "I didn't come to steal your virtue, I came to wake you for dinner." He ran a fingertip along her jawline. "The rest was your idea."

Indignation stiffened Gwen's spine but muddled her speech. "You—you . . . I was asleep, and you took advantage . . ."

"I certainly did," Luke agreed, then pulled her close for a hard, brief kiss. "And we both enjoyed every second of it." He rose gracefully. "White suits you," he commented, his gaze wandering over the soft folds of the robe, "but you might want to change into something a bit less informal for dinner, unless your object is to drive Bradley into a frenzy of desire."

Gwen rose, wrapping the robe more tightly about

her. "Don't worry about Bradley," she said icily. "He spent all afternoon sketching me in this robe."

The humor disappeared so swiftly from Luke's face, Gwen wondered if she had imagined its existence. His mouth was grim as he stepped toward her. "What?" The one word vibrated in the room.

"You heard me. I've agreed to let Bradley paint me."

"In that?" Luke's eyes dropped the length of the robe, then returned to her face.

"Yes, what of it?" Gwen tossed her head and turned to walk away from him. The silk of her robe floated around her legs and clung to her hips as she moved. When she reached the window, she turned and leaned back against the sill. Her stance was at once insolent and sensual. "What business is it of yours?"

"Don't play games unless you're prepared to lose," Luke warned softly.

"You're insufferable." The brown of her eyes grew molten.

"And you're a spoiled child."

"I'm not a child," Gwen retorted. "I make my own decisions. If I want to pose for Bradley in this robe or in a suit of armor or in a pair of diamond earrings and nothing else, that's nothing to do with you."

"I'd consider the diamond earrings carefully, Gwen." The soft tone of Luke's voice betrayed his rising temper. "If you try it, I'd have to break all of Bradley's fingers."

His calm promise of violence added fuel to Gwen's fire. "If that isn't typical male stupidity! If something doesn't work, kick it or swear at it! I thought you were more intelligent."

"Did you?" A glimmer of amusement returned to Luke's eyes. Reaching out, he gave her hair a sharp tug. "Too bad you were wrong."

"Men!" she expostulated, lifting her palms and eyes to the ceiling. "You're all the same."

"You speak, of course, from vast personal experience."

The sarcasm in his voice did not escape Gwen. "You're all arrogant, superior, selfish—"

"Beasts?" Luke suggested amiably.

"That'll do," she agreed with a nod.

"Glad to help." Luke sat back on the edge of the bed and watched her. The flickering lights of the setting sun accentuated the hollows and shadows of her face.

"You always think you know best and that women are too muddleheaded to decide things for themselves. All you do is give orders, orders, orders, and when you don't get your own way, you shout or sulk or, worse, patronize. I hate, loathe and despise being patronized!" Balling her hands into fists, Gwen thrust them into the pockets of her robe. "I don't like being told I'm cute in a tone of voice that means I'm stupid. I don't like being patted on the head like a puppy who can't learn to fetch. Then, after you've finished insulting my intelligence, you want to breathe all over me. Of course, I should be grateful for the attention because I'm such a sweet little simpleton." Unable to prevent herself any longer, Gwen gave the bedpost a hard slap. "I am not," she began, and her voice was low with fury, "I am *not* cold and unresponsive and sexually immature."

"Good Lord, child." Gwen, jolted by Luke's voice, blinked as she refocused on him. "What idiot ever told you that you were?"

Gwen stared at Luke in frozen silence.

"Your opinion of men obviously comes from the same source," he continued. "Your Michael must have been really convincing." Embarrassed, Gwen shrugged and turned back to the window. "Were you in love with him?"

The question caught her so off balance that she answered automatically. "No, but I thought I was, so it amounts to the same thing, I imagine."

"Bounced around a bit, were you?" His tone was surprisingly gentle as were the hands that descended to her shoulders.

"Oh, please." Quickly, Gwen moved away as she felt a strange, sweet ache. "Don't be kind to me. I can't fight you if you're kind."

"Is that what you want to do?" Luke took her shoulders firmly now and turned her around to face him. "Do you want to fight?" His eyes dropped to her lips. Gwen began to tremble.

"I think it's better if we do." Her voice was suddenly breathless. "I think fighting with you is safer."

"Safer than what?" he inquired. He smiled, a quick, flashing movement that was both charming and seductive. The room grew dim in the dusk, silhouetting them in the magic light of a dying day. "You are beautiful," he murmured, sliding his hand along the slope of her shoulders until his fingers traced her throat.

Mesmerized, Gwen stared up at him. "No, I—I'm not. My mouth's too wide, and my chin's pointed."

"Of course," Luke agreed as he drew her closer. "I see it now, you're quite an ugly little thing. It's a pity to waste velvet eyes and silken skin on such an unfortunate-looking creature."

"Please." Gwen turned her head, and his mouth brushed her cheek rather than her lips. "Don't kiss me. It confuses me—I don't know what to do."

"On the contrary, you seem to know precisely what to do."

"Luke, please." She caught her breath. "Please, when you kiss me, I forget everything, and I only want you to kiss me again."

"I'll be happy to do so."

"No, don't." Gwen pushed away and looked at him with huge, pleading eyes. "I'm frightened."

He studied her with quiet intensity. He watched her lip tremble, her teeth digging into it to halt the movement. The pulse in her neck throbbed under his palm. Letting out a long breath, he stepped back and slipped his hands into his pockets. His look was thoughtful. "I wonder, if I make love to you, would you lose that appealing air of innocence?"

"I'm not going to let you make love to me." Even to herself, Gwen's voice sounded shaky and unsure.

"Gwen, you're much too honest to make a statement like that, let alone believe it yourself." Luke turned and walked to the door. "I'll tell Anabelle you'll be down in a few minutes."

He closed the door behind him, and Gwen was left alone with her thoughts in the darkening room.

CHAPTER 6

Gwen endured Bradley's sketching for nearly an hour. His eyes were much sharper in his plain, harmless face than she had originally thought. And, she had discovered, he was a quiet tyrant. Once she had agreed to pose for him, he had taken over with mild but inescapable efficiency. He placed her on a white wrought-iron chair in the heart of the garden.

The morning was heavy and warm, with a hint of rain hovering despite the sunshine. A dragonfly darted past, zooming over a rosebush to her right. Gwen turned her head to watch its flight.

"Don't do that!" Bradley's beautifully modulated voice made Gwen guiltily jerk her head back. "I'm only sketching your face today," he reminded her. She murmured something unintelligible that had him smiling. "Now I understand why you work behind the scenes at *Style* and not in front of the camera." His pencil paused in midair. "You've never learned how to sit still!"

"I always feel as though I should be doing something," Gwen admitted. "How does anyone ever just sit like this? I had no idea how difficult it was."

"Where's your Southern languor?" Bradley asked, sketching in a stray wisp of hair. She would sit more quietly if he kept up a conversation, he decided, even though he did not particularly care for splitting his concentration between sketching and talking.

"Oh, I don't think I ever had it," Gwen told him. She brought up her foot to rest on the chair and laced her hands around her knee. Enjoying the heady perfumes of the garden, she took a deep breath. "And living in New York has made it worse. Although . . ." She paused, looking around her again, though this time remembering to move only her eyes. "There is something peaceful here, isn't there? I'm discovering how much I've missed that."

"Is your work very demanding?" Bradley asked, perfecting the line of her chin with a dash of his pencil.

"Hmm." Gwen shrugged and longed to take a good stretch. "There's always some deadline that no one could possibly meet that, of course, we meet. Then there are the models and photographers who need their artistic egos soothed—"

"Are you good at soothing artistic egos?" Bradley narrowed his eyes to find the perspective.

"Surprisingly, yes." She smiled at him. "And I like the challenge of meeting deadlines."

"I've never been good with deadlines," he murmured. "Move your chin, so." He gestured with a fingertip, and Gwen obeyed.

"No, some people aren't, but I have to be. When you're a monthly publication, you have no choice."

For a moment, Gwen fell silent, listening to the hum of bees around the azalea bushes in back of her. Somewhere near the house, a bird sent up a sudden, jubilant song. "Where are you from, Bradley?" she asked at length, turning her eyes back to him. He was a strange man, she thought, with his gangly body and wise eyes.

"Boston." His eyes went briefly to her, then back to his sketch pad. "Turn your head to the right a bit . . . There, good."

"Boston. I should have guessed. Your voice is very . . . elegant." Bradley chuckled. "How did you decide to become an artist?"

"It's my favorite mode of communication. I've always loved sketching. In school my teachers had to confiscate my sketchbooks. And some people are very impressed when they hear you're an artist."

Gwen laughed. "The last's not a real reason."

"Don't be too sure," Bradley murmured, involved with the curve of her cheek. "I enjoy flattery. Not everyone is as self-sufficient as you."

Forgetting his instructions, Gwen turned to him again. "Is that the way you see me?"

"Sometimes." He lifted a brow and motioned for her to turn away again. For a moment he studied her profile before beginning to draw again. "To be an artist, a good one, without the driving passion to be a great one, suits me perfectly." He smiled at her thoughtful expression. "It wouldn't suit you at all. You haven't the patience for it."

Gwen thought of the brisk, no-nonsense Gwen Lacrosse of *Style* magazine—a practical, efficient woman who knew her job and did it well, a woman who knew how to handle details and people, who was good at facts and figures. And yet . . . there was another Gwen Lacrosse who loved old, scented gardens and watched weepy movies on television, who hopped into hansom cabs in the rain. Michael had been attracted to the first Gwen but despaired of the second. She sighed. Perhaps she had never understood the mixture herself. She had not even questioned it. At least not until she had met Luke Powers.

Luke Powers. She didn't want to think about him. Things were not working out quite the way she had planned in that department. Worse yet, she wasn't at all sure they ever would.

Gwen tilted her head up to the sky. Bradley opened his mouth to remonstrate, then finding a new angle to his liking, continued sketching. The sun lit reddish sparks in her hair. She noticed that the clouds were rolling in from the west. A storm was probably brewing, she thought. It was still far off, hovering, taking its time. She had a feeling that it would strike when least expected. Though the day appeared to be sunny and pleasant, she felt the passion there, just below the surface. The air throbbed with it. In spite of the heat,

Gwen shivered involuntarily. Irresistibly, her eyes were drawn to the house and up.

Luke was watching her from the window of his room. She wondered how long he had been there, looking down with that quiet, direct expression that she had come to expect from him. His eyes never wavered as hers met them.

He stared without apology, without embarrassment. For the moment, Gwen found herself compelled to stare back. Even with the distance between them, she could feel the intrusion of his gaze. She stiffened against it.

As if sensing her response, Luke smiled . . . slowly, arrogantly, never shifting his eyes from hers. Gwen read the challenge in them. She tossed her head before turning away.

Bradley cocked a brow at Gwen's scowling face. "It appears," he said mildly, "that we're done for the day." He rose from his perch on a stone, unexpectedly graceful. "Tomorrow morning, I want you in the robe. I've a pretty good idea on the pose I want. I'm going in to see if I can charm Tillie out of a piece of that chocolate cake. Want some?"

Gwen smiled and shook her head. "No, it's a bit close to lunch for me. I think I'll give Mama a hand and do some weeding." She glanced down at the petunia bed. "She seems to be neglecting it a bit."

"Busy lady," Bradley said and, sticking the pencil behind his ear, sauntered down the path.

Busy lady? Gwen frowned after him. Her mother did not seem preoccupied . . . but *what* precisely was she doing? Perhaps it was just her way of intimating to Gwen that she, too, had a life, just as important as Gwen's big-city profession. Moving over to the petunia bed, Gwen knelt down and began to tug at stray weeds.

Anabelle had developed a habit of disappearing from time to time—that was something new. Unable to do otherwise, she glanced up at Luke's window again. He was gone. With a scowl, she went back to her weeding.

If only he would leave, she thought, everything would be fine. Her mother was a soft, gentle creature who trusted everyone. She simply had no defenses against a man like Luke Powers. And you do? she mocked herself. Swearing, Gwen tugged and unearthed a hapless petunia.

"Oh!" She stared down at the colorful blossom, foolishly guilty. A shadow fell across her, and she stiffened.

"Something upsetting you?" Luke asked. He crouched down beside her; taking the blossom from her hand, he tucked it behind her ear. Gwen remembered the rose and blushed before she could turn her face away.

"Go away. I'm busy," she said.

"I'm not." His voice was carelessly friendly. "I'll help."

"Don't you have work to do?" She shot him a scornful glance before ripping savagely at another weed.

"Not at the moment." Luke's tone was mild as he

felt his way among the flowers. His fingers were surprisingly deft. "The advantage of being self-employed is that you make your own hours—at least most of the time."

"Most of the time?" Gwen queried, curiously overcoming her dislike for this annoying man.

"When it works, you're chained to the typewriter, and that's that."

"Strange," Gwen mused aloud, forgetting to ignore him. "I can't picture you chained to anything. You seem so free. But it must be difficult putting all those words on paper, making the people inside your head walk and talk and think. Why did you decide to become a writer?"

"Because I have an affection for words," he said. "And because those people in my head are always scrambling to get out. Now I've answered your question frankly." Luke turned to her as he twirled a blade of grass between his fingers. "It's my turn to ask one. What were you thinking of when you were watching the sky?"

Gwen frowned. She wasn't at all sure she wanted to share her private thoughts with Luke Powers. "That we're in for some rain," she compromised. "Must you watch me that way?"

"Yes."

"You're impossible," she told him crossly.

"You're beautiful." His look was suddenly intense, shooting a quiver up her spine. He cupped her chin before she could turn away. "With the sunlight on your hair and your eyes misty, you were all I have ever dreamed of. I wanted you." His mouth drew closer to hers. His breath fluttered over her skin.

"Don't!" Gwen started to back away, but his fingers on her chin held her steady.

"Not so fast," Luke said softly.

His kiss was surprisingly gentle, brushing her mouth like a butterfly's wing. Instinctively, she parted her lips to receive his probing tongue. With a sigh, she succumbed to the mood of the waiting garden. Her passion had lain sleeping, like the threatened storm behind the layer of soft clouds. She trembled with desire as his fingers carefully traced the planes of her face. They caressed her cheekbones, the line of her jaw, the thick tousle of her hair at her temples, before he kissed her again. His tongue teased and tasted with only the slightest pressure. She gripped his shirt front tightly and moaned his name. Her skin was alive with him. Wanting, needing, she twined her arms around his neck and pulled him against her. Her mouth was avid, seeking.

For one blazing moment, the flame rose and consumed them both, as they embraced in the fragrant morning heat. Then he had drawn her away, and Gwen was staring up at him, trying to catch her breath.

"No." She shook her head, pressing her hands to her temples as she waited for her thoughts to steady. "No." Before she could turn and flee, Luke had sprung up, grabbing her wrist.

"No what?" His voice was deeper, but still calm.

"This isn't right." The words tumbled out of her as she tried to find reason. "Let me go."

"In a minute." Luke kept his hand on her wrist and stepped toward her. A sweeping gaze took in her frantic color and widened eyes. "You want it, and so do I."

"No, no, I don't!" She shot out the fierce denial and jerked her arm. Her wrist stayed in his grip.

"I don't remember your protesting too much!" he said mildly. She was annoyed to recognize amusement in his eyes. "Yes, I distinctly recall it was you who took matters to the boiling point."

"All right, all right. You win." She took a breath. "I did. I forgot, that's all."

He smiled. "Forgot what?"

Gwen narrowed her eyes at his amusement. It fanned her temper more than his anger would have. "Forgot that I don't like you," she tossed out. "Now let me go, my memory's back."

Luke laughed a joyous masculine laugh before he pulled Gwen back into his arms. "You tempt me to make you forget again, Gwenivere." He kissed her again, a hard and possessive kiss. It was over almost before it had begun, but her senses were already reeling from it. "Shall we go back to weeding?" he asked pleasantly, as he released her.

She drew herself straight, indignant, furious. "You can go . . ."

"Gwen!" Anabelle's soft voice cut off Gwen's suggestion. Her mother had drifted into the garden. "Oh, here you are, both of you. How nice."

"Hello, Anabelle." Luke gave her an easy smile. "We thought we'd give you a hand with the garden!"

"Oh?" She looked vaguely at her flowers, then her face brightened with a smile. "That's sweet, I'm sure I haven't been as diligent as I should be, but . . ." She trailed off, watching a bee swoop down on a rosebud. "Perhaps we can all get back to this later. Tillie's got lunch ready and insists on serving right away. It's her afternoon off, you know." She turned her smile on Gwen. "You'd better wash your hands, dear," she looked anxiously at Gwen, "and perhaps you should stay out of the sun for a while, you're a bit flushed."

Gwen could feel Luke grin without looking at him. "You're probably right," she mumbled. Detestable man! Why did he always succeed in confusing her?

Unaware of the fires raging in her daughter, Anabelle smilingly laid a hand on Gwen's cheek, but whatever she planned to say was distracted by the drone of a furry bee. "My, my," she said, watching it swoop greedily down on an azalea blossom. "He's certainly a big one." Having forgotten Tillie's instructions, she glanced back up at Gwen. "You were sitting for Bradley this morning, weren't you, dear?"

"Yes." Gwen made a face. "For almost two hours."

"Isn't that exciting?" Anabelle glanced up at Luke for his confirmation, then continued before he could comment. "A portrait painted by a real artist! I can hardly wait to see it when it's all finished! Why, I'll have to buy it, I suppose." Her blue eyes brightened. "Perhaps I'll hang it right over the mantel in the parlor. That is . . ." Another thought intruded, and she stopped her planning and rearranging to look at her daughter. "Unless you want it for you and your Michael."

"He isn't *my* Michael, Mama, I told you." Gwen stuck her hands in her pockets, wishing Luke would say something instead of simply watching her with those cool blue-gray eyes. Why was it never possible to tell what he was thinking? "And in any case, he'd never buy a painting from an unknown. He wouldn't be assured of the investment value," she added. She was sorry that a note of rancor slipped into her voice.

Luke's eyes remained cool, but Gwen saw his brow lift fractionally. He doesn't miss anything, she thought with a stab of resentment. Turning, she began to pull loose petals from an overbloomed rose.

"Oh, but surely, if it were a portrait of you . . ." Anabelle began. Observing her daughter's expression, she hastily changed her course. "I'm sure it's going to be just beautiful," she said brightly. She turned to Luke. "Don't you think so, Luke?"

"Undoubtedly," he agreed as Gwen gave the rose her fiercest attention. "Bradley has the raw material to work with. That is . . ." He paused and, unable to resist, Gwen looked over her shoulder to meet his eyes again. "If Gwenivere manages to hold still until it's finished."

Gwen's spine stiffened at the amusement in his voice, but before she could retort, Anabelle laughed gaily. "Oh, yes, Gwen's a ball of fire, I declare," she emoted. "Even as a youngster, flitting here and there, quicker than a minute. Why, I'd have to nearly chain her to a chair to braid her hair." She smiled in maternal memory, absently fluffing her own hair. "Then, at the end of the day, or most times long before, it looked as though I had never touched it! And her clothes!" She clucked her tongue and rolled her eyes. "Oh, what a time I used to have with torn knees and ripped seams."

"Mama." Gwen interrupted before Anabelle could launch into another speech on her girlhood. "I'm sure Luke's not interested in the state of my clothes."

He grinned at that, widely, irreverently. Gwen blushed to the roots of her hair. "On the contrary," he said as she groped around for something scathing and dignified to say. "I'm extremely interested." His eyes softened as he smiled at Anabelle. "It's all grist for my mill—just the sort of background material a writer needs."

"Why, yes, I suppose so." Gwen saw that her mother found this extremely profound. Anabelle lapsed into silence again, dreaming off into the middle distance. Luke grinned at Gwen over her head.

"And I've always had a fondness for little girls," he told her. "Particularly ones whose braids won't stay tied, and who regularly scrape their knees." He glanced down, letting his eyes run over Gwen's French-cut T-shirt and cinnamon-colored shorts. "I imagine over the years Anabelle was pretty busy administering first aid." His eyes traveled up on the same slow, casual journey before meeting hers.

"I didn't make a habit of falling down," Gwen began, feeling ridiculous.

Anabelle came out of her trance for a moment. "Oh, yes." She picked up on Luke's comment. "I don't think a day went by when I wasn't patching up some hurt. A fishhook in your hand one day . . ." She shuddered at the memory. "And a lump the size of a goose egg on your forehead the next. It was always one thing or another."

"Mama." Gwen crushed what was left of the rose between her fingers. "You make it sound as if I had been a walking disaster."

"You were just spirited, darling." Anabelle frowned a bit at the damaged rose, but made no comment. "Though there were times, I admit, I wasn't certain you'd live to grow up. But, of course, you have, so I probably shouldn't have worried so much."

"Mama." Gwen was suddenly touched. How difficult it must have been, she reflected, for such a young, dreamy woman to raise a lively youngster all on her own! How many sacrifices Anabelle must have made that Gwen had never even considered. Stepping over, Gwen put her hands on Anabelle's soft rounded shoulders. "I love you, and I'm terribly glad you're my mother."

With a sound of surprised pleasure, Anabelle framed Gwen's face and kissed both her cheeks. "What a sweet thing to hear, and from a grown daughter, too." She gave Gwen a quick, fragrant hug.

Over her mother's shoulder, Gwen saw that Luke was still watching them. His direct intensity made her feel self-conscious.

How do I really feel about him? she asked herself. And how can I feel anything, anything at all, when the woman I love most in the world stands between us?

She felt trapped, and something of her panic showed in her eyes.

Luke tilted his head. "You're very fortunate, Anabelle." He spoke to the mother, though his eyes remained on the daughter. "Love is very precious."

"Yes." She kissed Gwen's cheek again, then linked her arm through her daughter's. "I'm in a festive mood," she told them both, glowing. "I think we should be daring and have some wine with lunch." Her eyes widened. "*Lunch!* Oh, dear, Tillie will be furious! I completely forgot." She rested a hand against her heart as if to calm it. "I'll go smooth things along. Give me a minute." She assumed a businesslike air. "Then come right in. And see that you make a fuss over whatever she's fixed. We don't want to hurt her feelings any more than we have." She gave the final instructions as she swept back up the path and disappeared.

Gwen started to follow. Luke neatly cut off her retreat by taking her hand. "You'd better let her play diplomat first," he told her.

Gwen swung around to face him. "I don't want to be here with you."

Luke lifted a brow, letting his eyes play over her face. "Why not? I can't imagine more attractive circumstances. This lovely garden . . . A beautiful day . . . Tell me something," he continued, interrupting whatever retort she might have made. Casually, he tangled the fingers of his other hand in her hair. "What were you thinking of when you hugged your mother and looked at me?"

"That's none of your business." Gwen jerked her head, trying to free her hair from his curious fingers.

"Really?" He lifted and stroked a straying lock of her hair. Somewhere in the distant west, she heard the first rumbles of thunder. "I had the impression whatever was going through your mind at that moment was very much my business." He brought his eyes back down to hers and held them steady. "Why do you suppose I did?"

"I haven't the faintest idea," Gwen returned coolly. "Probably an author's overheated imagination."

Luke's smile moved slowly, touching his eyes seconds before it touched his lips. "I don't think so, Gwen. I prefer thinking of it as a writer's intuition."

"Or a man's overinflated ego," she shot back, lifting her hand to her hair in an attempt to remove his exploring fingers. "Would you stop that!" she demanded, trying to ignore the dancing of nerves at the back of her neck.

"Or a man's sensitivity to a woman," he countered, bringing her hand to his lips. He kissed her fingers one at a time until she regained the presence of mind to try to jerk free. Instead of releasing her, Luke simply laced fingers with hers. They stood, joined as carelessly as schoolchildren, while she frowned at him. The thunder came again, closer. "Sensitive enough to know when a woman who is attracted to me," he went on lazily, "is not willing to admit it."

Her eyes narrowed. "You're impossibly conceited."

"Hopelessly honest," he corrected. "Shall I prove it to you?"

Gwen lifted her chin. "There's nothing to prove." She knew the hopelessness of attempting to pull her hand from his. Casually, she looked past him to the sky. "The clouds are coming in. I don't want to get caught in the rain."

"We've got a minute," he said, without even glancing at the sky. He smiled. "I believe I make you nervous."

"Don't flatter yourself," she tossed back, and kept her hands calm in his.

"The pulse in your throat is hammering." His eyes dropped and lingered on it, further increasing its pace. "It's strangely attractive—"

"It always does when I'm annoyed," she said, fighting for poise as the sweep of his eyes from her throat to her face threatened to destroy her composure.

"I like you when you're annoyed. I like to watch the different expressions on your face and to see your eyes darken . . . but . . ." He trailed off, slipping his hands to her wrists. "At the moment, I believe it's nerves."

"Believe what you like." It was impossible to prevent her pulse from pounding against his fingers. She tried to calm her rebel blood. "You don't make me the least bit nervous."

"No?" His grin turned wolfish. Gwen braced for a struggle. "A difference of opinion," he observed. "And one I'm tempted to resolve." He drew her closer, letting his eyes rest on her mouth. Gwen knew he was baiting her and held her ground. She said nothing, waiting for him to make his move.

"At the moment, however, I'm starved." Luke

grinned, then gave her a quick, unexpected kiss on the nose. "And I'm too much of a coward to risk Tillie's bad temper." He dropped one of her hands, but kept the other companionably linked with his. "Let's eat," he suggested, ignoring Gwen's frown.

CHAPTER 7

Gwen noticed several small changes in Anabelle. There was an air of secrecy about her that Gwen found out of character. She disappears so often, Gwen thought as she seated herself in front of the vintage Steinway in the parlor. She's here one minute and gone the next. And she spends too much time with Luke Powers. There are too many discussions that stop abruptly when I walk in on them. They make me feel like an intruder. With little interest, she began to pick out a melody. The breeze came softly through the window, barely stirring the curtain. The scent of jasmine was elusive, teasing the senses.

I'm jealous, Gwen realized with a jolt of surprise. I expected Mama's undivided attention, and I'm not getting it. With a rueful laugh, Gwen began to play Chopin. Now when have I ever had Mama's undivided attention? She's always had her "visitors," her antiques, her flowers.

Thinking back over childhood memories, Gwen played with absentminded skill. She had forgotten how soothing the piano was to her. I haven't given myself enough time for this, she reflected. I should take a step back and look at where my life is going. I need to find out what's missing. Her fingers stilled on the last note, which floated quietly through the air and then vanished.

"Lovely," Luke said. "Really lovely."

Gwen suppressed the desire to jump at the sound of his voice. She forced herself to raise her eyes and meet his, struggling to keep the color from tinting her cheeks. It was difficult, after what she had said the evening before, to face him. She felt her defenses were shaky, her privacy invaded. He knew more of her now than she wanted him to.

"Thank you," she said politely. "I am, as Mama always said I would be, grateful for the music lessons she forced me to take."

"Forced?" To Gwen's consternation, Luke sat down on the stool beside her.

"As only she can." Gwen relieved a portion of her tension by giving her attention to another melody. "With quiet, unarguable insistence."

"Ah." Luke nodded in agreement. "And you didn't want to study piano?"

"No, I wanted to study crawfishing." She was stunned when he began to play along with her, picking out the melody on the treble keys. "I didn't know you played." The utter disbelief in her voice brought on his laugh.

"Believe it or not, I, too, had a mother." He gave Gwen his swift, conspiratorial grin. "I wanted to study rock skipping."

Totally disarmed, Gwen smiled back at him. Something passed between them. It was as strong and as real as the passion that had flared with their kiss, as gentle and soothing as the music drifting from the keys.

"Isn't that sweet." Anabelle stood in the doorway and beamed at both of them. "Duets are so charming."

"Mama." Gwen was relieved her voice did not tremble. "I looked for you earlier."

"Did you?" Anabelle smiled. "I'm sorry, dear, I've been busy with . . . this and that," she finished vaguely. "Aren't you sitting for Bradley today?"

"I've already given him his two hours this morning," Gwen answered. "It's lucky for me he wants the early light, or I'd be sitting all day. I thought perhaps you had something you'd like me to do or someplace you'd like me to take you. It's such a lovely day."

"Yes, it is, isn't it?" Anabelle agreed. Her eyes drifted momentarily to Luke's. Abruptly, her cheeks dimpled and her lips curved. "Why, as a matter of fact, darling, there *is* something you could do for me. Oh—" She paused and shook her head. "But it's so much trouble."

"I don't mind," Gwen interrupted, falling into a childhood trap.

"Well, if it really isn't a bother," Anabelle continued, beaming again. "I especially wanted some embroidery thread, very unusual shades, difficult to find, I'm afraid. There's a little shop in the French Market that carries them."

"In New Orleans?" Gwen's eyes widened.

"Oh, it is a bother, isn't it?" Anabelle sighed. "It's not important, dear. Not important at all," she added.

"It's not a bother, Mama," Gwen corrected, smiling at the old ruse. "Besides, I'd like to get into New Orleans while I'm home. I can be a tourist now."

"What a marvelous idea!" Anabelle enthused. "Wouldn't it be fun? Roaming through the Vieux Carré, wandering through the shops, listening to the music in Bourbon Street. Oh, and dinner at some lovely gallery restaurant. Yes." She clapped her hands together and glowed. "It's just the thing."

"It sounds perfect." Anabelle's childlike enthusiasm caused Gwen to smile. Shopping, she remembered, had always been Anabelle's favorite pastime. "I can't think of a better way to spend the day."

"Good. It's settled, then." She turned to Luke with a pleased smile. "You'll go with Gwen, won't you, dear? It wouldn't do for her to go all alone."

"Alone?" Gwen cut in, confused. "But, Mama, aren't you—?"

"It's such a long drive, too," Anabelle bubbled on. "I'm sure Gwen would love the company."

"No, Mama, I—"

"I'd love to." Luke easily overruled Gwen's objections. He gave Gwen an ironic smile. "I can't think of a better way to spend the day."

"Gwen, dear, I'm so glad you thought of it." The praise was given with a sigh as Anabelle moved over to pat Gwen's cheek.

Looking up into the ingenuous eyes, Gwen felt the familiar sensations of affection and frustration. "I'm very clever," she murmured, moving her lips into a semblance of a smile.

"Yes, of course you are," Anabelle agreed, and gave her a quick, loving hug. "I would change, though, darling. It wouldn't do to go into the city in those faded old jeans. Didn't I throw those out when you were fifteen? Yes, I'm sure I did. Well, run along and have fun," she ordered as she began to drift from the room. "I've just so much to do, I can't think of it all."

"Mama." Gwen called after her. Anabelle turned at the door, lifting her brows in acknowledgement. "The thread?"

"Thread?" Anabelle repeated blankly. "Oh, yes, of course. I'll write down the colors and the name of the shop." She shook her head with a self-deprecating smile. "My, my, I'm quite the scatterbrain. I'll go in right now and tell Tillie you won't be here for dinner. She gets so annoyed with me when I forget things. Do change those pants, Gwen," she added as she started down the hall.

"I'd hide them," Luke suggested confidentially. "She's liable to throw them out again."

Rising with what she hoped was dignity, Gwen answered, "If you'll excuse me?"

"Sure." Before she could move away, Luke took her hand in a light but possessive grip. "I'll meet you out front in twenty minutes. We'll take my car."

A dozen retorts trembled on Gwen's tongue and were dismissed. "Certainly. I'll try not to keep you waiting." She walked regally from the room.

The weather was perfect for a drive—sunny and cloudless, with a light breeze. Gwen had replaced her jeans with a snowy crepe de chine dress. It had a high, lacy neck and pleated bodice, its skirt flowing from a trim, tucked waist. She wore no jewelry. Her hair lay free on her shoulders. Hands primly folded in her lap, she answered Luke's easy conversation with polite, distant monosyllables. I'll get Mama's thread, she determined, have a token tour of the city and drive back as quickly as possible. I will be perfectly polite the entire time.

An hour later, Gwen found that maintaining her aloof sophistication was a difficult task. She had forgotten how much she loved the Vieux Carré. It was not just the exquisite iron grillwork balconies, the profusion of flowering plants, the charm of long wooden shutters and buildings that had stood for centuries. It was the subtle magic of the place. The air was soft and seemed freshly washed, its many scents ranging from flowery to spicy to the rich smell of the river.

"Fabulous, isn't it?" Luke asked as they stood on the curb of a street too narrow for anything but pedestrian traffic. "It's the most stable city I know."

"Stable?" Gwen repeated, intrigued enough to turn and face him directly.

"It doesn't change," he explained with a gesture of his hand. "It just continues on." Before she realized his intent, he laced his fingers with hers and began to walk. She tugged and was ignored.

"There's no reason to hold my hand," Gwen told him primly.

"Sure there is," he corrected, giving her a friendly smile. "I like to."

Gwen subsided into silence. Luke's palm was hard, the palm of a man used to doing manual labor. She remembered suddenly the feel of it caressing her throat. He sighed, turned and pulled her hard against him, covering her mouth in an unexpected and dizzying kiss. Gwen had no time to protest or respond before she was drawn away again. Along the crowded street, several people applauded.

Gwen and Luke walked past the many street artists in Jackson Square. They paused briefly to admire the chalk portraits of tourists, the oils of city scenes and the mysterious studies of the bayous. Gwen was torn between her desire to share her pleasure at returning to the city of her childhood and the feeling that she should ignore the dominating man by her side. She was not here to have a good time, she reminded herself sternly. She was here to do an errand. It was on the tip of her tongue to remind Luke of the purpose of their trip when she saw the magician. He was dressed in black, with spangles and a rakish beret and a flowing moustache.

"Oh, look!" Gwen pointed. "Isn't he wonderful?" She moved closer, unconsciously pulling Luke along by tightening her grip on his hand.

They watched brilliantly colored scarves appear from nowhere, huge bouquets of paper flowers grow from the magician's palm and coins sprout from the ears of onlookers. Two young clowns in whiteface entertained the stragglers by twisting balloons into giraffe and poodle shapes. Some distance away, guitarists sold their songs to passing tourists. Gwen could just hear their close-knit harmony.

Forgetting all her stern resolutions, she turned to grin at Luke. He dropped a bill into the cardboard box that served as the portable cash register for the magician. Reaching out, he pinched her chin between his thumb and forefinger. "I knew it wouldn't last too long."

"What wouldn't?" She brushed the hair from her eyes in a habitual gesture.

"You enjoy things too much to remain cool for long," he told her. "No, now don't do that," he ordered, running a finger down her nose as she frowned. He smiled, then brushed his lips over her fingertips. "Shall we be friends?"

Her hand, already warm from his, grew warmer at the kiss. She knew his charm was practiced, his smile a finely tuned weapon. She forced herself to be cautious.

"I don't know that I'd go as far as that," she replied, studying him with eyes that were warily amused.

"Fellow tourists?" he suggested. His thumb moved gently across her knuckles. "I'll buy you an ice cream cone."

Gwen knew she was losing to the smile and the persuasive voice. "Well . . ." It would do no harm to enjoy the day. No harm in enjoying the city, the magic . . . in enjoying him. "Two scoops," she demanded, answering his smile with her own.

They moved at an easy pace through the park, enjoying both shade and sun. All around was the soft, continuous cooing from hundreds of pigeons. They flocked along the ground, scattered when chased by children, sunned atop the statue of Andrew Jackson on a rearing horse. Here and there people sat or slept on curved black benches. A young girl sat in a patch of shade and played softly on a recorder.

They walked along the levee and looked at the brown waters of the Mississippi. Lazy music from calliopes provided a pleasant background as they talked of everything and of nothing. The bells of Saint Louis Cathedral chimed the hour. They laughed at the toddler who escaped from his mother and splashed in the cool waters of a fountain.

They walked along Bourbon Street, listening to

the tangled, continuous music that poured from open doors. Jazz and country and rock merged into one jumbled, compelling sound. They applauded the old man who danced in the street to the demanding strains of "Tiger Rag." They listened to the corner saxophone player whose lonely song brought Gwen to tears.

On a gallery overlooking a narrow street surging with people, they ate shrimp gumbo and drank cold, dry wine. They lingered over the leisurely meal, watching the sun slowly disappear. Pleasantly weary, Gwen toyed with the remains of her cheesecake and watched the first stars come out. Laughter rose from the street below. When she turned, she found Luke studying her over the rim of his glass.

"Why do you look at me like that?" Her smile was completely relaxed as she rested her chin on her palm.

"A remarkably foolish question," Luke answered as he set down his glass. "Why do you think?"

"I don't know." She took a deep breath. The scent of the city assailed her senses. "No one's ever looked at me quite the way you do. You can tell too much about people. It's not fair. You study them and steal their thoughts. It's not a very comfortable feeling."

Luke smiled, and his fingers were light on the back of her hand.

Gwen lifted an eyebrow, then strategically moved her hand out of reach. "You also have a way of making people say things. Yesterday I . . ." Gwen hesitated and twisted the stem of her glass between her fingers. "I said things to you I shouldn't have. It's disturbing to know you've revealed your emotions to someone else." She sipped her wine. "Michael always says I'm too open."

"Your emotions are beautiful." Gwen looked up, surprised at the tenderness in his voice. "Michael is a fool."

Quickly she shook her head. "Oh, no, he's really quite brilliant, and he never does anything foolish. He has an image to maintain. It's just that I was beginning to feel as if I were being molded into his conception of a proper attorney's wife."

"He asked you to marry him?" Luke asked, as he poured wine into both glasses.

"He was sure that I would. He was furious when I didn't jump at the offer." Gwen sighed and made a restless movement with her shoulders. "I kept seeing a long, narrow tunnel, very straight, no curves, no detours, no surprises. I guess I developed claustrophobia." She made a frustrated sound, wrinkling her nose. "There, you've done it again."

"I have?" He smiled as he leaned back in his seat. Moonlight spilled over her hair.

"I'm telling you things . . . things I've barely told myself. You always manage to find out what's in a person's mind, but you keep your own thoughts all tidy and tucked away."

"I put them in print," he corrected. "For anyone who cares to read them."

"Yes," she said slowly. "But how does one know if they're your real thoughts? Your books are interesting, but how do I know who you really are?"

"Do you want to?" There was a soft challenge in his voice.

Gwen hesitated, but the answer was already moving to her lips. "Yes, I do."

"But you're not quite sure." He rose, then held out his hand to her. "The wine's made you sleepy," he said, looking down into her heavy eyes. "Shall I take you home?"

"No." Gwen shook her head. "No, not yet." She slipped her hand back into his.

Luke drove down the magnolia-lined lane. The scent of the night was delicate, mixing with the fragrance of the woman who slept on his shoulder. After stopping the car, he turned his head and looked down at her. Gwen's mouth was soft and vulnerable in sleep. There was a moment's hesitation before he lifted her chin and drew away from her.

"Gwen." He moved his thumb gently over her lips. She gave a soft, pleased sigh. "Gwen," he said again with more firmness. Her lashes fluttered and opened. "We're home." He massaged her shoulders lightly, and she stretched under his hands.

"Did I fall asleep?" Her eyes were huge and dark as she smiled at him. "I didn't mean to."

"It's late."

"I know." She smiled sleepily. "I had fun. Thank you." On impulse, she bent forward and brushed her lips over his. His fingers tightened on her shoulders as he pulled away from her sharply. Gwen blinked in confusion. "Luke?"

"I have my limits," he said tersely. He made a quick, impatient sound as her face registered consternation. "I told you once, women are very soft and warm when they've been sleeping. I have a weakness for soft, warm women."

"I didn't mean to fall asleep," she murmured as his hand slipped around to cradle the back of her neck. Her head felt light, her limbs heavy.

A cloud drifted over the moon. The light shifted, dimmed and glowed again. He was watching her, studying each feature with absorption. She could feel his fingers on the base of her neck. They were hard and long, their strength obvious even in the gentle touch. She whispered, "What do you want?"

In answer, he bent slowly toward her. His mouth was easy, teasing the corners of hers, drifting to her closed lids, exploring the hollows of her cheeks. Passion lay simmering beneath the surface as he began to caress her body with slow, patient hands. He traced her parted lips with the tip of his tongue. "Beautiful," he murmured, moving his mouth to her ear. She shivered with pleasure as his thumb lingered on the point of her breast. "When I touch you, I feel your body melt under my hands." He met her mouth with a long, tender kiss. "What do I want?" he answered as he tasted the heated skin of her throat. "What I want more than anything at this moment is to make love with you. I want to take you slowly, until I know all of you."

She felt her body growing fluid, and her will flowed with it. "Will you make love with me?" She heard herself ask, heard the tone that was request rather than question. Luke's mouth paused on her skin. Slowly he tightened his grip on her hair, then drew her head back until their eyes met. For a moment, they hung suspended in silence with only the echo of her voice between them.

"No." His answer was cool and quick as a slap. Gwen jerked away from it and him and fumbled with the handle of the door. She stumbled out of the car, but before she could escape into the house, Luke captured her arms in a firm grip. "Wait a minute."

Shaking her head, Gwen pushed against him. "No, I want to go in. I didn't know what I was saying. It was crazy."

"You knew exactly what you were saying," Luke corrected, tightening his grasp.

Gwen wanted to deny it but found it impossible. She had wanted him, she knew she still wanted him. "All right, I knew what I was saying. Now will you let me go?"

"I won't apologize for touching you," he said.

"I'm not asking for apologies, Luke," she told him evenly. "I'm simply asking for my freedom." She realized uncomfortably that it was not freedom from his arms that she meant, but freedom from the power he held over her. The struggle inside her was reflected briefly in her face. Luke's frown deepened before he released her arms. "Thank you," she said.

She walked quickly inside the house before he could say another word.

CHAPTER 8

A yellow butterfly fluttered delicately over a pot of white impatiens. From the veranda, Gwen watched its dance until it skimmed away, light as the air. Sitting in the white porch rocker, dressed in a yellow sundress, Anabelle looked as fragile as the butterfly. Gwen studied her mother's soft pink cheeks and gentle blue eyes. Anabelle's small hands were busy with the domestic task of shelling peas, but her eyes were, as always, dreamy. Watching her, Gwen was swamped with waves of love and helplessness.

Who am I? she demanded of herself. Who am I to advise anyone on men? For a moment, Gwen wished desperately that she could seek from Anabelle advice for herself. Her own emotions were chaotic. She was terrified that her own feelings for Luke were approaching a dangerous level. Falling in love with a man like Luke was courting disaster. And yet, Gwen wondered unhappily, is it really possible for the mind to control the heart? In this case it must . . . there's no choice. I have to forget about last night. The sigh escaped before she could stop it. Priorities, she reminded herself. Gwen watched a bumblebee dive into a cluster of wisteria, then took a deep breath and turned to Anabelle. "Mama." Anabelle went on shelling peas, a misty smile on her lips. "Mama," Gwen repeated more sharply, placing a hand over her mother's.

"Oh, yes, dear?" Anabelle looked up with the open, expectant look of a child. "Did you say something?"

For an instant, Gwen teetered on the brink, then plunged. "Mama, don't you think twelve years is a terribly big gap?"

Gravely, Anabelle considered. "Why, I suppose it could be, Gwenivere, but then, as you grow older, twelve years is hardly any time at all." Her momentary seriousness vanished with a fresh smile. "Why, it seems like yesterday that you were twelve years old. I remember quite clearly when you fell out of that old cypress in the backyard and broke your arm. Such a brave child . . ." She began shelling peas again. "Never shed a tear. I cried enough for both of us, though."

"But, Mama." Valiantly Gwen tried to keep Anabelle's thoughts from straying. "Twelve years, when you're speaking of a man and a woman . . ." Anabelle failed to respond to the prompting, only nodding to indicate she was listening. "The age difference, Mama," Gwen blurted out. "Isn't twelve years a terribly wide age gap?"

"Sally Deumont's girls are nearly twelve years

apart," Anabelle stated with another series of nods. "I suppose having children that far apart has its drawbacks."

"No, Mama." Gwen ran both hands through her hair.

"And its advantages, certainly," Anabelle said soothingly, not wanting to be critical of an old friend.

"No, Mama, I don't mean that at all. I'm speaking of men and women . . . of relationships. Romantic relationships."

"Oh!" Anabelle blinked in surprise and smiled. "That's a different matter altogether, isn't it?" Gwen resisted grinding her teeth as her mother continued to shell peas for a moment in silence. "I'm surprised," Anabelle said at length, giving Gwen a look of gentle curiosity. "I'm surprised you would think that age and love had anything to do with each other. I've always thought of the heart as ageless."

The words caused Gwen to falter a moment. Slowly she leaned forward and took both her mother's hands in hers. "Mama, don't you think, sometimes, that love can blind people to what's right for them? Don't people often put themselves into a position where getting hurt is the only possible outcome?"

"Yes, of course." Anabelle shook her head, as if startled by the question. "That's part of life. If you never open yourself for pain, you never open yourself for joy. How empty life would be then. This Michael of yours," Anabelle continued with a light of concern in her eyes, "did he hurt you terribly?"

"No." Gwen released her mother's hands and rose

to walk the length of the veranda. "No, basically only my pride."

"That can happen by a fall off a horse," Anabelle stated. Abandoning her peas, she moved to join Gwen. "Darling, how young you are." She turned to face her, studying her with rare total concentration. "I sometimes forget that, because you're so much more practical and organized than I am. I suppose I always let you take care of me, much more than I took care of you."

"Oh, no, Mama," Gwen protested, but Anabelle placed a finger on her lips.

"It's true. I never like to look at the unpleasant side of things. I'm afraid I've always let you do that for me. In some ways you matured so quickly, but in others . . ." Anabelle sighed and slipped an arm around Gwen's waist. "Perhaps at last we've found something I can help you with."

"But, Mama, it's not me . . ." Gwen began, only to be ignored.

"Did you know I was only eighteen when I first saw your father? I fell instantly, wildly in love." The soft look in Anabelle's eyes halted Gwen's interruption. "Who would have thought his life would be so short? He never even got to see you. I always thought that the greatest tragedy. He would have been so proud to see himself in you." She sighed, then smiled at Gwen. "Ours was a first love, a desperate love, and often I've wondered if it would have withstood all the tests of time. I'll never know." Gwen remained silent, fascinated by a side of her mother she was seeing for the first time. "I learned so many things from that short, crowded marriage. I learned you must always accept love when it's offered, always give it when it's needed. There might not be a second chance. And I know, too, that until your heart's been broken, you never know the full beauty of love."

Gwen watched a squirrel dart across the lawn and scurry up a tree. It was an odd feeling, hearing her mother speak of being in love. She wondered if their relationship had blinded her from seeing Anabelle as a woman with needs and desires. Looking down, Gwen saw the smooth, untroubled skin of a woman at the peak of her beauty. There was still a youthful sweetness in the shape of the mouth, an impossible air of innocence in the eyes. Impulsively, Gwen asked the question that had lurked in her mind for years.

"Mama, why haven't you ever gotten married again?"

"I haven't wanted to," Anabelle answered instantly. She moved away with a swish of her skirts. "At first, I was too much in love with your father's memory, and later I was having too much fun raising you." She plucked a withered fuchsia bloom from a hanging basket and dropped it over the railing of the veranda. "I'm quite good with babies, you know. Later you became more and more independent, so I moved on to the next stage. I've had some admirers." She smiled, pleased with the thought. "I've simply never had the urge to settle down with any of them." In silence, Gwen watched Anabelle move from flower to flower. It occurred to her for the first time that her mother had probably enjoyed love affairs over the past twenty years. She had not been exclusively Gwen's dreamy, gentle mother but Anabelle Lacrosse, a lovely, desirable woman. For one brief moment, Gwen felt ridiculously like an orphan.

I'm being a fool, Gwen told herself, resting her head against the rail post. She's still the same person—I'm the one who's changing. I grew up, but I've kept her locked in a childhood image. It's time I let her out. But I can't bear to see her hurt, and I'm so afraid Luke will leave her wounded. He can't love her, not when he can kiss me the way he does. No . . . She closed her eyes. He wants me, but it has nothing to do with his heart. He wants me, but he turned away from me. Why else would he have done that, if not for her? A bright flash of jealousy both stunned and shamed her. With a shuddering sigh, she turned to find Anabelle studying her.

"You're not happy," her mother said simply.

"No." Gwen shook her head with the word.

"Confused?"

"Yes." Quickly she swallowed the tears that threatened to come.

"Men do that to us so easily." Anabelle smiled as if the prospect was not altogether unappealing. "Try a rare piece of advice from your mother, darling. Do nothing." With a little laugh, she tossed back a stray wisp of golden hair. "I know how difficult that is for you, but do try. Just let the pieces fall into place around you for a time. Sometimes doing nothing is doing everything."

"Mama." Gwen was forced to smile. "How can something so silly make so much sense?"

"Luke says I've an intuitive understanding," Anabelle replied with a glow of pride.

"He has a way with words," Gwen muttered.

"Tools of the trade." Luke spoke as the screen door swung shut behind him. His eyes met Gwen's. There was something intimate in the glance, something possessive. Even as the stirring began inside her, she lifted her chin in defense. A smile teased his mouth. "Guns primed, Gwenivere?"

"I'm a dead shot," she returned evenly.

"Oh dear." Anabelle moved lightly across the veranda and began to gather her peas. "You didn't tell me you were going hunting. I hope Tillie packed you a lunch."

Luke grinned over her head with such easy boyish charm, Gwen was helpless to resist. Her eyes warmed and her mouth softened as they shared the intimacy of a joke.

"Actually, I had fishing in mind," Luke countered, keeping his eyes on Gwen's. "I thought I'd walk down to Malon's cabin."

"That's nice." Anabelle straightened and smiled. "Malon still brings up fresh fish," she told Gwen. "You run along, too, darling. You know he would be hurt if you didn't visit."

"Oh, well, I . . ." Seeing the amusement on Luke's face, Gwen continued smoothly, "I'll visit him, Mama, another time. I told Tillie I'd help her do some canning."

"Nonsense." Anabelle flitted to the screen door, beaming at Luke as he held it open for her. "Thank you, darling," she said before giving Gwen a look over her shoulder. "You're on vacation. That's no time to be standing in a hot kitchen over boiling tomatoes. Run along and have fun. She's always loved to fish," she added to Luke before she stepped inside. "Tell Malon I'd adore some fresh shrimp." The door closed behind her. Gwen had the odd feeling that she had just been pushed gently out of the way. Luke gave her slim blue jeans and plain white T-shirt a cursory glance.

"Looks like you're dressed for fishing," he said with a nod. "Let's go."

"I have no intention of going anywhere with you." Gwen dusted her hands on her hips and started to move by him. She was brought up short by his hand on her arm. They stood side by side. Gwen let her eyes rest on his imprisoning hand and then slid them slowly to meet his. It was her most disdainful stare. "I beg your pardon?" she said icily. To her dismay, Luke burst out laughing. The warm, deep tones of it caused a bird to dart from the lawn to the shelter of a tree. "Let me go, you . . . you . . ."

"Wasn't it 'beast' before?" he asked as he began to assist her down the stairs.

"You are the most outrageous man." She continued to struggle as she trotted to keep pace.

"Thanks."

Gwen dug in her heels and managed to persuade Luke to stop. Staring up at him, she took a long, deep breath. "You are the most arrogant, officious, egotistical, thick-skinned man I have ever met."

"You forgot unreasonable, tyrannical and incredibly attractive. Really, Gwen, you surprise me. I thought you had more imagination. Are those your best insults?"

"Off the cuff, yes." She sniffed and tried not to respond to the humor in his eyes. "If you'll give me a little time, I can be more articulate."

"Don't trouble, I got the idea." He released her arm, held up one hand in the air, and the other out to her. "Truce?"

Gwen's guard relaxed before she realized it. Her hand moved to meet his.

"Truce," she agreed, with only a token trace of reluctance.

"Until . . . ?" he asked as he rubbed his thumb lightly across the back of her hand.

"Until I decide to be annoyed with you again." Gwen smiled, tossing back her curls as she enjoyed his laugh. It was, she decided, the most pleasing, infectious laugh she had ever heard.

"Well, will you fish with me?" he asked.

"Perhaps I will." For a moment she pursed her lips in thought. When she smiled again, it was the smile of challenge. "Ten bucks says I catch a bigger fish than you."

"Done." Casually, Luke laced his fingers through hers. This time Gwen made no objection.

Gwen knew every twist of the river and every turn of the paths in the bayou. Automatically, she moved north toward Malon's cabin. They walked under cascading moss and filtered sunlight.

"Do you really know how to can tomatoes, Gwenivere?" Luke asked as he bent under a low-hanging branch.

"Certainly, and anything else that comes out of a garden. When you're poor, a garden can mean the difference between eating or not."

"I've never known poor people who eat with Georgian silver," Luke commented dryly.

"Heirlooms." Gwen gave a sigh and a shrug. "Mama always considered heirlooms a sacred trust. One can't sell a sacred trust. Nor," she added with a wry smile, "can one comfortably wear or eat a sacred trust. Mama loves that house, it's her Camelot. She's a woman who needs a Camelot."

"And Gwenivere doesn't?" A great egret, startled by their intrusion, unfolded himself from the water and rose into the sky. Gwen felt an old, familiar stir of pleasure as she watched.

"I suppose I've always wanted to find my own. Heirlooms belong to someone else first. I'd nearly forgotten the scent of wild jasmine," she murmured as the fragrance drifted to her.

There was a dreamlike stillness around them. Beside them, the stream moved on its lackadaisical journey to the Gulf. Its water mirrored the moss dripping trees. Gwen tossed a pebble and watched the ripples spread and vanish. "I spent most of my leisure time out here when I was younger," she said. "I felt more at home here than inside my own house. There was never any real privacy there, with strangers always coming and going. I never wanted to share my kingdom with anyone before. . . ."

She could feel Luke's big hand tighten his grasp on hers. He met her eyes with perfect understanding.

CHAPTER 9

Malon's cabin hung over the water. It was built of split logs with a low, wide A roof and a porch that doubled as a dock for his pirogue. On a small, spare patch of grass beside the cabin, half a dozen chickens clucked and waddled. Somewhere deep in the marsh, a woodpecker drummed. A scratchy recording of music by Saint-Saëns came from the cabin to compete with the drumming and clucking. Stretched lengthwise on a narrow railing above the water, a tabby cat slept.

"It's just the same," Gwen murmured. She was unaware of the relief in her voice or the pleasure that lit her face. She smiled up at Luke and pulled him quickly across the lawn and up the three wooden steps. "Raphael," she said to the snoozing cat. Lazily he opened one eye, made a disinterested noise and shut it again.

"Affectionate as ever," Gwen remarked. "I was afraid he'd forget me."

"Raphael is too old to forget anything."

Gwen turned quickly at the sound of the voice. Malon stood in the cabin doorway, a mortar and pestle in his hand. He was a small man, barely taller than Gwen herself, but with powerful arms and shoulders. His middle had not gone to flesh with age, but remained as flat as a boxer's, as he had indeed once been. His hair was white, thick and curly, his face brown and lined, his eyes were a faded blue under dark brows. His age was a mystery. The bayou had been his home for an unspecified number of years. He took from the stream what he needed and was content. He had both a passionate love and a deep respect for the bayou. These he had passed on to the young girl who had found his cabin more than fifteen years before. Gwen checked the impulse to run into his arms.

"Hello, Malon. How are you?"

"Comme ci, comme ça." He gave a tiny shrug, then set down his mortar and pestle. He nodded a greeting to Luke before concentrating on Gwen. For a full minute she stood silent under his scrutiny. At length he said, "Let me see your hands." Obediently, Gwen held them out. "Soft," Malon said with a snort. "Lady's hands now, *hein?* Why didn't you get a lady's figure in New York, too?"

"I could only afford the hands. I'm still saving up for the rest. And Tillie's still pressing your shirts, I see." Gwen ran an experimental finger over the faded but crisp material of his cotton shirt. "When are you going to marry her?"

"I'm too young to get married," he said. "I have not finished sowing wild oats."

Gwen laughed and laid her cheek against his. "Oh, I've missed you, Malon." He answered her laugh and gave her one quick, bruising and unexpected hug. From the outset, they had spoken in Cajun French, a dialect that Gwen used again without the slightest thought. She closed her eyes a moment, enjoying the strength in his burly arms, the feel of his leathery cheek against hers, the scent of woodsmoke and herbs that was his personal cologne. She realized suddenly why she had not come to see him earlier. He had been the one constant male figure in her life. She had been afraid she would find him changed.

"Everything's the same," she murmured.

"But you." There was a smile in his voice, and she heard it.

"I should have come sooner." For the first time since she had known him, Gwen dared kiss his cheek.

"You are forgiven," he said.

Gwen was suddenly conscious of Luke beside her. She flushed. "I'm sorry," she said to him, "I—I didn't realize that we were rambling on in French."

Luke smiled while absently scratching Raphael's ears. "You don't have to apologize—I enjoyed it."

Gwen forced her thoughts into order. She would not fall under the charm of that smile again. "Do you speak French?" she asked with casual interest.

"No. But I still enjoyed it." She had the uncomfortable feeling he knew precisely how deeply his smile affected her. He turned his clear, calm eyes to Malon. "Anabelle says she'd like some shrimp."

"I go shrimping tomorrow," Malon answered with an agreeable nod. "Your book goes well?"

"Well enough."

"So, you take the day off, *hein?* You take this one fishing?" A jerk of his thumb in Gwen's direction accompanied the question.

"Thought I might," Luke replied without glancing at her.

Malon shrugged and sniffed. "Use t'be she knew which end of the pole to hold and which to put in the water, but that was before she went up there." A snap of his head indicated "up there." Even a town twenty miles from Lafitte was regarded with suspicion.

"Perhaps she remembers," Luke suggested. "She seems reasonably intelligent."

"She was raised good," Malon added, softening a bit. "Her papa was a good boy. She has his face. She don't favor her mama."

Gwen straightened her shoulders and raised her brows ever so slightly. "*She* remembers *everything.* My mother can outfish both of you in her sleep."

"Poo-yie!" Malon shook his hand and wrist as if he had touched something hot. "This city girl, she scare me out of my shoe. You take her. Me, I'm too old to fight with mean women."

"A minute ago you were too young to get married," Gwen reminded him.

"Yes, it's a good age I have." He smiled contentedly. "*Allez,* I have medicine to make. Take the poles and the pirogue and bring me a fish for my dinner." Without another word, he walked into the cabin, letting the screen door slam shut behind him.

"He hasn't changed," Gwen stated, trying to sound indignant.

"No," Luke agreed, taking two fishing poles and putting them across his shoulder. "He's still crazy about you." After stepping into the pirogue, he held out a hand to her. With the ease of experience, Gwen settled into the canoe. Soundlessly, Raphael leaped from rail to boat and fell instantly back to sleep.

"He doesn't want to miss the fun," Gwen explained.

Luke poled away from the dock. "Tell me, Gwenivere," he asked, "how do you come to speak the dialect so fluently? Anabelle can barely read a French menu." Sunshine dappled their heads as they passed under a canopy of trees.

"Tillie taught me." Gwen leaned her head back and let the warm sunlight play on her face. She remembered Malon saying long ago that his pirogue could ride on a film of dew. "I've spoken the coastal dialect for as long as I can remember. For the most part, the people here treat outsiders as beneath their notice; it's a very closed society. But I speak Cajun—therefore, I *am* Cajun. I'm curious, though, why Malon accepts you. It's obvious that you're on easy terms."

"I don't speak Cajun." Luke stood in the pirogue

and poled down the river as if born to it. "But we speak the same language nonetheless."

They cleared the trees and drifted into a ghost forest shadowed by stumps of cypress. The boat moved through floating mats of hyacinths. Tiny baby crawfish clung to the clumped roots, while a fat cottonmouth disappeared into the lavender blooms. The winding river was teeming with life. Gwen watched a marsh raccoon fishing from the sloping bank.

"How is it," Gwen mused aloud, "that a Pulitzer Prize winner speaks the same language as a Louisiana *traiteur?*"

"Traiteur?" Luke repeated, meeting the frank curiosity in her eyes.

"Folk doctor. Malon fishes and trades and lumbers sometimes, but primarily he's the local *traiteur.* He cures snakebites, illness and spells. Spells are his specialty."

"Hmm. Did you ever wonder why he lives here, alone with his cat, his music and his books?" Gwen did not answer, content to watch Luke pole through the scattered stumps. "He's been to Rome and London and Budapest, but he lives here. He's driven tanks, broken horses, boxed and flown planes. Now he fishes and cures spells. He knows how to fix a carburetor, how to play classical guitar and how to cure snakebites. He does as he pleases and no more. He's the most successful man I know."

"How did you find out so much about him in such a short time?"

"I asked," Luke told her simply.

"No. No, it's not as easy as that." Gwen made a frustrated gesture with her hand. "People tell you things, I don't know why. I've told you things I have no business telling you, and I tell you before I realize it." She examined his face. "And worse, you don't always need to be told, you know. You see people much too clearly."

He smiled down at her. "Does it make you uncomfortable that I know who you are?"

The river widened. Gwen's pout became a frown. "Yes, I think it does. It makes me feel defenseless, the same way I felt when I first saw Bradley's sketches."

"An invasion of privacy?"

"Privacy's important to me," Gwen admitted.

"I understand," Luke leaned on the pole. "You grew up having to share your home with strangers, having to share Anabelle. The result is a desire for privacy and independence. I apologize for invading your privacy, but, after all, it's partly my profession."

"Are we all characters to you?" Gwen asked as she baited her hook and cast her line.

"Some more than others," he returned dryly, casting his line on the opposite side of the boat from hers.

Gwen shook her head. "You know," she began, then settled back, stretching her legs and crossing them, "I'm finding it very hard not to like you."

At the other end of the canoe, Luke mirrored her position. "I'm a very charming person."

"Unfortunately, that's true." With a contented sigh, Gwen closed her eyes. "You're not at all how I pictured you."

"Oh?"

"You look more like a woodchopper than a world-renowned writer."

Luke grinned. "And how should a world-renowned writer look?"

"Several different ways, I suppose. Intellectual, with small glasses and narrow shoulders. Or prominent . . ."

"Heaven forbid."

"Or prominent," Gwen continued, ignoring him. "Wearing a well-cut suit and with just a hint of a paunch. Dashing, maybe, with a faint scar along the jawline. Or Byronic . . ."

"Oh, good Lord."

"With a romantic pallor and tragic eyes."

"It's difficult to maintain a pallor in California."

"The trouble is, you're too physical." Gwen was enjoying the gentle drift of the boat and the warm fingers of sun. "What's your new book about?"

"A man and a woman."

"It's been done before," Gwen commented as she opened her eyes.

Luke smiled. His legs made a friendly tangle with hers. "It's *all* been done before, child. It's simply that each person believes his is a fresh experience."

Gwen tilted her head, waiting for his explanation.

Luke obliged. "Endless numbers of symphonies are composed on the same eighty-eight keys." He closed his eyes, and Gwen took the opportunity to study him.

"Will you let me read it?" she asked suddenly. "Or are you temperamental and sensitive?"

"I'm only temperamental when it's to my advantage," Luke told her lazily, opening one eye. "How's your spelling?"

"Comme ci, comme ça," Gwen grinned across at him.

"You can proof my rough draft, my spelling's only half that good."

"That's generous of you." Abruptly she let out a cry. "Oh, I've got one!" Instantly she was sitting up, giving all her attention to the fish on the end of her line. Her face was animated as she tossed her hair back with an impatient jerk of her head. There was competence in her hands and a gleam of challenge in her eyes. "Eight pounds easy," she announced as she plopped the defeated fish on deck. "And that was just for practice." Raphael roused himself to inspect the first catch, then curled up beside Gwen's hip and went back to sleep.

The silence lay comfortably between them. There was no need for conversation or small talk. Dragonflies streaked by now and then with a flash of color and a quick buzz. Occasionally birds called to each other. It seemed natural to Gwen to loll drowsily across from Luke under the hazy sun. Her legs crossed over his with absent camaraderie. The shadows lengthened. Still they lingered, drifting among the stumps of once-towering cypress.

"The sun'll be gone in a couple of hours," Luke commented. Gwen made an unintelligible sound of agreement. "We should be heading back." The boat rocked gently as Luke got to his feet.

Under the cover of gold-tipped lashes, Gwen watched him. He stretched, and muscles rippled. His eyes were clear and light, an arresting contrast to the burnished tone of his skin. They flicked over her as she lay still, too comfortable to stir herself. She knew that he was aware of her scrutiny.

"You owe me ten dollars," she reminded him smiling.

"A small price to pay for the afternoon." The water sighed as the boat glided over it. "Did you know you have five pale gold freckles on your nose?"

Gwen laughed as she stretched her arms luxuriously over her head. "I believe you're quite mad."

He watched her as the lashes shadowed her cheeks and her mouth sweetened with a smile. "I begin to be sure of it," he murmured.

It wasn't until the pirogue bumped noiselessly against its home dock that Gwen stirred again. The thin wisps of clouds were pink now with the setting sun, and there was a coolness in the air.

"Mmm." Her sigh was filled with the simple pleasure of the moment. "What a lovely ride."

"Next time, you pole," Luke stated. He watched Raphael stand, stretch and leap nimbly onto the dock and then joined him. After securing the boat, he offered a hand to Gwen.

"I suppose that's only fair." Gwen stood in one fluid

movement. As nimbly as Raphael, she leaped onto the dock. She tilted back her head to give Luke a flippant grin, but found her lips captured by his.

One hand tangled in her hair while his other pressed into the small of her back, demanding she come closer. His mouth was desperate in its need for possession. There was a tension in him, a whisper of power held tightly in check. Gwen's pulses hammered at the thought of it unleashed. There was no gentleness in the mouth that claimed hers nor in the arms that held her, and she asked for none. There was a wild, restless thing in her that cried for release. She explored the strength of his arms, then the softness of his hair, as she plunged deeper into sensations she could no longer measure. Touching him, she felt there were no limits to the power flooding her. What filled her was more than the quick heat of passion, more than a transient surge of desire. It was an all-consuming need to be his. She wanted to travel where only he could take her and to learn what only he could teach her. Then Luke's hands were on her shoulders, pushing her away.

"Gwen," he began in a voice roughened with desire.

"No, don't talk," she murmured, and pulled his mouth back to hers. It was his taste, and his taste only, that could satisfy her growing hunger. She was famished, only now aware that she had fasted all her life. For a soaring, blinding moment, his mouth bruised hers; then he wrenched away. He held her shoulders in a crushing grip, but Gwen felt no pain as his eyes met hers. She could only stare. Her confusion, her need, her willingness, were plain on her face. Luke's oath was savage and swift as he turned away.

"You should know better than to look at a man like that."

Gwen heard the harsh journey of air in and out of his lungs. Her fingers shook as she ran them nervously through her hair. "I—I don't know how I looked."

"Malleable," Luke muttered. He stared down at the sluggish river before turning back to her. "Pliant, willing and outrageously innocent. Do you know how difficult it is to resist the untouched, the uncorrupted?"

Helplessly, Gwen shook her head. "No, I. . . ."

"Of course you don't," Luke cut in sharply. She winced at his tone, and he let out a long breath. "Good heavens, how easy it is to forget what a child you are."

"I'm not, I . . ." Gwen shook her head in mute denial. "It happened so fast, I didn't think. I just . . ."

"I can hardly deny that it's my fault." His tone had cooled, and its marked disinterest had the edge of a knife. "You're an extraordinary creature, part will-o'-the-wisp, part Amazon, and I have a problem keeping my hands off you. Knowing I can have you is not exactly an incentive to restrain myself."

His matter-of-fact tone scraped at Gwen's raw pride, even as it tripped her temper. "You're hateful."

"Agreed," Luke said with a brief nod. "But still, I think, civilized enough not to take advantage of an innocent girl."

"I am not . . ." Gwen managed before she felt the need to swallow. "I am not an innocent girl, I'm a grown woman!"

"As you wish. Do you still want me to take advantage of you?" Luke's tone was agreeable now.

"No!" Impatiently, she brushed at the hair on her forehead. "I mean, it wouldn't be . . . Certainly not!"

"In that case . . ." Taking her arm, Luke firmly guided Gwen inside Malon's cabin.

CHAPTER 10

Knocking on Luke's door was not the easiest thing Gwen had ever done, but it was necessary. She felt it necessary to prove to herself that she would not succumb to a newly discovered weakness again. She was a grown woman, capable of handling herself. She had asked to read Luke's manuscript, had agreed to proof it. She would not back down because of a kiss or a moment of madness. Still, Gwen braced herself as she lifted her knuckles to the wood. She held her breath.

"Come in."

These simple, ordinary words from inside the room caught at her heart. Letting out her breath slowly, she arranged her features in casual, almost indifferent lines and opened the door. Luke did not even bother to look up.

Reference books were piled on the table and scattered over the floor. Papers—typewritten, handwritten, crumpled and smooth—were strewn everywhere. On the table in the midst of the chaos was a battered portable typewriter. There sat the creator of the havoc, frowning at the keys while he pounded on them. The curtains were still drawn, closing out the late-morning sun, and the bed was a tangle of sheets. Everywhere were books, papers, folders.

"What a mess," Gwen murmured involuntarily. At her voice, Luke glanced up. There was at first a crease of annoyance between his brows, then a look of mild surprise before all was smoothed away.

"Hello," he said easily. He did not rise, but leaned back in his chair to look at her.

Gwen advanced, stepping over books and around papers on the journey. "This is incredible." She lifted her hand to gesture around the room, then dropped it to her side. "How do you live like this?"

Luke looked around, shrugged and met the curiosity in her eyes. "I don't, I work like this. If you've come to tidy up, I'll tell you the same thing I told the girl Anabelle used to send up here. Mess with my papers, and I'll toss you out the window."

Amused, Gwen stuck her hands in her pockets and nudged a book out of her way with her toe. "So, you're temperamental after all." This, she felt, was a trait she could understand and deal with.

"If you like," he agreed. "This way, if I lose something, I can only swear at myself, not at some hapless maid or well-meaning secretary. I have an aversion for well-meaning secretaries. What can I do for you? I'm afraid the coffee's cold."

The formality in his tone made it clear this was his domain. Gwen schooled her voice to sound briskly professional. “You said yesterday you'd like me to proof your manuscript. I'd be glad to do it. If,” she added with a glance around the room, “you can find it.”

He smiled his charming, irresistible smile. Gwen hardened herself against it. “Are you an organized soul, Gwenivere? I've always admired organization as long as it doesn't infringe on my habits. Sit,” he invited with a gesture of his hand.

Gwen stepped over two dictionaries and an encyclopedia. “Would you mind if I opened the drapes first?” she asked.

“If you wish,” he answered as he reached for a pile of typewritten pages. “Just don't get domestic.”

“Nothing could be further from my mind,” she assured him, and had the pleasure of seeing him wince at the brilliance of the sunlight that streamed into the room. “There,” she said, adopting the tone of a nursery school teacher, “isn't that better?”

“Sit.”

Gwen did so after removing a pile of magazines from the chair across from him.

“You look older with your hair up,” Luke commented mildly. “Nearly sixteen.”

A fire lit in her eyes, but she managed to keep her voice cool. “Do you mind if I get started?”

“Not at all.” Luke handed her a stack of typewritten material. “You'll find a pencil and a dictionary somewhere. Do as much as you like, just be quiet about it.”

Gwen's mouth opened to retort, but as he was typing

again, she closed it. After locating a pencil under a pile of discarded magazines, she picked up the first page. She refused to admit that the project excited her, that she wanted the job because it meant sharing something with him. Dismissing such thoughts, she resolved to read with objective professionalism. Minutes later, her pencil was forgotten—she was enthralled.

Time passed. Gwen no longer heard the clicking of the typewriter. Dust motes danced in the insistent sunlight, but Gwen was unaware of them. Luke's characters were flesh and blood to her. She felt she knew them, cared about them. She was even unaware that her eyes had filled with tears. She felt as the woman in Luke's story felt; desperately in love, confused, proud, vulnerable. She wept for the beauty of the words and the despair of the heroine. Suddenly, she lifted her eyes.

Luke had stopped typing, but for how long, she did not know. She blinked to clear her vision. He was watching her. His eyes were intent and searching, his mouth unsmiling. Helplessly Gwen stared back, letting the tears fall freely. Her weakness frightened her. He was not touching her, not speaking to her, yet her whole body felt attuned to him. She opened her mouth, but no words came. She shook her head, but he neither moved nor spoke. Knowing her only defense was escape, Gwen stood and darted from the room.

The bayou offered a haven, so she abandoned the house and fled toward it. She had calmed herself considerably by the time she neared Malon's cabin. Taking long, deep breaths, Gwen slowed her steps. It would not do to have Malon see her out of breath and distressed. As she rounded the last bend in the path, she saw Malon stepping from his pirogue onto the dock. Already, she felt reason returning.

"A good catch?" she asked, grateful she could smile at him without effort.

"Not bad," he answered with typical understatement. "Did you come for dinner?"

"Dinner?" Gwen repeated, glancing automatically at the sun. "Is it so late?" Could the afternoon have gone so swiftly? she wondered.

"It is late enough because I'm hungry," Malon replied. "We'll cook up some shrimp and eat, then you can take your mama her share. Can you still make coffee?"

"Of course I can still make coffee—just don't tell Tillie." Gwen followed him inside, letting the screen door slam behind them.

Before long the cabin was filled with the pungent scent of shrimp gumbo cooking and the quiet strains of Chopin. Raphael sunned on the windowsill, leaving the humans to deal with the domestic chores. Gwen felt the tension draining from her system. She ate, surprised at her appetite until she recalled she had eaten nothing since breakfast.

"You still like my cooking, *hein?*" Pleased, Malon spooned more gumbo onto her plate.

"I just didn't want to hurt your feelings," Gwen told him between bites. Malon watched her clean her plate and chuckled. With a contented sigh, Gwen sat back. "I haven't eaten that much in two years."

"That's why you're skinny." Malon leaned back, too, and lit a strong French cigarette. Gwen remembered the scent as well as she remembered the tastes. She had been twelve—curious and ultimately sick—when she persuaded Malon to let her try one. He had offered no sympathy and no lecture. Grinning at the memory, Gwen watched the thin column of smoke rise.

"Now you feel better," Malon commented. At his statement, she shifted her eyes back to his. Instantly, she saw he was not referring to her hunger. Her shoulders lifted and then fell with her sigh.

"Some. I needed to come here—it's helped. I'm having trouble understanding myself, and there's . . . well, there's this man."

"There is bound to be," Malon agreed, blowing a series of smoke rings. "You are a woman."

"Yes, but not a very smart one. I don't know very much about men. And he's nothing like the men I've known in any case." She turned to Malon. "The trouble is . . ." She made a small, frustrated sound and walked to the window. "The trouble is, I'm becoming more involved, more emotionally involved with . . . this man than I can afford to."

"'Afford to,'" he repeated with a snort. "What do you mean, 'afford to'? Emotions cost you nothing."

"Oh, Malon." When she turned back to him, her eyes were unhappy. "Sometimes they cost everything. I'm beginning to need him, beginning to feel an—an attachment that can lead nowhere."

"And why can it lead nowhere?"

"Because I need love." After running a hand through her hair, Gwen paced the width of the cabin.

"So does everyone," Malon told her, carefully crushing out his cigarette.

"But he doesn't love me," she said miserably. Her hands made a futile gesture. "He doesn't love me, yet I can't stop thinking about him. When I'm with him, I forget everything else. It's wrong, he's involved with someone else, and . . . Oh, Malon, it's so complicated." Her voice faltered away.

"Life is not simple, little girl," he said, reverting to her childhood title, "but we live it." Rising, he moved toward her, then patted her cheek. "Complications provide spice."

"Right now," she said with a small smile, "I'd rather be bland."

"Did you come for advice or for sympathy?" His eyes were small and sharp, his palm rough. He smelled of fish and tobacco. Gwen felt the ground was more solid where he stood.

"I came to be with you," she told him softly, "because you are the only father I have." Slipping her arms around his waist, she rested her head on one of his powerful shoulders. She felt his wide hand stroke her hair. "Malon," she murmured. "I don't want to be in love with him."

"So, do you come for an antilove potion? Do you want a snakeskin for his pillow?"

Gwen laughed and tilted back her head. "No."

"Good. I like him. I would feel bad putting a hex on him."

She realized Malon had known all along she had been speaking of Luke. Always she had been as clear as a piece of glass to him. Still, she was more comfortable with him than with anyone else. Gwen studied him, wondering what secrets he held behind the small blue eyes. "Malon, you never told me you'd been to Budapest."

"You never asked."

She smiled and relaxed. "If I asked now, would you tell me?"

"I'll tell you while you do the dishes."

Bradley frowned at his canvas, then at his model. "You're not giving me the spark," he complained as he pushed the fisherman's cap further back on his head.

Three nights of fitful sleep had dimmed Gwen's spark considerably. She sat, as Bradley had directed her, in the smoothly worn U formed by two branches of an ancient oak. She wore the robe he had chosen, with a magnolia tucked behind her ear. Following his instructions, she had left her hair free and kept her makeup light. Because of their size and color, her eyes dominated the picture. But they did not, as Bradley had anticipated, hold the light he had seen before. There was a listlessness in the set of her shoulders, a moodiness in the set of her mouth.

"Gwen," Bradley said with exaggerated patience, "depression is not the mood we're seeking."

"I'm sorry, Bradley." Gwen shrugged and sent him a weary smile. "I haven't been sleeping well."

"Warm milk," Monica Wilkins stated from her perch on a three-legged stool. She was painting, with quiet diligence, a tidy clump of asters. "Always helps me."

Gwen wanted to wrinkle her nose at the thought, but instead she answered politely. "Maybe I'll try that next time."

"Don't scald it, though," Monica warned as she perfected her image of a petal.

"No, I won't," Gwen assured her with equal gravity.

"Now that we've got that settled . . ." Bradley began, in such a martyrlike voice that Gwen laughed.

"I'm sorry, Bradley, I'm afraid I'm a terrible model."

"Nonsense," Bradley said. "You've just got to relax."

"Wine," Monica announced, still peering critically at her asters.

"I beg your pardon?" Bradley turned his head and frowned.

"Wine," Monica repeated. "A nice glass of wine would relax her beautifully."

"Yes, I suppose it might, if we had any." Bradley adjusted the brim of his cap and studied the tip of his brush.

"I have," Monica told him in her wispy voice.

"Have what?"

Gwen's eyes went back to Bradley. I'm beginning to feel as though I was at a tennis match, she thought, lifting a hand to the base of her neck.

"Wine," Monica answered, carefully adding a vein to a pale green leaf. "I have a thermos of white wine in my bag. It's nicely chilled."

"How clever of you," Bradley told her admiringly.

"Thank you." Monica blushed. "You're certainly welcome to it, if you think it might help." Carefully she opened a bulky macramé sack and pulled out a red thermos.

"Monica, I'm in your debt." Gallantly, Bradley bowed over the thermos. Monica let out what sounded suspiciously like a giggle before she went back to her asters.

"Bradley, I really don't think this is necessary," Gwen began.

"Just the thing to put you into the mood," he disagreed as he unscrewed the thermos lid. Wine poured, light and golden, into the plastic cup.

"But Bradley, I hardly drink at all."

"Glad to hear it." He held out the cup. "Bad for your health."

"Bradley," Gwen began again, trying to keep her voice firm. "It's barely ten o'clock in the morning."

"Yes, drink up, the light will be wrong soon."

"Oh, good grief." Defeated, Gwen lifted the plastic cup to her lips and sipped. With a sigh, she sipped again. "This is crazy," she muttered into the wine.

"What's that, Gwen?" Monica called out.

"I said this is lovely," Gwen amended. "Thank you, Monica."

"Glad to help." As the women exchanged smiles, Bradley tipped more wine into the cup.

"Drink it up," he ordered, like a parent urging medicine on a child. "We don't want to lose the light."

Obediently, Gwen tilted the cup. When she handed

it back to Bradley, she heaved a huge sigh. "Am I relaxed?" she asked. There was a pleasant lightness near the top of her head. "My, it's gotten warm, hasn't it?" She smiled at no one in particular as Bradley replaced the lid on the thermos.

"I hope I haven't overdone it," he muttered to Monica.

"One never knows about people's metabolisms," Monica said. With a noncommittal grunt, Bradley returned to his canvas.

"Now look this way, love," he ordered as Gwen's attention wandered. "Remember, I want contrasts. I see the delicacy of your bone structure, the femininity in the pose, but I want to see character in your face. I want spirit—no, more—I want challenge in your eyes. Dare the onlooker to touch the untouched."

"Untouched," Gwen murmured as her memory stirred. "I'm not a child," she asserted, and straightened her shoulders.

"No," Bradley agreed as he studied her closely. "Yes, yes, that's perfect!" He grabbed his brush. Glancing over his shoulder, he caught sight of Luke approaching, and then he gave his full attention to his work. "Ah, the mouth's perfect," he muttered, "just between sulky and a pout. Don't change it, don't change a thing. Bless you, Monica!"

Bradley worked feverishly, unaware that the wine was a far less potent stimulant to his model than the man who now stood beside him. It was his presence that brought the rush of color to her cheeks, that brightened her eyes with challenge and made her mouth grow soft, sulky and inviting. Luke's own face was inscrutable as he watched. Though he stood in quiet observation, there was an air of alertness about him. Bradley muttered as he worked. A crow cawed monotonously in the distance.

A myriad of thoughts and feelings rushed through Gwen's mind. Longing warred fiercely with pride. Luke had infuriated her, charmed her, laughed at her, rejected her. I will not fall in love with him, she told herself. I will not allow it to happen. *He won't make a fool of me again.*

"Magnificent," Bradley murmured.

"Yes, it is." Luke slipped his hands into his pockets as he studied the portrait. "You've caught her."

"It's rare," Bradley muttered, touching up the shadows of Gwen's cheeks in the portrait. "Her looks are just a bonus. It's that aura of innocence mixed with the hint of banked fires. Incredible combination. Every man who sees this portrait will want her."

A flash of irritation crossed Luke's face as he lifted his eyes to Gwen's. "Yes, I imagine so."

"I'm calling it *The Virgin Temptress.* It suits, don't you think?"

"Hmm."

Taking this as full agreement, Bradley lapsed back into unintelligible mutters. Abruptly, he put down his brush and began packing his equipment. "You did beautifully," he told Gwen. "We're losing the morning light. We should start a bit earlier, I think. Three more good sittings should do it now."

"I'll walk back with you, Bradley." Monica rose.

"I've done about all I can do on this one." Gathering up her paints, easel and stool, she started after Bradley.

Gwen slipped down from her seat in the fork of the tree with a quick flutter of white. As her bare feet touched the grass, the wine spun dizzily in her head. Instinctively she rested her hand against the tree for support. Watching her, Luke lifted a brow in speculation. With exaggerated care, she straightened, swallowed the odd dryness in her throat and started to walk. Her legs felt strangely weak. It was her intention to walk past Luke with icy dignity, but he stopped her easily with a hand on her arm.

"Are you all right?"

The sun had the wine bubbling inside her. Clearing her throat, Gwen spoke distinctly. "Of course. I am just fine."

Luke placed two fingers under her chin and lifted it. He studied her upturned face. Humor leaped into his eyes. "Why, Gwenivere, you're sloshed."

Knowing the truth of his statement only stiffened her dignity. "I have no idea what you are talking about. If you would kindly remove your hand from my face, I would greatly appreciate it."

"Sure. But don't blame me if you fall on it once the support's gone." Luke dropped his hand, and Gwen swayed dangerously. She gripped Luke's shirt to right herself.

"If you will excuse me," she said regally, but neither moved nor dropped her hand. Heaving a deep sigh, Gwen raised her face again and frowned. "I'm waiting for you to stand still."

"Oh. Sorry. May one ask how you came to be in this condition?"

"Relaxed," Gwen corrected.

"I beg your pardon?"

"That's what I am. It was either wine or warm milk. Monica's a whiz at these things. I'm not too fond of warm milk, and there wasn't any handy in any case."

"No, I can see it might be difficult to come by," Luke agreed, slipping a supporting arm around her waist as she began to weave her way across the lawn.

"I only had a topful, you know."

"That should do it."

"Oh, dear." Gwen stopped abruptly. "I've stepped on a bee." She sat down in a floating film of white. "I suppose the poor little thing will go off and die." Lifting her foot, she frowned at the small welt on the ball of her foot.

"Happily bombed, I should think." Luke sat down and took her foot in his hand. "Hurt?" he asked as he drew out the stinger.

"No, I don't feel anything."

"Small wonder. I think it might be wise to tell Bradley you don't want to be quite so relaxed at ten in the morning."

"He's very serious about his art," Gwen said confidentially. "He believes I'll become immoral."

"A distinct possibility if you continue to relax before noon," Luke agreed dryly. "But I believe you mean 'immortal.'"

"Do you think so, too?" Gwen lifted her face to

the sun. "I really thought he and Monica were macadamias."

"What?"

"Nuts." Gwen lay back in the grass and shut her eyes. "I think it would be rather sweet if they fell in love, don't you?"

"Adorable."

"You're just cynical because you've been in love so many times."

"Have I?" He traced a finger over her ankle as he watched the sun highlight her hair. "Why do you say that?"

"Your books. You know how women think, how they feel. When I was reading yesterday, I hurt because it was too real, too personal." The robe shifted lightly with her sigh. "I imagine you've made love with dozens of women."

"Making love and being in love are entirely separate things."

Gwen opened her eyes. "Sometimes," she agreed. "For some people."

"You're a romantic," Luke told her with a shrug. "Only a romantic can wear floating white or toss flowers to the stars or believe a magician's illusions."

"How odd." Gwen's voice was genuinely puzzled as she closed her eyes again. "I've never thought of myself as a romantic. Is it wrong?"

"No." The word was quick and faintly annoyed. Luke rose and stared down at her. Her hair was spread out under her, glinting with golden lights. The robe crossed lightly over her breasts, making an inviting shadow.

Swearing under his breath, he bent and scooped her into his arms.

"Mmm, you're very strong." Her head spun gently, so she rested it against his shoulder. "I noticed that the first day, when I watched you chop down the tree. Michael lifts weights."

"Good for Michael."

"No, actually, he strained his back." With a giggle, Gwen snuggled deeper into the curve of his shoulder. "Michael isn't very physical, you see. He plays bridge." Gwen lifted her face and smiled cheerfully. "I'm quite hopeless at bridge. Michael says my mind needs discipline."

"I simply must meet this Michael."

"He has fifty-seven ties, you know."

"Yes, I imagine he does."

"His shoes are always shined," Gwen added wistfully, and traced Luke's jawline with her fingertip. "I really must try to be more tidy. He tells me continually that the image a person projects is important, but I tend to forget. Feeding pigeons in the park isn't good for a corporate image."

"What is?"

"Opera," she said instantly. "German opera particularly, but I fall asleep. I like to watch murder mysteries on the late-night TV."

"Philistine," Luke concluded as his mouth twitched into a smile.

"Exactly," Gwen agreed, feeling more cheerful than she had in weeks. "Your face is leaner than his, too, and he never forgets to shave."

"Good for Michael," Luke mumbled again as he mounted the porch steps.

"He never made me feel the way you do." At these words Luke stopped and stared down into Gwen's eyes. Cushioned by the wine, Gwen met his look with a gentle smile. "Why do you suppose that is?"

Luke's voice was edged with roughness. "Can you really be so utterly guileless?"

She considered the question, then shrugged. "I don't know. I suppose so. Do you want me to be?"

For a moment, Luke's arms tightened, shifting her closer against him. In immediate response, Gwen closed her eyes and offered her mouth. When his lips brushed over her brow, she sighed and cuddled closer. "Sometimes you're a very nice man," she murmured.

"Am I?" He frowned down at her. "Let's say sometimes I remember there are a few basic rules. At the moment, I'm finding my memory unfortunately clear."

"A very nice man," Gwen repeated, and kissed a spot under his jaw. With a yawn, she settled comfortably against him. "But I won't fall in love with you."

Luke looked down at her quiet face with its aureole of soft curls. "A wise decision," he said softly, and carried her into the house.

CHAPTER 11

It was dark when Gwen awoke. Disoriented, she stared at the dim shapes of furniture and the pale silver moonlight. It was a knock at the door that had awakened her, and it came again, soft and insistent. Brushing her hair from her face, she sat up. The room spun once, then settled. Gwen moaned quietly and swallowed before she rose to answer the knock. In the hallway the light was bright. She put her hand over her eyes to shield them.

"Oh, darling, I'm sorry to wake you." Anabelle gave a sympathetic sigh. "I know how these headaches are."

"Headaches?" Gwen repeated, gingerly uncovering her eyes.

"Yes, Luke told me all about it. Did you take some aspirin?"

"Aspirin?" Gwen searched her memory. Abruptly, color rushed to her cheeks. "Oh!"

Taking this as an affirmative response, Anabelle smiled. "Are you feeling better now?"

"I haven't got a headache," Gwen murmured.

"Oh, I'm so glad, because you have a phone call." Anabelle smiled more brightly. "It's from New York, so I really thought it best to wake you. It's that Michael of yours. He has a lovely voice."

"Michael," Gwen echoed softly. She sighed, wishing she could return to the comforting darkness of her room. She felt only weariness at the sound of his name. Glancing down, she saw she still wore the white robe. She could clearly remember her conversation with Luke and, more disturbing, the feel of his arms as he carried her.

"You really shouldn't keep him waiting, darling." Anabelle interrupted Gwen's thoughts with gentle prompting. "It's long-distance."

"No, of course not." Gwen followed her mother to the foot of the stairs.

"I'll just run along and have Tillie warm up some dinner for you." Anabelle retreated tactfully, leaving Gwen staring down at the waiting receiver. She took a deep breath, blew it out and picked up the phone.

"Hello, Michael."

"Gwen—I was beginning to think I'd been left on hold." His voice was even, well pitched and annoyed.

"I'm sorry." The apology was automatic, and immediately, she swore at herself for giving it. Why does he always intimidate me? she demanded silently of herself. "I was busy," she added in a firmer voice. "I wasn't expecting to hear from you."

"I hope it's a pleasant surprise," he replied. From the tone of his voice, Gwen knew he had already concluded it was. "I've been busy myself," he went on without bothering to hear her answer. "Right up to my chin in a lawsuit against Delron Corporation. Tricky business. It's had me chained to my desk."

"I'm sorry to hear that, Michael," Gwen said. Glancing up, she saw Luke coming down the steps. *Oh, perfect,* she thought in despair. She feigned unconcern with a faint nod of greeting, but when he stopped and leaned against the newel post, she frowned. "Do you mind?" she whispered sharply to Luke.

"No, not a bit." He smiled but made no effort to move. "Say hello for me."

Her eyes narrowed into furious slits. "You're horrible, absolutely horrible."

"What?" came Michael's puzzled voice. "What did you say?"

"Oh, nothing," Gwen said sharply.

"For heaven's sake, Gwen, I'm simply trying to tell you about the Delron case. You needn't get testy."

"I am not testy. Why did you call, Michael?"

"To see when you'd be coming home, sweetheart. I miss you." He was using his quiet, persuasive tone, and Gwen sighed. Closing her eyes, she rested the receiver against her forehead a moment.

"Does he always make you feel guilty?" Luke asked conversationally. Gwen jerked up her chin and glared.

"Shut up," she ordered, furious that he could read her so accurately.

"What?" Michael's voice shouted through the receiver. Luke gave a quick laugh at the outraged voice. "We must have a bad connection," he concluded.

"Must have," Gwen muttered. Taking a deep breath, Gwen decided to clear the air once and for all. "Michael, I . . ."

"I thought I'd given you enough time to cool off," Michael said pleasantly.

"Cool off?"

"It was foolish of us to fight that way, sweetheart. Of course I know you didn't mean the things you said."

"I didn't?"

"You know you have a tendency to say rash things when you're in a temper," Michael reminded her in a patient, forgiving tone. "Of course," he went on, "I suppose I was partially to blame."

"You were?" Gwen struggled to keep her voice quiet and reasonable. "How could you be partially to blame for my temper?" Glancing up, she saw Luke still watching her.

"I'm afraid I rushed you. You simply weren't ready for a sudden proposal."

"Michael, we've been seeing each other for nearly a year," Gwen reminded him, pushing her fingers through her hair in irritation. The gesture caused the V of her bodice to widen enticingly.

"Of course, sweetheart," he said soothingly. "But I should have prepared you."

"*Prepared me?* I don't want to be prepared, Michael, do you understand? I want to be surprised. And if you call me sweetheart again in that patronizing voice, I'm going to scream."

"Now, now, Gwen, don't get upset. I'm more than willing to forgive and forget."

"Oh." Gwen swallowed her rage. "Oh, that's generous of you, Michael. I don't know what to say."

"Just say when you'll be back, sweetheart. We'll have a nice celebration dinner and set the date. Tiffany's has some lovely rings. You can take your pick."

"Michael," Gwen said, "please listen to me. Really listen this time. I'm not what you want. . . . I can't be what you want. If I tried, I'd shrivel up inside. Please, I do care about you, but don't ask me to be someone I'm not."

"I don't know what you're talking about, Gwen," he interrupted. "I'm not asking you—"

"Michael," Gwen said, cutting him off. "I just can't go through all this again. I did mean the things I said, but I don't want to have to say them all again. I'm not good for you, Michael. Find someone who knows how to fix vodka martinis for twenty."

"You're talking nonsense." It was his cool attorney's voice, and Gwen closed her eyes, knowing arguments were futile. "We'll straighten all this out when you get home."

"No, Michael," she said, knowing he wouldn't hear.

"Give me a call and I'll meet your plane. Goodbye, Gwen."

"Goodbye, Michael," she murmured, even while she replaced the receiver. She felt a wave of sorrow and guilt. Lifting her eyes, she met Luke's. There was no amusement in them now, only understanding. She felt that amusement would have been easier to handle. "I'd appreciate it very much," she said quietly, "if you wouldn't say anything just now." She walked past him and up the stairs while he looked after her.

Gwen stood on her balcony under a moonlit sky. Moss-draped cypress trees appeared ghostly and tipped with silver. There was a bird singing in a sweet, clear voice, and she wondered if it was a nightingale. The time seemed right for nightingales. She sighed, remembering that Luke had called her a romantic. Perhaps he was right. But it was not the soft night or the song of a bird that kept her out of bed and on the balcony.

Of course you can't sleep, she berated herself silently. How can you expect to sleep at night when you slept all afternoon? Color rushed to her cheeks as she recalled the reason for her peaceful midday nap. I certainly managed to make a first-class fool of myself. Did he have to be there? Couldn't I have stumbled into the house without an audience? Why can I never be cool and dignified around him?

And then the call from Michael. Gwen lifted her hand to the base of her neck and tried to massage away the tension. Again she played over the telephone conversation in her mind, attempting to find some way she could have made her feelings clearer. It's all been said before, she reminded herself, but he doesn't listen. *He forgives me.* With a quiet laugh, Gwen pressed her fingers to her eyes. He forgives me but thinks nothing of the cruel things he said. He doesn't even love me. He loves the woman he'd like me to be.

As she watched, a star shivered and fell in a speeding arc of light. Gwen caught her breath at the fleeting flash from heaven. Abruptly her thoughts centered on Luke. With him, she had felt a meteoric intensity, a brilliant heat. But she knew she could not hold him any more than the night sky could hold the trailing shimmer of light. Feeling a sudden chill, Gwen slipped back into her room. The middle of the night's a bad time for thinking, she decided. I'd be much better off if I went downstairs and tried some of Monica's detestable warm milk.

Gwen moved quickly down the hall, not bothering to switch on a light. She knew her way, just as she knew which steps creaked and which boards moaned. An unexpected sound made her whirl around as she reached the head of the stairs.

"Mama!" Stunned, Gwen watched her mother creep down the third-floor staircase. Anabelle started at Gwen's voice, and her hand fluttered to her heart.

"Gwenivere, you scared the wits out of me!" Anabelle's soft bosom rose with her breath. Her hair was charmingly disordered around her face. The robe she wore was frilly, pink and feminine. "Whatever are you doing out here in the dark?"

"I couldn't sleep." Gwen moved closer and caught the familiar scent of lilac. "Mama . . ."

"Of course, you're probably starving." Anabelle

gave a sympathetic cluck. "It doesn't do to miss meals, you know."

"Mama, what were you doing upstairs?"

"Upstairs?" Anabelle repeated, then glanced back over her shoulder. "Oh, why, I was just up with Luke." She smiled, not noticing Gwen's draining color.

"W-with Luke?"

"Yes." She made a token gesture of tidying her hair. "He's such a marvelous, generous man."

Gwen gently took her mother's hand. "Mama." She bit her lip to steady her voice and took a deep breath. "Are you certain this is what you want?"

"Is what what I want, darling?"

"This—this relationship with Luke," Gwen managed to get out, although the words hurt her throat.

"Oh, Gwen, I simply couldn't get along without Luke." She gave Gwen's icy hand a squeeze. "Goodness, you're cold. You'd best get back to bed, dear. Is there anything I can get for you?"

"No," Gwen answered quietly. "No, there's nothing." She gave Anabelle a quick, desperate hug. "Please, you go back to bed, I'll be fine."

"All right, dear." Anabelle kissed her brow in a way Gwen recognized from childhood. Satisfied that there was no fever, Anabelle patted her cheek. "Good night, Gwen."

"Good night, Mama," Gwen murmured, watching her disappear down the hall.

Gwen waited until the sound of the closing door had echoed into silence before she let out a shuddering breath. Face it, Gwen, you've been falling for your mother's man. For a moment, she merely stared down at her empty hands. Doing nothing wasn't enough, she reflected. I could have stopped it. . . . I didn't want to stop it. There's nothing to do now but get untangled while I still can. It's time to face things head-on. Lifting her chin, she began to climb the stairs to the third floor.

Without giving herself a chance to think any further, she knocked at Luke's door.

"Yes?" The reply was curt and immediate.

Refusing to give in to the urge to turn and run, Gwen twisted the knob and pushed open Luke's door. He was, as he had been before, seated in the midst of his own disorder. He was hitting the keys of the typewriter in a quick, staccato rhythm, and his eyes were intent and concentrated. Faded, low-slung jeans were his only concession to modesty. The faintest hint of lilac drifted through the air. Moistening her lips, Gwen kept her eyes from the tousled sheets of the bed.

I am in love with him, she realized suddenly, and simultaneously remembered it was impossible for her to be so. I'll have to find a way to fall out of love with him, she told herself, warding off a brief stab of misery. I'll have to start now. Keeping her head high, she closed the door behind her and leaned against it.

"Luke?"

"Hmm?" He glanced up absently, his fingers still working the keys. His expression altered as he focused on her. His hands lay still. "What are you doing here?"

There was such sharp impatience in his voice that Gwen bit her lip.

"I'm sorry to interrupt your work. I need to talk to you."

"At this hour of the night?" His tone was politely incredulous. "Run along, Gwen, I'm busy."

Gwen swallowed her pride. "Luke, please. It's important."

"So's my sanity," he muttered, without changing rhythm.

She ran a hand through her hair. *Sanity,* she thought desperately, I must have lost mine the moment he put down that ax and walked toward me. "You're making this very difficult."

"I?" he tossed back furiously. "I make it difficult? Do you know how you look at me? Do you know how many times I've found myself alone with you when you're half-dressed?" Instinctively, Gwen reached for the low neckline of her robe. "Contrary to popular opinion," he continued as he rose and strode to a small table across the room, "I am a mortal man given to normal instincts." There was a decanter of brandy on the table, and he poured himself a hefty glass. "Damn it, I want you. Haven't I made that clear enough?"

His tone was rough. Gwen felt the tears burn in her throat. When she spoke, her voice was thick with them. "I'm sorry, I didn't mean . . ." She broke off with a helpless shrug.

"For God's sake, don't cry," he said impatiently. "I'm in no mood to give you a few comforting kisses and send you along. If I touch you now, you won't leave here tonight." His eyes met hers. She swallowed even the thought of tears. "I'm not in a civilized mood, Gwen. I told you once that I know my limit. Well, I've reached it." He lifted the decanter and poured again.

Temptation fluttered along her skin. He wanted her, she could almost taste his desire. How easy it would be to take just one small step . . . to steal a night, a moment. The night would be full and rich. *But the morning would be empty.* Gwen's eyes dropped, and she struggled with her own heart. When his passion was spent, she knew her love would starve. Love has found another fool, she thought resignedly. It's best to do this quickly.

"This isn't easy for me," Gwen told him quietly. Though she fought for calm, her eyes were tragic as they met his. "I need to talk to you about Mama."

Luke turned and walked to the French doors. Tossing them open, he stared out into the night. "What about her?"

"I was wrong to interfere." Gwen shut her eyes tight and struggled to strengthen her voice. "It was wrong of me to come here thinking I had any say in whom my mother becomes involved with."

Luke swore and whirled back to face her. She watched him struggle with temper. "You are an idiot. Anabelle is a beautiful woman—"

"Please," Gwen interrupted swiftly, "let me finish. I need to say this, and it's so difficult. I'd like to say it all at once." She still stood with her back to the door, poised for escape. Luke shrugged, dropped back into his chair and signaled for her to continue. "It isn't up to me to decide what's right for my mother, it's not my right to interfere. You're good for her, I can't deny it." Gwen's breath trembled before she could steady it. "And I can't deny I'm attracted to you, but it's nothing that can't be resolved by a bit of distance. I think—I think if you and I just stay out of each other's way for the rest of my visit, everything will work out."

"Oh, do you?" Luke gave a quick laugh as he set down his glass. "That's an amazing piece of logic." He rubbed the bridge of his nose between his thumb and forefinger. Gwen frowned at the action, finding it somehow out of character.

"I'm leaving next week," Gwen told him. "There's no need for me to stay, and I've left several things undone back in New York." Hurriedly, she turned to the door.

"Gwen." Luke's voice stopped her, but she could not bear to turn and face him again. "Don't waste yourself on Michael."

"I don't intend to," she answered in a choked voice. Blind with tears, she opened the door and plunged into the darkness.

CHAPTER 12

Gwen dressed with care. She stretched out the process, dawdling over the buttons of her pale lavender blouse. After another sleepless night, Gwen knew she could not survive even a few more days in the same house with Luke. She could not be sophisticated, mature or philosophical about love. She went to her closet and pulled out her suitcase.

When two women love the same man, she mused, one of them has to lose. If it were anyone else, I could fight her. She opened the first case. How does a daughter fight her own mother? Even if she wins, she loses. I haven't really lost, she reflected as she moved to her dresser and pulled open a drawer. You have to have something first to lose it. I never had Luke.

Gwen packed methodically, using the task as a diversion. She refused to speculate on what she would do when she returned to New York. While packing, she had no past and no future, only the present. She would have to face the shambles of her life soon enough.

"Gwen." Anabelle knocked quickly and stuck her head into the room. "I wonder if you've seen . . . Oh!" She opened the door all the way when she saw Gwen's half-packed cases. "What's this?"

Gwen moistened her lips and strove for casualness. "I've got to get back to New York."

"Oh." There was disappointment in the single syllable. "But you just got here. Are you going back to Michael?"

"No, Mama, I'm not going back to Michael."

"I see." She paused a moment. "Is there some trouble at your office?"

The excuse was so perfect, agreement trembled on Gwen's tongue. Regretably, the lie would not form on her lips. "No."

Anabelle tilted her head at her daughter's tone, then quietly closed the door at her back. "You know I don't like to pry, Gwen, and I know you're a very private person, but . . ." Anabelle sighed before she walked over to sit on Gwen's bed. "I really think you'd better tell me what this is all about."

"Oh, Mama." Gwen turned away and rested both palms on her dresser. "It's such an awful mess."

"It can't be as bad as all that." Anabelle folded her hands neatly in her lap. "Just tell me straight out, it's the best way."

Gwen took a breath and held it. "I'm in love with Luke," she said quickly, then expelled the breath in one swift whoosh.

"And . . ." Anabelle prompted.

Gwen's eyes flew to the mirror in search of her mother's. "Mama, I said I was in love with Luke."

"Yes, darling, I heard that part. I'm waiting for the part about the dreadful mess."

"Mama." Gingerly, Gwen turned around. Anabelle smiled patiently. "It's not just an infatuation or a crush, I'm really in love with him."

"Oh, yes, well, that's nice."

"I don't think you understand." Gwen covered her face with her hands for a moment and then dropped them. "I even wanted him to—to make love with me."

Anabelle blushed a soft, gentle pink and brushed at her skirts. "Yes, well . . . I'm sure that's quite natural. I don't believe you and I ever had a talk about . . . ah, the birds and the bees."

"Oh, good grief, Mama," Gwen said impatiently. "I don't need a lecture on sex. I know all about that."

"Oh?" Anabelle lifted her brows in maternal censure. "I see."

"No, I don't mean . . ." Gwen stopped in frustration. How did this conversation get away from me? she wondered. "Mama, please, this is hard enough. I came home to get rid of the man, and before I knew it, I was involved with him. I didn't plan it, I didn't want it. I'd never, never do anything to hurt you, and I was wrong because years don't mean a thing, and no one has the right to choose for anyone else. Now I have to go away because I love you both so terribly, don't you see?" Gwen ended on a note of despair and dropped down at Anabelle's feet.

Anabelle stared down at the tragic face thoughtfully. "Perhaps I will in a minute," she answered, furrowing her brow. "No, actually, I don't think I will. Why don't you try again? Start with the part about your coming here to get rid of Luke. I believe that's where I got confused."

Gwen sniffled and accepted Anabelle's lace hankie. "I wanted to make him go away because I thought it was wrong for you to have an affair with him. But it was none of my—"

"A what?" Anabelle interrupted. Her hand paused on its journey to smooth Gwen's curls. *"An affair?"* she repeated, blinking rapidly. "An affair? Luke and I?" To Gwen's amazement, Anabelle tossed back her head and laughed. It was a young, gay sound. "How delightful! Darling, darling, how flattering. My, my." She smiled into space, her cheeks rosy with pleasure. "Such a handsome young man, too. He must be—" she stopped and fluttered her lashes "—well, a year or two younger than I." She laughed again and clapped her hands together as Gwen looked on. Bending down, she kissed her daughter soundly. "Thank you, sweet, sweet child. I don't know when I've had a nicer present."

"Now *I* don't understand." Gwen wiped a lingering tear from her lashes. "Are you saying you and Luke aren't lovers?"

"Oh, my." Anabelle rolled her eyes. "How very blunt you are."

"Mama, please, I'll go mad in a moment." Briefly, Gwen pressed her fingers to her eyes. Rising, she began to pace the room. "You talked and talked about him in all your letters. You said he'd changed your life. You said he was the most wonderful man you'd ever met. You couldn't get along without him. And just last night you were coming out of his room in the middle of the night. And you've been acting strangely." Gwen whirled around and paced in the other direction. "You can't deny it. Locking your door and practically pushing me out of the house on the flimsiest of excuses."

"Oh, dear." Anabelle clucked her tongue and touched a hand to her hair. "I begin to see. I suppose it was silly of me to keep it a secret." Standing, Anabelle took a blouse from Gwen's suitcase, shook it out and walked to the closet. "Yes, it's obviously my fault. But then, I wanted to surprise you. Poor darling, no wonder you've been so unhappy and confused. I'm afraid I thought you were brooding over Michael, but it wasn't him at all, was it? Luke makes much better sense, I'm sure." Carefully, Anabelle hung up the blouse. "Now, when I think back on it, I can see how you might think so." She moved back to the suitcase while Gwen prayed for patience. "Luke and I aren't having an affair, though I do thank you for the kind thought, dear. We are, however, collaborating in a sense. Why don't you sit down?"

"I think," Gwen said, "I'm going to scream any minute."

"Always so impatient," Anabelle sighed. "Well, this is a bit embarrassing. I feel so foolish." She placed her hands on her cheeks as they grew warm. "Oh, I do hope you won't laugh at me. I'm . . . I'm writing a book." The confession came out in a swift jumble of words.

"What?" Gwen exclaimed, touching her hand to her ear to check her hearing.

"I've always wanted to, but I never thought I could until Luke encouraged me." Excitement joined the embarrassment in Anabelle's voice. "I've always had such pretty stories in my head, but I never had the courage to write them down. Luke says—" Anabelle lifted her chin and glowed proudly "—he says I have a natural talent."

"Talent?" Gwen echoed as she sank onto the bed.

"Isn't that lovely of him?" Anabelle enthused. She shook out one of Gwen's packed dresses and moved toward the closet. "He's given me so much help, so much time and encouragement! He doesn't even mind if I pop up to his room and try out an idea! Why, just last night he stopped his own work to listen to me."

Remembering the conclusions she had drawn, Gwen shut her eyes. "Oh, good grief! Why didn't you tell me?"

"I wanted to surprise you. And to be honest, I felt you'd think I was being silly." She began neatly to put away Gwen's lingerie. "My, what a pretty chemise. New York has such wonderful shops. Then there's the money."

"Money," Gwen repeated. Opening her eyes, she tried valiantly to follow her mother's winding train of thought. "What money?"

"Luke thinks I should sell the manuscript when I'm finished. It's—well, it's a bit crass, don't you think?"

"Oh, Mama." Gwen could only close her eyes again.

"I am sorry about not telling you and about locking my door so you wouldn't catch me writing. And about shooing you out of the house so that I could finish up. You aren't angry with me, are you?"

"No, no, I'm not angry." Gwen stared up at Anabelle's glowing face and then buried her own in her hands and laughed. "Oh, help! What a fool I've made of myself!" She rose quickly and embraced her mother. "I'm proud of you, Mama. Very proud."

"You haven't read it yet," Anabelle reminded her.

"I don't have to read it to be proud of you. And I don't think you're silly, I think you're marvelous." Drawing away slightly, she studied Anabelle's face. "Luke's right," she said, kissing both of her mother's cheeks. "You are a beautiful woman."

"Did he say that?" Anabelle dimpled. "How sweet." After patting Gwen's shoulder, she moved to the door. "I think we've solved everything nicely. Come down after you're unpacked, and I'll let you read my first chapters."

"Mama." Gwen shook her head. "I can't stay. . . ."

"Oh, Luke." Anabelle beamed as she opened the door. "How lucky. You'll never believe the mess Gwen and I have just straightened out."

"Oh?" Luke looked past Anabelle to Gwen, then studied the open cases on her bed. "Going somewhere?"

"Yes."

"No," Anabelle said simultaneously. "Not anymore.

She was going back to New York, but we solved everything nicely."

"Mama," Gwen said warningly, and stepped forward.

"I've confessed all," she told Luke with a bright smile. "Gwen knows all about my secret hobby. The poor darling thought you and I were having a romance."

"Weren't we?" Luke lifted her hand to his lips.

"Oh, you devil." Anabelle patted his cheek, highly pleased. "I must get along now, but I'm sure Luke will want to hear what you told me about being in love with him."

"Mama!" The sharp retort emerged as a tragic whisper.

"I'd close the door," Anabelle suggested to Luke. "Gwen favors her privacy."

"I'll do that," Luke agreed, and kissed her hand again. With a delighted blush and flutter, she disappeared.

"A truly marvelous woman," Luke commented, quietly closing the door and turning the key. He turned it over in his palm a moment, studying it, then slipped it into his pocket. Gwen decided it was better strategy not to comment. "Now, suppose you tell me what you told Anabelle about being in love with me."

Looking into his calm eyes, Gwen knew it wasn't going to be easy. Temper would not work as long as he had the key. It was vital that she remain as calm as he. "I owe you an apology," she said as she casually moved to her closet. Taking the dress Anabelle had just replaced, Gwen folded it and laid it back in the suitcase.

Luke continued to stand by the door, watching her movements. “For what, precisely?”

Gwen bit the underside of her lip hard and moved back to the closet. “For the things I said about you and Mama.”

“You’re apologizing for believing we were having an affair?” Luke smiled at her for the first time, and although she heard it in his voice, she did not turn to see it. “I took it as a compliment.”

Turning slowly, Gwen decided to brazen it out. It was impossible, she decided, to be any more humiliated than she already was. “I’m well aware that I’ve made a fool of myself. And I know that I deserve to feel every bit as ridiculous as I feel. As I look back, I believe that you decided on the very first day to teach me a lesson. You never admitted you were having an affair with my mother, you simply told me it was none of my business. I felt differently at the time.” Gwen paused to catch her breath, and Luke moved into the room to lean comfortably on one of the bedposts. “I was wrong and you were right. It wasn’t any of my business, and you succeeded in teaching me a lesson just by letting me draw my own conclusions. These were helped along by Mama’s unusual behavior and her affection for you. You could, of course, have saved me a great deal of anxiety and humiliation by explaining things, but you chose to make your point. Point taken, Mr. Powers,” she continued as she worked herself up into a temper. “I’ve been put in my place by an expert. Now, I'd like you to get out of here and leave me alone. If there's one thing I want above all else, it's never to see you again. I can only be thankful we live on opposite ends of the continent."

Luke waited a moment while she tore two skirts out of her closet and heaved them into the case. "Can I get a copy of that speech for my files?"

Gwen whirled, eyes flaming. "You unfeeling, pompous boor! I've done all the groveling I'm going to do. What more do you want?"

"Was that groveling?" he asked, lifting a brow in interest. "Fascinating. What I want," he continued, "is for you to elaborate on the statement Anabelle made before she left the room. I found it very interesting."

"You want it all, don't you?" Gwen snapped, slamming the lid on her first case. "All right, then, I'll give it to you. It makes little difference at this point." She took a breath to help the words come quickly. "I love you. What will you do now that you know?" she demanded, keeping her head high. "Write it into one of your books for comic relief?"

Luke considered a moment and then shrugged. "No. I rather think I'll marry you."

In stunned silence, Gwen stared at him. "I don't think that's very funny."

"No, I doubt marriage is a funny business. I'm sure it has its moments, though. We'll have to find out." Straightening, he walked over and put his hands on her shoulders. "Soon."

"Don't touch me," she whispered, and tried to jerk out of his hold.

"Oh, yes, I'll touch you." He turned Gwen to face him. "I'll do much more than touch you. Idiot," he said roughly when he saw her tear-drenched eyes. "Are you so blind you can't see what you've put me through? I wanted you from the first moment I saw you. You stood there smiling at me, and I felt as though someone had hit me with a blunt instrument. I wanted to teach you a lesson, all right, but I didn't expect to learn one. I didn't expect some skinny kid to tangle herself up in my mind so that I couldn't get her out." He pulled her close as she stared up at him, dry-eyed and fascinated. "I love you to the edge of madness," he murmured before his mouth crushed hers.

It's a dream, Gwen thought dazedly as his mouth roamed her face, teasing her skin. It must be a dream. She threw her arms around his neck and clung, praying never to wake up. "Luke," she managed before her mouth was silenced again. "Tell me you mean it," she begged as he tasted her neck. "Please tell me you mean it."

"Look at me," he ordered, taking her chin in his hand. She did, and found her answer. Joy bubbled inside her and escaped in laughter. Laughing with her, Luke rested his brow against hers. "I believe I've surprised you."

"Oh, Luke." She buried her face in his shoulder, holding him as if she would never let him go. "I'm not surprised, I'm delirious." She sighed, weak from laughter, dizzy with love. "How did this happen?"

"I haven't the faintest idea." He brushed his lips

over the top of her head. "Falling in love with you was not in my plans."

"Why not?" she demanded, rubbing her cheek against his. "I'm a very nice person."

"You're a child," he corrected, lost in the scent of her hair. "Do you realize what we were doing when I was your age?" He gave a quick, mystified laugh. "I was working on my second novel, and you were drawing pictures with your Crayolas."

"It's twelve years, not twenty," Gwen countered, slipping her hands under his shirt to feel the warmth of his back. "And you can hardly make an issue out of an age difference, particularly a twelve-year age difference, after all this. You don't have any double standards, do you?" she asked, lifting a brow.

Luke gave her hair a brief tug. "It's not just the years. You're so innocent, so unspoiled. Wanting you was driving me mad, then loving you only made it worse." He kissed her lightly behind the ear, and she shivered with pleasure. "Even up to last night I was determined not to take advantage of that innocence. Part of me still wants to leave you that way."

"I hope the rest of you has more sense," Gwen tossed back her head to look up at him.

"I'm serious."

"So am I." She ran a fingertip along his jawline. "Buy Bradley's portrait, if you want an image."

"I already have." He smiled, caught her fingers in his and kissed them. "You don't think I'd let anyone else have it, do you?"

"Have me, too." Amusement vanished from his face as she pressed against him. "I'm a woman, Luke, not a child or an image. I love you, and I want you." Rising on her toes, she met his mouth. His hands sought her, possessed her, while she trembled with excitement. Her love seemed to expand, surrounding her until there was nothing else. She pressed closer, offering everything. It was he who drew away.

"Gwen." Luke let out a long breath and shook his head. "It's difficult to remember that you're Anabelle's daughter and that she trusts me."

"I'm trying to make it impossible," she countered. She could feel the speed of his heartbeat against hers, and reveled in a new sense of power. "Aren't you going to corrupt me?"

"Undoubtedly," he agreed. Framing her face with his hands, he kissed her nose. "After we're married."

"Oh." Gwen pouted a moment, then shrugged. "That's sensible, I suppose. Michael was always sensible, too."

Luke's eyes narrowed at the mischief in hers. "That," he said distinctly, "was a low blow. Do you know how very near I came to pulling the phone out of the wall last night when I heard you talking to him?"

"Did you?" Gwen's face illuminated at the thought. "Were you jealous?"

"That's one way of putting it," Luke agreed.

"Well," Gwen considered carefully, trying not to smile, "I suppose I can understand that. As I said, he's a very sensible man. It's all right, though, I'm sure you're every bit as sensible as Michael."

Luke studied her carefully, but Gwen managed to keep the smile a mere hint on her lips. "Are you challenging me to kiss you into insensibility?"

"Oh, yes," she agreed, and closed her eyes. "Please do."

"I never could resist a dare," Luke murmured, drawing her into his arms.

Island *of* Flowers

CHAPTER 1

Laine's arrival at Honolulu International Airport was traditional. She would have preferred to melt through the crowd, but it appeared traveling tourist class categorized her as just that. Golden-skinned girls with ivory smiles and vivid sarongs bestowed brilliant colored leis. Accepting both a kiss and floral necklace, Laine wove through the milling crowd and searched for an information desk. The girth of a fellow passenger hampered her journey. His yellow and orange flowered shirt and the twin cameras which joined the lei around his neck attested to his determination to enjoy his vacation. Under different circumstances, his appearance would have nudged at her humor, but the tension in Laine's stomach stifled any amusement. She had not stood on American soil in fifteen years. The ripe land with cliffs and beaches which she had seen as the plane descended brought no sense of homecoming.

The America Laine pictured came in sporadic patches of memory and through the perspective of a child of seven. America was a gnarled elm tree guarding her bedroom window. It was a spread of green grass where buttercups scattered gold. It was a mailbox at the end of a long, winding lane. But most of all, America was the man who had taken her to imaginary African jungles and desert islands. However, there were orchids instead of daisies. The graceful palms and spreading ferns of Honolulu were as foreign to Laine as the father she had traveled half the world to find. It seemed a lifetime ago that divorce had pulled her away from her roots.

Laine felt a quiet desperation that the address she had found among her mother's papers would lead to emptiness. The age of the small, creased piece of paper was unknown to her. Neither did she know if Captain James Simmons still lived on the island of Kauai. There had only been the address tossed in among her mother's bills. There had been no correspondence, nothing to indicate the address was still a vital one. To write to her father was the practical thing to do, and Laine had struggled with indecision for nearly a week. Ultimately, she had rejected a letter in favor of a personal meeting. Her hoard of money would barely see her through a week of food and lodging, and though she knew the trip was impetuous, she had not been able to prevent herself. Threading through her doubts was the shimmering strand of fear that rejection waited for her at the end of her journey.

There was no reason to expect anything else, she

lectured herself. *Why should the man who had left her fatherless during her growing-up years care about the woman she had become?* Relaxing the grip on the handle of her handbag, Laine reasserted her vow to accept whatever waited at her journey's end. She had learned long ago to adjust to whatever life offered. She concealed her feelings with the habit developed during her adolescence.

Quickly, she adjusted the white, soft-brimmed hat over a halo of flaxen curls. She lifted her chin. No one would have guessed her underlying anxiety as she moved with unconscious grace through the crowds. She looked elegantly aloof in her inherited traveling suit of ice blue silk, altered to fit her slight figure rather than her mother's ample curves.

The girl at the information desk was deep in an enjoyable conversation with a man. Standing to one side, Laine watched the encounter with detached interest. The man was dark and intimidatingly tall. Her pupils would undoubtedly have called him *séduisant.* His rugged features were surrounded by black hair in curling disorder, while his bronzed skin proved him no stranger to the Hawaiian sun. There was something rakish in his profile, some basic sensuality which Laine recognized but did not fully comprehend. She thought perhaps his nose had been broken at one time, but rather than spoiling the appeal of the profile, the lack of symmetry added to it. His dress was casual, the jeans well worn and frayed at the cuffs, and a denim work shirt exposed a hard chest and corded arms.

Vaguely irritated, Laine studied him. She observed

the easy flow of charm, the indolent stance at the counter, the tease of a smile on his mouth. *I've seen his type before,* she thought with a surge of resentment, *hovering around Vanessa like a crow around carrion.* She remembered, too, that when her mother's beauty had become only a shadow, the flock had left for younger prey. At that moment, Laine could feel only gratitude that her contact with men had been limited.

He turned and encountered Laine's stare. One dark brow rose as he lingered over his survey of her. She was too unreasonably angry with him to look away. The simplicity of her suit shouted its exclusiveness, revealing the tender elegance of young curves. The hat half shaded a fragile, faintly aristocratic face with well-defined planes, straight nose, unsmiling mouth and morning-sky eyes. Her lashes were thick and gold, and he took them as too long for authenticity. He assessed her as a cool, self-possessed woman, recognizing only the borrowed varnish.

Slowly, and with deliberate insolence, he smiled. Laine kept her gaze steady and struggled to defeat a blush. The clerk, seeing her companion's transfer of attention, shifted her eyes in Laine's direction and banished a scowl.

"May I help you?" Dutifully, she affixed her occupational smile. Ignoring the hovering male, Laine stepped up to the counter.

"Thank you. I need transportation to Kauai. Could you tell me how to arrange it?" A whisper of France lingered in her voice.

"Of course, there's a charter leaving for Kauai

in . . ." The clerk glanced at her watch and smiled again. "Twenty minutes."

"I'm leaving right now." Laine glanced over and gave the loitering man a brief stare. She noted that his eyes were as green as Chinese jade. "No use hanging around the airport, and," he continued as his smile became a grin, "my Cub's not as crowded or expensive as the charter."

Laine's disdainful lift of brow and dismissing survey had been successful before, but did not work this time. "Do you have a plane?" she asked coldly.

"Yeah, I've got a plane." His hands were thrust in his pockets, and in his slouch against the counter, he still managed to tower over her. "I can always use the loose change from picking up island hoppers."

"Dillon," the clerk began, but he interrupted her with another grin and a jerk of his head.

"Rose'll vouch for me. I run for Canyon Airlines on Kauai." He presented Rose with a wide smile. She shuffled papers.

"Dillon . . . Mr. O'Brian is a fine pilot." Rose cleared her throat and sent Dillon a telling glance. "If you'd rather not wait for the scheduled charter, I can guarantee that your flight will be equally enjoyable with him."

Studying his irreverent smile and amused eyes, Laine was of the opinion that the trip would be something less than enjoyable. However, her funds were low, and she knew she must conserve what she had.

"Very well, Mr. O'Brian, I will engage your services." He held out his hand, palm up, and Laine dropped her eyes to it. Infuriated by his rudeness, she brought her eyes back to his. "If you will tell me your rate, Mr. O'Brian, I shall be happy to pay you when we land."

"Your baggage check," he countered, smiling. "Just part of the service, lady."

Bending her head to conceal her blush, Laine fumbled through her purse for the ticket.

"O.K., let's go." He took both the stub and her arm, propelling her away as he called over his shoulder in farewell to the information clerk, "See you next time, Rose."

"Welcome to Hawaii," Rose stated out of habit, then, with a sigh, pouted after Dillon's back.

Unused to being so firmly guided, and hampered by a stride a fraction of his, Laine struggled to maintain her composure while she trotted beside him. "Mr. O'Brian, I hope I don't have to jog to Kauai." He stopped and grinned at her. She tried, and failed, not to pant. His grin, she discovered, was a strange and powerful weapon, and one for which she had not yet developed a defense.

"Thought you were in a hurry, Miss . . ." He glanced at her ticket, and she watched the grin vanish. When his eyes lifted, all remnants of humor had fled. His mouth was grim. She would have retreated from the waves of hostility had not his grip on her arm prevented her. "Laine Simmons?" It was more accusation than question.

"Yes, you've read it correctly," she said.

Dillon's eyes narrowed. She found her cool façade

melting with disconcerting speed. "You're going to see James Simmons?"

Her eyes widened. For an instant, a flash of hope flickered on her face. But his expression remained set and hostile. She smothered the impulse to ask hundreds of questions as she felt his tightening fingers bruise her arm.

"I don't know how that concerns you, Mr. O'Brian," she began, "but yes. Do you know my father?" She faltered over the final word, finding the novelty of its use bittersweet.

"Yes, I know him . . . a great deal better than you do. Well, Duchess—" he released her as if the contact was offensive "—I doubt if fifteen years late is better than never, but we'll see. Canyon Airlines is at your disposal." He inclined his head and gave Laine a half bow. "The trip's on the house. I can hardly charge the owner's prodigal daughter." Dillon retrieved her luggage and stalked from the terminal in thunderous silence. In the wake of the storm, Laine followed, stunned by his hostility and by his information.

Her father owned an airline. She remembered James Simmons only as a pilot, with the dream of his own planes a distant fantasy. When had the dream become reality? Why did this man, who was currently tossing her mother's elegant luggage like so many duffel bags into a small, streamlined plane, turn such hostility on her at the discovery of her name? How did he know fifteen years had spanned her separation from her father? She opened her mouth to question Dillon as he rounded the nose of the plane. She shut it again as he turned and captured her with his angry stare.

"Up you go, Duchess. We've got twenty-eight minutes to endure each other's company." His hands went to her waist, and he hoisted her as if she were no more burden than a feather pillow. He eased his long frame into the seat beside her. She became uncomfortably aware of his virility and attempted to ignore him by giving intense concentration to the buckling of her safety belt. Beneath her lashes, she watched as he flicked at the controls before the engine roared to life.

The sea opened beneath them. Beaches lay white against its verge, dotted with sun worshipers. Mountains rose, jagged and primitive, the eternal rulers of the islands. As they gained height, the colors in the scene below became so intense that they seemed artificial. Soon the shades blended. Browns, greens and blues softened with distance. Flashes of scarlet and yellow merged before fading. The plane soared with a surge of power, then its wings tilted as it made a curving arch and hurtled into the sky.

"Kauai is a natural paradise," Dillon began in the tone of a tour guide. He leaned back in his seat and lit a cigarette. "It offers, on the North Shore, the Wailua River which ends at Fern Grotto. The foliage is exceptional. There are miles of beaches, fields of cane and pineapple. Opeakea Falls, Hanalei Bay and Na Pali Coast are also worth seeing. On the South Shore," he continued, while Laine adopted the air of attentive listener, "we have Kokie State Park and Waimea Canyon. There are tropical trees and flowers at Olopia and

Menehune Gardens. Water sports are exceptional almost anywhere around the island. Why the devil did you come?"

The question, so abrupt on the tail of his mechanical recital, caused Laine to jolt in her seat and stare. "To . . . to see my father."

"Took your own sweet time about it," Dillon muttered and drew hard on his cigarette. He turned again and gave her a slow, intimate survey. "I guess you were pretty busy attending that elegant finishing school."

Laine frowned, thinking of the boarding school which had been both home and refuge for nearly fifteen years. She decided Dillon O'Brian was crazed. There was no use contradicting a lunatic. "I'm glad you approve," she returned coolly. "A pity you missed the experience. It's amazing what can be done with rough edges."

"No thanks, Duchess." He blew out a stream of smoke. "I prefer a bit of honest crudeness."

"You appear to have an adequate supply."

"I get by. Island life can be a bit uncivilized at times." His smile was thin. "I doubt if it's going to suit your tastes."

"I can be very adaptable, Mr. O'Brian." She moved her shoulders with gentle elegance. "I can also overlook a certain amount of discourtesy for short periods of time. Twenty-eight minutes is just under my limit."

"Terrific. Tell me, Miss Simmons," he continued with exaggerated respect, "how is life on the Continent?"

"Marvelous." Deliberately, she tilted her head and

looked at him from under the brim of her hat. "The French are so cosmopolitan, so urbane. One feels so . . ." Attempting to copy her mother's easy polish, she gestured and gave the next word the French expression. "*Chez soi* with people of one's own inclinations."

"Very true." The tone was ironic. Dillon kept his eyes on the open sky as he spoke. "I doubt if you'll find many people of your own inclinations on Kauai."

"Perhaps not." Laine pushed the thought of her father aside and tossed her head. "Then again, I may find the island as agreeable as I find Paris."

"I'm sure you found the men agreeable." Dillon crushed out his cigarette with one quick thrust. Laine found his fresh anger rewarding. The memory of the pitifully few men with whom she had had close contact caused her to force back a laugh. Only a small smile escaped.

"The men of my acquaintance—" she apologized mentally to elderly Father Rennier "—are men of elegance and culture and breeding. They are men of high intellect and discerning tastes who possess the manners and sensitivity which I currently find lacking in their American counterparts."

"Is that so?" Dillon questioned softly.

"That, Mr. O'Brian," said Laine firmly, "is quite so."

"Well, we wouldn't want to spoil our record." Switching over to automatic pilot, he turned in his seat and captured her. Mouth bruised mouth before she realized his intent.

She was locked in his arms, her struggles prevented by his strength and by her own dazed senses. She was overwhelmed by the scent and taste and feel of him. He increased the intimacy, parting her lips with his tongue. To escape from sensations more acute than she had thought possible, she clutched at his shirt.

Dillon lifted his face, and his brows drew straight at her look of stunned, young vulnerability. She could only stare, her eyes filled with confused new knowledge. Pulling away, he switched back to manual control and gave his attention to the sky. "It seems your French lovers haven't prepared you for American technique."

Stung, and furious with the weakness she had just discovered, Laine turned in her seat and faced him. "Your technique, Mr. O'Brian, is as crude as the rest of you."

He grinned and shrugged. "Be grateful, Duchess, that I didn't simply shove you out the door. I've been fighting the inclination for twenty minutes."

"You would be wise to suppress such inclinations," Laine snapped, feeling her temper bubbling at an alarming speed. *I will not lose it,* she told herself. She would not give this detestable man the satisfaction of seeing how thoroughly he had unnerved her.

The plane dipped into an abrupt nosedive. The sea hurtled toward them at a terrifying rate as the small steel bird performed a series of somersaults. The sky and sea were a mass of interchangeable blues with the white of clouds and the white of breakers no longer separate. Laine clutched at her seat, squeezing her eyes shut as the sea and sky whirled in her brain. Protest was impossible. She had lost both her voice and her heart at the first circle. She clung and prayed for her stomach to remain stationary. The plane leveled, then cruised right side up, but inside her head the world still revolved. Laine heard her companion laugh wholeheartedly.

"You can open your eyes now, Miss Simmons. We'll be landing in a minute."

Turning to him, Laine erupted with a long, detailed analysis of his character. At length, she realized she was stating her opinion in French. She took a deep breath. "You, Mr. O'Brian," she finished in frigid English, "are the most detestable man I have ever met."

"Thank you, Duchess." Pleased, he began to hum.

Laine forced herself to keep her eyes open as Dillon began his descent. There was a brief impression of greens and browns melding with blue, and again the swift rise of mountains before they were bouncing on asphalt and gliding to a stop. Dazed, she surveyed the hangars and lines of aircraft, Piper Cubs and cabin planes, twin engines and passenger jets. *There's some mistake,* she thought. *This cannot belong to my father.*

"Don't get any ideas, Duchess," Dillon remarked, noting her astonished stare. His mouth tightened. "You've forfeited your share. And even if the captain was inclined to be generous, his partner would make things very difficult. You're going to have to look someplace else for an easy ride."

He jumped to the ground as Laine stared at him with disbelief. Disengaging her belt, she prepared to lower herself to the ground. His hands gripped her waist before her feet made contact. For a moment, he held her suspended. With their faces only inches apart, Laine found his eyes her jailer. She had never known eyes so green or so compelling.

"Watch your step," he commanded, then dropped her to the ground.

Laine stepped back, retreating from the hostility in his voice. Gathering her courage, she lifted her chin and held her ground. "Mr. O'Brian, would you please tell me where I might find my father?"

He stared for a moment, and she thought he would simply refuse and leave her. Abruptly, he gestured toward a small white building. "His office is in there," he barked before he turned to stride away.

CHAPTER 2

The building which Laine approached was a midsize hut. Fanning palms and flaming anthurium skirted its entrance. Hands trembling, Laine entered. She felt as though her knees might dissolve under her, as though the pounding of her heart would burst through her head. What would she say to the man who had left her floundering in loneliness for fifteen years? What words were there to bridge the gap and express the need which had never died? Would she need to ask questions, or could she forget the whys and just accept?

Laine's image of James Simmons was as clear and vivid as yesterday. It was not dimmed by the shadows of time. *He would be older,* she reminded herself. *She was older as well.* She was not a child trailing after an idol, but a woman meeting her father. They were neither one the same as they had been. Perhaps that in itself would be an advantage.

The outer room of the hut was deserted. Laine had a vague impression of wicker furnishings and woven mats. She stared around her, feeling alone and unsure. Like a ghost of the past, his voice reached out, booming through an open doorway. Approaching the sound, Laine watched as her father talked on the phone at his desk.

She could see the alterations which age had made on his face, but her memory had been accurate. The sun had darkened his skin and laid its lines upon it, but his features were no stranger to her. His thick brows were gray now, but still prominent over his brown eyes. The nose was still strong and straight over the long, thin mouth. His hair remained full, though as gray as his brows, and she watched as he reached up in a well-remembered gesture and tugged his fingers through it.

She pressed her lips together as he replaced the receiver, then swallowing, Laine spoke in soft memory. "Hello, Cap."

He twisted his head, and she watched surprise flood his face. His eyes ran a quick gamut of emotions, and somewhere between the beginning and the end she saw the pain. He stood, and she noted with a small sense of shock that he was shorter than her child's perspective had made him.

"Laine?" The question was hesitant, colored by a reserve which crushed her impulse to rush toward him. She sensed immediately that his arms would not be open to receive her, and this rejection threatened to destroy her tentative smile.

"It's good to see you." Hating the inanity, she stepped into the room and held out her hand.

After a moment, he accepted it. He held her hand briefly, then released it. "You've grown up." His survey was slow, his smile touching only his mouth. "You've the look of your mother. No more pigtails?"

The smile illuminated her face with such swift impact, her father's expression warmed. "Not for some time. There was no one to pull them." Reserve settled over him again. Feeling the chill, Laine fumbled for some new line of conversation. "You've got your airport; you must be very happy. I'd like to see more of it."

"We'll arrange it." His tone was polite and impersonal, whipping across her face like the sting of a lash.

Laine wandered to a window and stared out through a mist of tears. "It's very impressive."

"Thank you, we're pretty proud of it." He cleared his throat and studied her back. "How long will you be in Hawaii?"

She gripped the windowsill and tried to match his tone. Even at their worst, her fears had not prepared her for this degree of pain. "A few weeks perhaps, I have no definite plans. I came . . . I came straight here." Turning, Laine began to fill the void with chatter. "I'm sure there are things I should see since I'm here. The pilot who flew me over said Kauai was beautiful, gardens and . . ." She tried and failed to remember the specifics of Dillon's speech. "And parks." She settled on a generality, keeping her smile fixed. "Perhaps you could recommend a hotel?"

He was searching her face, and Laine struggled to

keep her smile from dissolving. "You're welcome to stay with me while you're here."

Burying her pride, she agreed. She knew she could not afford to stay anywhere else. "That's kind of you. I should like that."

He nodded and shuffled some papers on his desk. "How's your mother?"

"She died," Laine murmured. "Three months ago."

Cap glanced up sharply. Laine watched the pain flicker over his face. He sat down. "I'm sorry, Laine. Was she ill?"

"There was . . ." She swallowed. "There was a car accident."

"I see." He cleared his throat, and his tone was again impersonal. "If you had written, I would have flown over and helped you."

"Would you?" She shook her head and turned back to the window. She remembered the panic, the numbness, the mountain of debts, the auction of every valuable. "I managed well enough."

"Laine, why did you come?" Though his voice had softened, he remained behind the barrier of his desk.

"To see my father." Her words were devoid of emotion.

"Cap." At the voice Laine turned, watching as Dillon's form filled the doorway. His glance scanned her before returning to Cap. "Chambers is leaving for the mainland. He wants to see you before he takes off."

"All right. Laine," Cap turned and gestured awkwardly, "this is Dillon O'Brian, my partner. Dillon, this is my daughter."

"We've met." Dillon smiled briefly.

Laine managed a nod. "Yes, Mr. O'Brian was kind enough to fly me from Oahu. It was a most . . . fascinating journey."

"That's fine then." Cap moved to Dillon and clasped a hand to his shoulder. "Run Laine to the house, will you, and see she settles in? I'm sure she must be tired."

Laine watched, excluded from the mystery of masculine understanding as looks were exchanged. Dillon nodded. "My pleasure."

"I'll be home in a couple of hours." Cap turned and regarded Laine in awkward silence.

"All right." Her smile was beginning to hurt her cheeks, so Laine let it die. "Thank you." Cap hesitated, then walked through the door leaving her staring at emptiness. *I will not cry,* she ordered herself. *Not in front of this man.* If she had nothing else left, she had her pride.

"Whenever you're ready, Miss Simmons."

Brushing past Dillon, Laine glanced back over her shoulder. "I hope you drive a car with more discretion than you fly a plane, Mr. O'Brian."

He gave an enigmatic shrug. "Why don't we find out?"

Her bags were sitting outside. She glanced down at them, then up at Dillon. "You seem to have anticipated me."

"I had hoped," he began as he tossed the bags into the rear of a sleek compact, "to pack both them and you back to where you came from, but that is obviously impossible now." He opened his door, slid into the driver's seat and started the engine. Laine slipped in beside him, unaided. Releasing the brake, he shot forward with a speed which jerked her against the cushions.

"What did you say to him?" Dillon demanded, not bothering with preliminaries as he maneuvered skillfully through the airport traffic.

"Being my father's business partner does not entitle you to an account of his personal conversations with me," Laine answered. Her voice was clipped and resentful.

"Listen, Duchess, I'm not about to stand by while you drop into Cap's life and stir up trouble. I didn't like the way he looked when I walked in on you. I gave you ten minutes, and you managed to hurt him. Don't make me stop the car and persuade you to tell me." He paused and lowered his voice. "You'd find my methods unrefined." The threat vibrated in his softly spoken words.

Suddenly Laine found herself too tired to argue. Nights with only patches of sleep, days crowded with pressures and anxiety, and the long, tedious journey had taken their toll. With a weary gesture, she pulled off her hat. Resting her head against the seat, she closed her eyes. "Mr. O'Brian, it was not my intention to hurt my father. In the ten minutes you allowed, we said remarkably little. Perhaps it was the news that my mother had died which upset him, but that is something he would have learned eventually at any rate." Her tone was hollow, and he glanced at her, surprised by the sudden frailty of her unframed face. Her hair was soft and pale against her ivory skin. For the first time, he saw the smudges of mauve haunting her eyes.

"How long ago?"

Laine opened her eyes in confusion as she detected a whisper of sympathy in his voice. "Three months." She sighed and turned to face Dillon more directly. "She ran her car into a telephone pole. They tell me she died instantly." *And painlessly,* she added to herself, *anesthetized with several quarts of vintage champagne.*

Dillon lapsed into silence, and she was grateful that he ignored the need for any trite words of sympathy. She had had enough of those already and found his silence more comforting. She studied his profile, the bronzed chiseled lines and unyielding mouth, before she turned her attention back to the scenery.

The scent of the Pacific lingered in the air. The water was a sparkling blue against the crystal beaches. Screw pines rose from the sand and accepted the lazy breeze, and monkeypods, wide and domelike, spread their shade in invitation. As they drove inland, Laine caught only brief glimpses of the sea. The landscape was a myriad of colors against a rich velvet green. Sun fell in waves of light, offering its warmth so that flowers did not strain to it, but rather basked lazily in its glory.

Dillon turned up a drive which was flanked by two sturdy palms. As they approached the house, Laine felt the first stir of pleasure. It was simple, its lines basic and clean, its walls cool and white. It stood two stories square, sturdy despite its large expanses of glass.

Watching the windows wink in the sun, Laine felt her first welcoming.

"It's lovely."

"Not as fancy as you might have expected," Dillon countered as he halted at the end of the drive, "but Cap likes it." The brief truce was obviously at an end. He eased from the car and gave his attention to her luggage.

Without comment, Laine opened her door and slipped out. Shading her eyes from the sun, she stood for a moment and studied her father's home. A set of stairs led to a circling porch. Dillon climbed them, nudged the front door open and strode into the house. Laine entered unescorted.

"Close my door; flies are not welcome."

Laine glanced up and saw, with stunned admiration, an enormous woman step as lightly down the staircase as a young girl. Her girth was wrapped in a colorful, flowing muumuu. Her glossy black hair was pulled tight and secured at the back of her head. Her skin was unlined, the color of dark honey. Her eyes were jet, set deep and widely spaced. Her age might have been anywhere from thirty to sixty. The image of an island priestess, she took a long, uninhibited survey of Laine when she reached the foot of the stairs.

"Who is this?" she asked Dillon as she folded her thick arms over a tumbling bosom.

"This is Cap's daughter." Setting down the bags, he leaned on the banister and watched the exchange.

"Cap Simmons's daughter." Her mouth pursed

and her eyes narrowed. "Pretty thing, but too pale and skinny. Don't you eat?" She circled Laine's arm between her thumb and forefinger.

"Why, yes, I . . ."

"Not enough," she interrupted and fingered a sunlit curl with interest. "Mmm, very nice, very pretty. Why do you wear it so short?"

"I . . ."

"You should have come years ago, but you are here now." Nodding, she patted Laine's cheek. "You are tired. I will fix your room."

"Thank you. I . . ."

"Then you eat," she ordered, and hefted Laine's two cases up the stairs.

"That was Miri," Dillon volunteered and tucked his hands in his pockets. "She runs the house."

"Yes, I see." Unable to prevent herself, Laine lifted her hand to her hair and wondered over the length. "Shouldn't you have taken the bags up for her?"

"Miri could carry me up the stairs without breaking stride. Besides, I know better than to interfere with what she considers her duties. Come on." He grabbed her arm and pulled her down the hall. "I'll fix you a drink."

With casual familiarity, Dillon moved to a double-doored cabinet. Laine flexed her arm and surveyed the cream-walled room. Simplicity reigned here as its outer shell had indicated, and she appreciated Miri's obvious diligence with polish and broom. There was, she noted with a sigh, no room for a woman here. The furnishings shouted with masculinity, a masculinity which was well established and comfortable in its solitary state.

"What'll you have?" Dillon's question brought Laine back from her musings. She shook her head and dropped her hat on a small table. It looked frivolous and totally out of place.

"Nothing, thank you."

"Suit yourself." He poured a measure of liquor into a glass and dropped down on a chair. "We're not given to formalities around here, Duchess. While you're in residence, you'll have to cope with a more basic form of existence."

She inclined her head, laying her purse beside her hat. "Perhaps one may still wash one's hands before dinner?"

"Sure," he returned, ignoring the sarcasm. "We're big on water."

"And where, Mr. O'Brian, do you live?"

"Here." He stretched his legs and gave a satisfied smile at her frown. "For a week or two. I'm having some repairs done to my house."

"How unfortunate," Laine commented and wandered the room. "For both of us."

"You'll survive, Duchess." He toasted her with his glass. "I'm sure you've had plenty of experience in surviving."

"Yes, I have, Mr. O'Brian, but I have a feeling you know nothing about it."

"You've got guts, lady, I'll give you that." He tossed back his drink and scowled as she turned to face him.

"Your opinion is duly noted and filed."

"Did you come for more money? Is it possible you're that greedy?" He rose in one smooth motion and crossed the room, grabbing her shoulders before she could back away from his mercurial temper. "Haven't you squeezed enough out of him? Never giving anything in return. Never even disturbing yourself to answer one of his letters. Letting the years pile up without any acknowledgment. What the devil do you want from him now?"

Dillon stopped abruptly. The color had drained from her face, leaving it like white marble. Her eyes were dazed with shock. She swayed as though her joints had melted, and he held her upright, staring at her in sudden confusion. "What's the matter with you?"

"I . . . Mr. O'Brian, I think I would like that drink now, if you don't mind."

His frown deepened, and he led her to a chair before moving off to pour her a drink. Laine accepted with a murmured thanks, then shuddered at the unfamiliar burn of brandy. The room steadied, and she felt the mists clearing.

"Mr. O'Brian, I . . . am I to understand . . ." She stopped and shut her eyes a moment. "Are you saying my father wrote to me?"

"You know very well he did." The retort was both swift and annoyed. "He came to the islands right after you and your mother left him, and he wrote you regularly until five years ago when he gave up. He still sent money," Dillon added, flicking on his lighter. "Oh yes, the money kept right on coming until you turned twenty-one last year."

"You're lying!"

Dillon looked over in astonishment as she rose from her chair. Her cheeks were flaming, her eyes flashing. "Well, well, it appears the ice maiden has melted." He blew out a stream of smoke and spoke mildly. "I never lie, Duchess. I find the truth more interesting."

"He never wrote to me. Never!" She walked to where Dillon sat. "Not once in all those years. All the letters I sent came back because he had moved away without even telling me where."

Slowly, Dillon crushed out his cigarette and rose to face her. "Do you expect me to buy that? You're selling to the wrong person, Miss Simmons. I saw the letters Cap sent, *and* the checks every month." He ran a finger down the lapel of her suit. "You seem to have put them to good use."

"I tell you I never received any letters." Laine knocked his hand away and tilted her head back to meet his eyes. "I have not had one word from my father since I was seven years old."

"Miss Simmons, I mailed more than one letter myself, though I was tempted to chuck them into the Pacific. Presents, too; dolls in the early years. You must have quite a collection of porcelain dolls. Then there was the jewelry. I remember the eighteenth birthday present very clearly. Opal earrings shaped like flowers."

"Earrings," Laine whispered. Feeling the room

tilt again, she dug her teeth into her lip and shook her head.

"That's right." His voice was rough as he moved to pour himself another drink. "And they all went to the same place: 17 rue de la Concorde, Paris."

Her color ebbed again, and she lifted a hand to her temple. "My mother's address," she murmured, and turned away to sit before her legs gave way. "I was in school; my mother lived there."

"Yes." Dillon took a quick sip and settled on the sofa again. "Your education was both lengthy and expensive."

Laine thought for a moment of the boarding school with its plain, wholesome food, cotton sheets and leaking roof. She pressed her fingers to her eyes. "I was not aware that my father was paying for my schooling."

"Just who did you think was paying for your French pinafores and art lessons?"

She sighed, stung by the sharpness of his tone. Her hands fluttered briefly before she dropped them into her lap. "Vanessa . . . my mother said she had an income. I never questioned her. She must have kept my father's letters from me."

Laine's voice was dull, and Dillon moved with sudden impatience. "Is that the tune you're going to play to Cap? You make it very convincing."

"No, Mr. O'Brian. It hardly matters at this point, does it? In any case, I doubt that he would believe me any more than you do. I will keep my visit brief, then return to France." She lifted her brandy and stared into the amber liquid, wondering if it was responsible for her numbness. “I would like a week or two. I would appreciate it if you would not mention this discussion to my father; it would only complicate matters.”

Dillon gave a short laugh and sipped from his drink. “I have no intention of telling him any part of this little fairy tale.”

“Your word, Mr. O’Brian.” Surprised by the anxiety in her voice, Dillon glanced up. “I want your word.” She met his eyes without wavering.

“My word, Miss Simmons,” he agreed at length.

Nodding, she rose and lifted her hat and bag from the table. “I would like to go up to my room now. I’m very tired.”

He was frowning into his drink. Laine, without a backward glance, walked to her room.

CHAPTER 3

Laine faced the woman in the mirror. She saw a pale face, dominated by wide, shadowed eyes. Reaching for her rouge, she placed borrowed color on her cheeks.

She had known her mother's faults: the egotism, the shallowness. As a child, it had been easy to overlook the flaws and prize the sporadic, exciting visits with the vibrant, fairy-tale woman. Ice-cream parfaits and party dresses were such a contrast to home-spun uniforms and porridge. As Laine had grown older, the visits had become further spaced and shorter. It became routine for her to spend her vacations from school with the nuns. She had begun to see, through the objectivity of distance, her mother's desperation for youth, her selfish grip on her own beauty. A grown daughter with firm limbs and unlined skin had been more of an obstacle than an accomplishment. A grown daughter was a reminder of one's own mortality.

She was always afraid of losing, Laine thought. Her looks, her youth, her friends, her men. All the creams and potions. She sighed and shut her eyes. All the dyes and lotions. There had been a collection of porcelain dolls, Laine remembered. Vanessa's dolls, or so she had thought. Twelve porcelain dolls, each from a different country. She thought of how beautiful the Spanish doll had been with its high comb and mantilla. And the earrings . . . Laine tossed down her brush and whirled around the room. Those lovely opal earrings that looked so fragile in Vanessa's ears. I remember seeing her wear them, just as I remember listing them and the twelve porcelain dolls for auction. *How much more that was mine did she keep from me?* Blindly, Laine stared out her window. The incredible array of island blossoms might not have existed.

What kind of woman was she to keep what was mine for her own pleasure? To let me think, year after year, that my father had forgotten me? She kept me from him, even from his words on paper. I resent her for that, how I resent her for that. Not for the money, but for the lies and the loss. She must have used the checks to keep her apartment in Paris, and for all those clothes and all those parties. Laine shut her eyes tight on waves of outrage. At least I know now why she took me with her to France: as an insurance policy. She lived off me for nearly fifteen years, and even then it wasn't enough. Laine felt tears squeezing through her closed lids. Oh, how Cap must hate me. How he must hate me for the ingratitude and the coldness. He would never believe me. She sighed, remembering her father's reaction to her appearance. *"You've the look of your mother."* Opening her eyes, she walked back and studied her face in the mirror.

It was true, she decided as she ran her fingertips along her cheeks. The resemblance was there in the bone structure, in the coloring. Laine frowned, finding no pleasure in her inheritance. He's only to look at me to see her. He's only to look at me to remember. He'll think as Dillon O'Brian thinks. How could I expect anything else? For a few moments, Laine and her reflection merely stared at one another. But perhaps, she mused, her bottom lip thrust forward in thought, with a week or two I might salvage something of what used to be, some portion of the friendship. I would be content with that. But he must not think I've come for money, so I must be careful he not find out how little I have left. More than anything, I shall have to be careful around Mr. O'Brian.

Detestable man, she thought on a fresh flurry of anger. He is surely the most ill-bred, mannerless man I have ever met. He's worse, much worse, than any of Vanessa's hangers-on. At least they managed to wear a light coat of respectability. Cap probably picked him up off the beach out of pity and made him his partner. He has insolent eyes, she added, lifting her brush and tugging it through her hair. Always looking at you as if he knew how you would feel in his arms. He's nothing but a womanizer. Tossing down the brush, she glared at the woman in the glass. He's just an unrefined, arrogant womanizer. Look at the way he behaved on the plane.

The glare faded as she lifted a finger to rub it over her lips. The memory of their turbulent capture flooded back. You've been kissed before, she lectured, shaking her head against the echoing sensations. *Not like that,* a small voice insisted. *Never like that.*

"Oh, the devil with Dillon O'Brian!" she muttered aloud, and just barely resisted the urge to slam her bedroom door on her way out.

Laine hesitated at the sound of masculine voices. It was a new sound for one generally accustomed to female company, and she found it pleasant. There was a mixture of deep blends, her father's booming drum tones and Dillon's laconic drawl. She heard a laugh, an appealing, uninhibited rumble, and she frowned as she recognized it as Dillon's. Quietly, she came down the rest of the steps and moved to the doorway.

"Then, when I took out the carburetor, he stared at it, muttered a stream of incantations and shook his head. I ended up fixing it myself."

"And a lot quicker than the Maui mechanic or any other would have." Cap's rich chuckle reached Laine as she stepped into the doorway.

They were seated easily. Dillon was sprawled on the sofa, her father in a chair. Pipe smoke rose from the tray beside him. Both were relaxed and so content in each other's company that Laine felt the urge to back away and leave them undisturbed. She felt like an intruder into some long established routine. With a swift pang of envy, she took a step in retreat.

Her movement caught Dillon's attention. Before she could leave, his eyes held her motionless just as effectively as if his arms had reached out to capture her. She had changed from the sophisticated suit she had worn for the flight into a simple white dress from her own wardrobe. Unadorned and ingenue, it emphasized her youth and her slender innocence. Following the direction of Dillon's unsmiling survey, Cap saw Laine and rose. As he stood, his ease transformed into awkwardness.

"Hello, Laine. Have you settled in all right?"

Laine forced herself to shift her attention from Dillon to her father. "Yes, thank you." The moistening of her lips was the first outward sign of nerves. "The room is lovely. I'm sorry. Did I interrupt?" Her hands fluttered once, then were joined loosely as if to keep them still.

"No . . . ah, come in and sit down. Just a little shop talk."

She hesitated again before stepping into the room.

"Would you like a drink?" Cap moved to the bar and jiggled glasses. Dillon remained silent and seated.

"No, nothing, thank you." Laine tried a smile. "Your home is beautiful. I can see the beach from my window." Taking the remaining seat on the sofa, Laine kept as much distance between herself and Dillon as possible. "It must be marvelous being close enough to swim when the mood strikes you."

"I don't get to the water as much as I used to." Cap settled down again, tapping his pipe against the tray. "Used to scuba some. Now, Dillon's the one for it." Laine heard the affection in his voice and caught it again in his smiling glance at the man beside her.

"I find the sea and the sky have a lot in common," Dillon commented, reaching forward to lift his drink from the table. "Freedom and challenge." He sent Cap an easy smile. "I taught Cap to explore the fathoms; he taught me to fly."

"I suppose I'm more of a land creature," Laine replied, forcing herself to meet his gaze levelly. "I haven't much experience in the air or on the sea."

Dillon swirled his drink idly, but his eyes held challenge. "You do swim, don't you?"

"I manage."

"Fine." He took another swallow of his drink. "I'll teach you to snorkel." Setting down the glass, he resumed his relaxed position. "Tomorrow. We'll get an early start."

His arrogance shot up Laine's spine like a rod. Her tone became cool and dismissive. "I wouldn't presume to impose on your time, Mr. O'Brian."

Unaffected by the frost in her voice, Dillon continued. "No trouble. I've got nothing scheduled until the afternoon. You've got some extra gear around, haven't you, Cap?"

"Sure, in the back room." Hurt by the apparent relief in his voice, Laine shut her eyes briefly. "You'll enjoy yourself, Laine. Dillon's a fine teacher, and he knows these waters."

Laine gave Dillon a polite smile, hoping he could read between the lines. "I'm sure you know how much I appreciate your time, Mr. O'Brian."

The lifting of his brows indicated that their silent communication was proceeding with perfect understanding. "No more than I your company, Miss Simmons."

"Dinner." Miri's abrupt announcement startled Laine. "You." She pointed an accusing finger at Laine, then crooked it in a commanding gesture. "Come eat, and don't pick at your food. Too skinny," she muttered and whisked away in a flurry of brilliant colors.

Laine's arm was captured as they followed in the wake of Miri's waves. Dillon slowed her progress until they were alone in the corridor. "My compliments on your entrance. You were the picture of the pure young virgin."

"I have no doubt you would like to offer me to the nearest volcano god, Mr. O'Brian, but perhaps you would allow me to have my last meal in peace."

"Miss Simmons." He bowed with exaggerated gallantry and increased his hold on her arm. "Even I can stir myself on occasion to escort a lady into dinner."

"Perhaps with a great deal of concentration, you could accomplish this spectacular feat without breaking my arm."

Laine gritted her teeth as they entered the glass-enclosed dining room. Dillon pulled out her chair. She glanced coldly up at him. "Thank you, Mr. O'Brian," she murmured as she slid into her seat. Detestable man!

Inclining his head politely, Dillon rounded the table and dropped into a chair. "Hey, Cap, that little cabin plane we've been using on the Maui run is running a bit rough. I want to have a look at it before it goes up again."

"Hmm. What do you think's the problem?"

There began a technical, and to Laine unintelligible, discussion. Miri entered, placing a steaming tray of fish in front of Laine with a meaningful thump. To assure she had not been misunderstood, Miri pointed a finger at the platter, then at Laine's empty plate before she swirled from the room.

The conversation had turned to the intricacies of fuel systems by the time Laine had eaten all she could of Miri's fish. Her silence during the meal had been almost complete as the men enjoyed their mutual interest. She saw, as she watched him, that her father's lack of courtesy was not deliberate, but rather the result of years of living alone. He was, she decided, a man comfortable with men and out of his depth with feminine company. Though she felt Dillon's rudeness was intentional, it was her father's unconscious slight which stung.

"You will excuse me?" Laine rose during a brief lull in the conversation. She felt a fresh surge of regret as she read the discomfort in her father's eyes. "I'm a bit tired. Please." She managed a smile as she started to rise. "Don't disturb yourself, I know the way." As she turned to go, she could almost hear the room sigh with relief at her exit.

Later that evening, Laine felt stifled in her room. The house was quiet. The tropical moon had risen and she could see the curtains flutter with the gentle whispers of perfumed air. Unable to bear the loneliness of the four walls any longer, she stole quietly downstairs and into the night. As she wandered without regard for destination, she could hear the night birds call to each other, piercing the stillness with a strange, foreign music. She listened to the sea's murmur and slipped off her shoes to walk across the fine layer of sand to meet it.

The water fringed in a wide arch, frothing against the sands and lapping back into the womb of midnight blue. Its surface winked with mirrored stars. Laine breathed deeply of its scent, mingling with the flowered air.

But this paradise was not for her. Dillon and her father had banished her. It was the same story all over again. She remembered how often she had been excluded on her visits to her mother's home in Paris. *Again an intruder,* Laine decided, and wondered if she had either the strength or the will to pursue the smiling masquerade for even a week of her father's company. Her place was not with him any more than it had been with Vanessa. Dropping to the sand, Laine brought her knees to her chest and wept for the years of loss.

"I don't have a handkerchief, so you'll have to cope without one."

At the sound of Dillon's voice, Laine shuddered and hugged her knees tighter. "Please, go away."

"What's the problem, Duchess?" His voice was rough and impatient. If she had had more experience, Laine might have recognized a masculine discomfort with feminine tears. "If things aren't going as planned, sitting on the beach and crying isn't going to help. Especially if there's no one around to sympathize."

"Go away," she repeated, keeping her face buried. "I want you to leave me alone. I want to be alone."

"You might as well get used to it," he returned carelessly. "I intend to keep a close eye on you until you're back in Europe. Cap's too soft to hold out against the sweet, innocent routine for long."

Laine sprang up and launched herself at him. He staggered a moment as the small missile caught him off guard. "He's my father, do you understand? My *father.* I have a right to be with him. I have a right to know him." With useless fury, she beat her fists against his chest. He weathered the attack with some surprise before he caught her arms and dragged her, still swinging, against him.

"There's quite a temper under the ice! You can always try the routine about not getting his letters—that should further your campaign."

"I don't want his pity, do you hear?" She pushed and shoved and struck out while Dillon held her with minimum effort. "I would rather have his hate than his disinterest, but I would rather have his disinterest than his pity."

"Hold still, blast it," he ordered, losing patience with the battle. "You're not going to get hurt."

"I will not hold still," Laine flung back. "I am not a puppy who washed up on his doorstep and needs to be dried off and given a corner and a pat on the head. I *will* have my two weeks, and I won't let you spoil it for me." She tossed back her head. Tears fell freely, but her eyes now held fury rather than sorrow. "Let me go! I don't want you to touch me." She began to battle with new enthusiasm, kicking and nearly throwing them both onto the sand.

"All right, that's enough." Swiftly, he used his arms to band, his mouth to silence.

He was drawing her into a whirlpool, spinning and spinning, until all sense of time and existence was lost in the current. She would taste the salt of her own tears mixed with some tangy, vital flavor which belonged to him. She felt a swift heat rise to her skin and fought against it as desperately as she fought against his imprisoning arms. His mouth took hers once more, enticing her to give what she did not yet understand. All at once she lost all resistance, all sense of self. She went limp in his arms, her lips softening in surrender. Dillon drew her away and without even being aware of what she was doing, Laine dropped her head to his chest. She trembled as she felt his hand brush lightly through her hair, and nestled closer to him. Suddenly warm and no longer alone, she shut her eyes and let the gamut of emotions run its course.

"Just who are you, Laine Simmons?" Dillon drew her away again. He closed a firm hand under her chin as she stubbornly fought to keep her head lowered. "Look at me," he commanded. The order was absolute. With his eyes narrowed, he examined her without mercy.

Her eyes were wide and brimming, the tears trembling down her cheeks and clinging to her lashes. All layers of her borrowed sophistication had been stripped away, leaving only the vulnerability. His search ended on an impatient oath. "Ice, then fire, now tears. No, don't," he commanded as she struggled to lower her head again. "I'm not in the mood to test my resistance." He let out a deep breath and shook his head. "You're going to be nothing but trouble, I should have seen that from the first look. But you're here, and we're going to have to come to terms."

"Mr. O'Brian . . ."

"Dillon, for pity's sake. Let's not be any more ridiculous than necessary."

"Dillon," Laine repeated, sniffling and despising herself. "I don't think I can discuss terms with any coherence tonight. If you would just let me go, we could draw up a contract tomorrow."

"No, the terms are simple because they're all mine."

"That sounds exceedingly reasonable." She was pleased that irony replaced tears.

"While you're here," Dillon continued mildly, "we're going to be together like shadow and shade. I'm your guardian angel until you go back to the Left Bank. If you make a wrong move with Cap, I'm coming down on you so fast you won't be able to blink those little-girl eyes."

"Is my father so helpless he needs protection from his own daughter?" She brushed furiously at her lingering tears.

"There isn't a man alive who doesn't need protection from you, Duchess." Tilting his head, he studied her damp, glowing face. "If you're an operator, you're a good one. If you're not, I'll apologize when the time comes."

"You may keep your apology and have it for breakfast. With any luck, you'll strangle on it."

Dillon threw back his head and laughed, the same appealing rumble Laine had heard earlier. Outraged both with the laughter and its effect on her, she swung back her hand to slap his face.

"Oh, no." Dillon grabbed her wrist. "Don't spoil it. I'd just have to hit you back, and you look fabulous when you're spitting fire. It's much more to my taste than the cool mademoiselle from Paris. Listen, Laine." He took an exaggerated breath to control his laughter, and she found herself struggling to deal with the stir caused by the way her name sounded on his lips. "Let's try a truce, at least in public. Privately, we can have a round a night, with or without gloves."

"That should suit you well enough." Laine wriggled out of his loosened hold and tossed her head. "You have a considerable advantage—given your weight and strength."

"Yeah." Dillon grinned and moved his shoulders. "Learn to live with it. Come on." He took her hand in a friendly gesture which nonplussed her. "Into bed; you've got to get up early tomorrow. I don't like to lose the morning."

"I'm not going with you tomorrow." She tugged her hand away and planted her bare heels in the sand. "You'll probably attempt to drown me, then hide my body in some cove."

Dillon sighed in mock exasperation. "Laine, if

I have to drag you out of bed in the morning, you're going to find yourself learning a great deal more than snorkeling. Now, are you going to walk back to the house, or do I carry you?"

"If they could bottle your arrogance, Dillon O'Brian, there would be no shortage of fuel in this country!"

With this, Laine turned and fled. Dillon watched until the darkness shrouded her white figure. Then he bent down to retrieve her shoes.

CHAPTER 4

The morning was golden. As usual, Laine woke early. For a moment, she blinked in puzzlement. Cool green walls had replaced her white ones, louvered shades hung where she expected faded striped curtains. Instead of her desk stood a plain mahogany bureau topped with a vase of scarlet blossoms. But it was the silence which most confused her. There were no giggles, no rushing feet outside her door. The quiet was broken only by a bird who sang his morning song outside her window. Memory flooded back. With a sigh, Laine lay back against the pillow and wished she could go to sleep again. The habit of early rising was too ingrained. She rose, showered and dressed.

A friend had persuaded her to accept the loan of a swimsuit, and Laine studied the two tiny pieces. She slipped on what had been described as a modified bikini. The silvery blue was flattering, highlighting her subtle curves, but no amount of adjustment could result in more substantial coverage. There was definitely too much of her and too little suit.

"Silly," Laine muttered and adjusted the halter strings a last time. "Women wear these things all the time, and I've hardly the shape for drawing attention."

Skinny. With a grimace, she recalled Miri's judgment. Laine gave the top a last, hopeless tug. *I don't think all the fish in the Pacific are going to change this inadequacy.* Pulling on white jeans and a scarlet scoop-necked top, she reminded herself that cleavage was not what she needed for dealing with Dillon O'Brian.

As she wandered downstairs, Laine heard the stirrings which accompany an awakening house. She moved quietly, half afraid she would disturb the routine. In the dining room, the sun poured like liquid gold through the windows. Standing in its pool, Laine stared out at soft ferns and brilliant poppies. Charmed by the scene, she decided she would let nothing spoil the perfection of the day. There would be time enough later, on some drizzling French morning, to think of rejections and humiliations, but today the sun was bright and filled with promise.

"So, you are ready for breakfast." Miri glided in from the adjoining kitchen. She managed to look graceful despite her size, and regal despite the glaring flowered muumuu.

"Good morning, Miri." Laine gave her the first smile of the day and gestured toward the sky. "It's beautiful."

"It will bring some color to your skin." Miri sniffed and ran a finger down Laine's arm. "Red if you aren't careful. Now, sit and I will put flesh on your skinny bones." Imperiously, she tapped the back of a chair, and Laine obeyed.

"Miri, have you worked for my father long?"

"Ten years." Miri shook her head and poured steaming coffee into a cup. "Too long a time for a man not to have a wife. Your mother," she continued, narrowing her dark eyes, "she was skinny too?"

"Well, no, I wouldn't say . . . That is . . ." Laine hesitated in an attempt to gauge Miri's estimation of a suitable shape.

Rich laughter shot out. Miri's bosom trembled under pink and orange flowers. "You don't want to say she was not as much woman as Miri." She ran her hands over her well-padded hips. "You're a pretty girl," she said unexpectedly and patted Laine's flaxen curls. "Your eyes are too young to be sad." As Laine stared up at her, speechless under the unfamiliar affection, Miri sighed. "I will bring your breakfast, and you will eat what I give you."

"Make it two, Miri." Dillon strolled in, bronzed and confident in cutoff denims and a plain white T-shirt. "Morning, Duchess. Sleep well?" He dropped into the chair opposite Laine and poured himself a cup of coffee. His movements were easy, without any early-morning lethargy, and his eyes were completely alert. Laine concluded that Dillon O'Brian was one of those rare creatures who moved from sleep to wakefulness instantly. It also occurred to her, in one insistent flash, that he was not only the most attractive man she had ever known, but the most compelling. Struggling against an unexplained longing, Laine tried to mirror his casualness.

"Good morning, Dillon. It appears it's going to be another lovely day."

"We've a large supply of them on this side of the island."

"On this side?" Laine watched as he ran a hand through his hair, sending it into a state of appealing confusion.

"Mmm. On the windward slopes it rains almost every day." He downed half his coffee in one movement, and Laine found herself staring at his long, brown fingers. They looked strong and competent against the cream-colored earthenware. Suddenly, she remembered the feel of them on her chin. "Something wrong?"

"What?" Blinking, she brought her attention back to his face. "No, I was just thinking . . . I'll have to tour the island while I'm here," she improvised, rushing through the words. "Is your . . . is your home near here?"

"Not far." Dillon lifted his cup again, studying her over its rim. Laine began to stir her own coffee as if the task required enormous concentration. She had no intention of drinking it, having had her first—and, she vowed, last—encounter with American coffee aboard the plane.

"Breakfast," Miri announced, gliding into the room with a heaping tray. "You will eat." With brows drawn, she began piling portions onto Laine's plate. "And then you go out so I can clean my house. You!" She shook a large spoon at Dillon who was filling his own plate with obvious appreciation. "Don't bring any sand back with you to dirty my floors."

He responded with a quick Hawaiian phrase and a cocky grin. Miri's laughter echoed after her as she moved from the room and into the kitchen.

"Dillon," Laine began, staring at the amount of food on her plate, "I could never eat all of this."

He forked a mouthful of eggs and shrugged. "Better make a stab at it. Miri's decided to fatten you up, and even if you couldn't use it—and you can," he added as he buttered a piece of toast, "Miri is not a lady to cross. Pretend it's bouillabaisse or escargots."

The last was stated with a tangible edge, and Laine stiffened. Instinctively, she put up her defenses. "I have no complaints on the quality of the food, but on the quantity."

Dillon shrugged. Annoyed, Laine attacked her breakfast. The meal progressed without conversation. Fifteen minutes later, she searched for the power to lift yet another forkful of eggs. With a sound of impatience, Dillon rose and pulled her from her chair.

"You look like you'll keel over if you shovel in one more bite. I'll give you a break and get you out before Miri comes back."

Laine gritted her teeth, hoping it would help her to be humble. "Thank you."

As Dillon pulled Laine down the hall toward the front door, Cap descended the stairs. All three stopped as he glanced down from man to woman. "Good morning. It should be a fine day for your snorkeling lesson, Laine."

"Yes, I'm looking forward to it." She smiled, straining for a naturalness she was unable to feel in his presence.

"That's good. Dillon's right at home in the water." Cap's smile gained warmth as he turned to the man by her side. "When you come in this afternoon, take a look at the new twin-engine. I think the modifications you specified worked out well."

"Sure. I'm going to do a bit of work on that cabin plane. Keep Tinker away from it, will you?"

Cap chuckled as they enjoyed some personal joke. When he turned to Laine, he had a remnant of his smile and a polite nod. "I'll see you tonight. Have a good time."

"Yes, thank you." She watched him move away and, for a moment, her heart lifted to her eyes. Looking back, she found Dillon studying her. His expression was indrawn and brooding.

"Come on," he said with sudden briskness as he captured her hand. "Let's get started." He lifted a faded, long-stringed bag and tossed it over his shoulder as they passed through the front door. "Where's your suit?"

"I have it on." Preferring to trot alongside rather than be dragged, Laine scrambled to keep pace.

The path he took was a well-worn dirt track. Along its borders, flowers and ferns crept to encroach on the walkway. Laine wondered if there was another place on earth where colors had such clarity or where green had so many shades. The vanilla-scented blossoms of heliotrope added a tang to the moist sea air. With a high call, a skylark streaked across the sky and disappeared. Laine and Dillon walked in silence as the sun poured unfiltered over their heads.

After a ten-minute jog, Laine said breathlessly, "I do hope it isn't much farther. I haven't run the decathlon for years."

Dillon turned, and she braced herself for his irritated retort. Instead, he began to walk at a more moderate pace. Pleased, Laine allowed herself a small smile. She felt even a minor victory in dealing with Dillon O'Brian was an accomplishment. Moments later, she forgot her triumph.

The bay was secluded, sheltered by palms and laced with satin-petaled hibiscus. In the exotic beauty of Kauai, it was a stunning diamond. The water might have dripped from the sky that morning. It shone and glimmered like a multitude of fresh raindrops.

With a cry of pleasure, Laine began to pull Dillon through the circling palms and into the white heat of sun and sand. "Oh, it's beautiful!" She turned two quick circles as if to insure encompassing all the new wonders. "It's perfect, absolutely perfect."

She watched his smile flash like a brisk wind. It chased away the clouds and, for one precious moment, there was understanding rather than tension between them. It flowed from man to woman with an ease which was as unexpected as it was soothing. His frown returned abruptly, and Dillon crouched to rummage through the bag. He pulled out snorkels and masks.

"Snorkeling's easy once you learn to relax and breathe properly. It's important to be both relaxed and alert." He began to instruct in simple terms, explaining breathing techniques and adjusting Laine's mask.

"There is no need to be quite so didactic," she said at length, irked by his patronizing tone and frowning face. "I assure you, I have a working brain. Most things don't have to be repeated more than four or five times before I grasp the meaning."

"Fine." He handed her both snorkel and mask. "Let's try it in the water." Pulling off his shirt, he dropped it on the canvas bag. He stood above her adjusting the strap on his own mask.

A fine mat of black hair lay against his bronzed chest. His skin was stretched tight over his rib cage, then tapered down to a narrow waist. The faded denim hung low over his lean hips. With some astonishment, Laine felt an ache start in her stomach and move warmly through her veins. She dropped her eyes to an intense study of the sand.

"Take off your clothes." Laine's eyes widened. She took a quick step in retreat. "Unless you intend to swim in them," Dillon added. His lips twitched before he turned and moved toward the water.

Embarrassed, Laine did her best to emulate his casualness. Shyly, she stripped off her top. Pulling off her jeans, she folded both and followed Dillon toward the bay. He waited for her, water lapping over his thighs. His eyes traveled over every inch of her exposed skin before they rested on her face.

"Stay close," he commanded when she stood beside him. "We'll skim the surface for a bit until you get the hang of it." He pulled the mask down over her eyes and adjusted it.

Easily, they moved along the shallows where sunlight struck the soft bottom and sea lettuce danced and swayed. Forgetting her instructions, Laine breathed water instead of air and surfaced choking.

"What happened?" Dillon demanded, as Laine coughed and sputtered. "You're going to have to pay more attention to what you're doing," he warned. Giving her a sturdy thump on the back, he pulled her mask back over her eyes. "Ready?" he asked.

After three deep breaths, Laine managed to speak. "Yes." She submerged.

Little by little, she explored deeper water, swimming by Dillon's side. He moved through the water as a bird moves through the air, with inherent ease and confidence. Before long, Laine learned to translate his aquatic hand signals and began to improvise her own.

They were joined in the liquid world by curious fish. As Laine stared into round, lidless eyes, she wondered who had come to gape at whom.

The sun flickered through with ethereal light. It nurtured the sea grass and caused shells and smooth rocks to glisten. It was a silent world, and although the sea bottom teemed with life, it was somehow private and free. Pale pink fingers of coral grouped together to form a hiding place for vivid blue fish. Laine watched in fascination as a hermit crab slid out of its borrowed shell and scurried away. There was a pair of orange starfish clinging contentedly to a rock, and a sea urchin nestled in spiny solitude.

Laine enjoyed isolation with this strange, moody man. She did not pause to appraise the pleasure she took in sharing her new experiences with him. The change in their relationship had been so smooth and so swift, she had not even been aware of it. They were, for a moment, only man and woman cloaked in a world of water and sunlight. On impulse, she lifted a large cone shaped shell from its bed, its resident long since evicted. First holding it out for Dillon to view, she swam toward the dancing light on the surface.

Shaking her head as she broke water, Laine splattered Dillon's mask with sundrops. Laughing, she pushed her own mask to the top of her head and stood in the waist-high water. "Oh, that was wonderful! I've never seen anything like it." She pushed damp tendrils behind her ears. "All those colors, and so many shades of blue and green molded together. It feels . . . it feels as if there were nothing else in the world but yourself and where you are."

Excitement had kissed her cheeks with color, her eyes stealing the blue from the sea. Her hair was dark gold, clinging in a sleek cap to her head. Now, without the softening of curls, her face seemed more delicately sculptured, the planes and hollows more fragile. Dillon watched her in smiling silence, pushing his own mask atop his head.

"I've never done anything like that before. I could have stayed down there forever. There's so much to see, so much to touch. Look what I found. It's beautiful." She held the shell in both hands, tracing a finger over its amber lines. "What is it?"

Dillon took it for a moment, turning it over in his hands before giving it back to her. "A music volute. You'll find scores of shells around the island."

"May I keep it? Does this place belong to anyone?"

Dillon laughed, enjoying her enthusiasm. "This is a private bay, but I know the owner. I don't think he'd mind."

"Will I hear the sea? They say you can." Laine lifted the shell to her ear. At the low, drifting echo, her eyes widened in wonder. *"Oh, c'est incroyable."* In her excitement, she reverted to French, not only in speech, but in mannerisms. Her eyes locked on his as one hand held the shell to her ear and the other gestured with her words. *"On entend le bruit de la mer. C'est merveilleux! Dillon, écoute."*

She offered the shell, wanting to share her discovery. He laughed as she had heard him laugh with her father. "Sorry, Duchess, you lost me a few sentences back."

"Oh, how silly. I wasn't thinking. I haven't spoken English in so long." She brushed at her damp hair and offered him a smile. "It's marvelous, I can really hear the sea." Her words faltered as his eyes lost their amusement. They were darkened by an emotion which caused her heart to jump and pound furiously against her ribs. Her mind shouted quickly to retreat, but her body and will melted as his arms slid around her. Her mouth lifted of its own accord to surrender to his.

For the first time, she felt a man's hands roam over her naked skin. There was nothing between them but the satin rivulets of water which clung to their bodies. Under the streaming gold sun, her heart opened, and she gave. She accepted the demands of his mouth, moved with the caresses of his hands until she thought they would never become separate. She wanted only for them to remain one until the sun died, and the world was still.

Dillon released her slowly, his arms lingering, as if reluctant to relinquish possession. Her sigh was mixed with pleasure and the despair of losing a newly discovered treasure. "I would swear," he muttered, staring down into her face, "you're either a first-rate actress or one step out of a nunnery."

Immediately, the helpless color rose, and Laine

turned to escape to the sand of the beach. "Hold on." Taking her arm, Dillon turned her to face him. His brows drew close as he studied her blush. "That's a feat I haven't seen in years. Duchess, you amaze me. Either way," he continued, and his smile held mockery but lacked its former malice, "calculated or innocent, you amaze me. Again," he said simply and drew her into his arms.

This time the kiss was gentle and teasing. But she had less defense against tenderness than passion, and her body was pliant to his instruction. Her hands tightened on his shoulders, feeling the ripple of muscles under her palms as he drew every drop of response from her mouth. With no knowledge of seduction, she became a temptress by her very innocence. Dillon drew her away and gave her clouded eyes and swollen mouth a long examination.

"You're a powerful lady," he said at length, then let out a quick breath. "Let's sit in the sun awhile." Without waiting for her answer, he took her hand and moved toward the beach.

On the sand, he spread a large beach towel and dropped onto it. When Laine hesitated, he pulled her down to join him. "I don't bite, Laine, I only nibble." Drawing a cigarette from the bag beside them, he lit it, then leaned back on his elbows. His skin gleamed with water and sun.

Feeling awkward, Laine sat very still with the shell in her hands. She tried not only to understand what she had felt in Dillon's arms, but why she had felt it. It had been important, and somehow, she felt certain it would remain important for the rest of her life. It was a gift that did not yet have a name. Suddenly, she felt as happy as when the shell had spoken in her ear. Glancing at it, Laine smiled with unrestrained joy.

"You treat that shell as though it were your firstborn." Twisting her head, she saw Dillon grinning. She decided she had never been happier.

"It is my first souvenir, and I've never dived for sunken treasure before."

"Just think of all the sharks you had to push out of the way to get your hands on it." He blew smoke at the sky as she wrinkled her nose at him.

"Perhaps you're only jealous because you didn't get one of your own. I suppose it was selfish of me not to have gotten one for you."

"I'll survive."

"You don't find shells in Paris," she commented, feeling at ease and strangely fresh. "The children will treasure it as much as they would gold doubloons."

"Children?"

Laine was examining her prize, exploring its smooth surface with her fingers. "My students at school. Most of them have never seen anything like this except in pictures."

"You teach?"

Much too engrossed in discovering every angle of the shell, Laine missed the incredulity in his voice. She answered absently, "Yes, English to the French students and French to the English girls who board there. After I graduated, I stayed on as staff. There was really nowhere else to go, and it had always been home in any case. Dillon, do you suppose I could come back sometime and find one or two others, a different type perhaps? The girls would be fascinated; they get so little entertainment."

"Where was your mother?"

"What?" In the transfer of her attention, she saw he was sitting up and staring at her with hard, probing eyes. "What did you say?" she asked again, confused by his change of tone.

"I said, where was your mother?"

"When . . . when I was in school? She was in Paris." The sudden anger in his tone threw her into turmoil. She searched for a way to change the topic. "I would like to see the airport again; do you think I . . ."

"Stop it."

Laine jerked at the harsh command, then quickly tried to slip into her armor. "There's no need to shout. I'm quite capable of hearing you from this distance."

"Don't pull that royal routine on me, Duchess. I want some answers." He flicked away his cigarette. Laine saw both the determination and fury in his face.

"I'm sorry, Dillon." Rising and stepping out of reach, Laine remained outwardly calm. "I'm really not in the mood for a cross-examination."

With a muttered oath, Dillon swung to his feet and captured her arms with a swiftness which left her stunned. "You can be a frosty little number. You switch on and off so fast, I can't make up my mind which is the charade. Just who the devil are you?"

"I'm tired of telling you who I am," she answered quietly. "I don't know what you want me to say; I don't know what you want me to be."

Her answer and her mild tone seemed only to make him more angry. He tightened his hold and gave her a quick shake. "What was this last routine of yours?"

She was yanked against him in a sudden blaze of fury, but before punishment could be meted out, someone called his name. With a soft oath Dillon released her, and turned as a figure emerged from a narrow tunnel of palms.

Laine's first thought was that a spirit from the island was drifting through the shelter and across the sand. Her skin was tawny gold and smooth against a sarong of scarlet and midnight blue. A full ebony carpet of hair fell to her waist, flowing gently with her graceful movements. Almond-shaped amber eyes were fringed with dark velvet. A sultry smile flitted across an exotic and perfect face. She lifted a hand in greeting, and Dillon answered.

"Hello, Orchid."

Her mortality was established in Laine's mind as the beautiful apparition lifted her lips and brushed Dillon's. "Miri said you'd gone snorkeling, so I knew you'd be here." Her voice flowed like soft music.

"Laine Simmons, Orchid King." Dillon's introductions were casual. Laine murmured a response, feeling suddenly as inadequate as a shadow faced with the sun. "Laine's Cap's daughter."

"Oh, I see." Laine was subjected to a more lengthy survey. She saw speculation beneath the practiced smile. "How nice you're visiting at last. Are you staying long?"

"A week or two." Laine regained her poise and met Orchid's eyes. "Do you live on the island?"

"Yes, though I'm off it as often as not. I'm a flight attendant. I'm just back from the mainland, and I've got a few days. I wanted to trade the sky for the sea. I hope you're going back in." She smiled up at Dillon and tucked a hand through his arm. "I would love some company."

Laine watched his charm flow. It seemed he need do nothing but smile to work his own particular magic. "Sure, I've got a couple of hours."

"I think I'll just go back to the house," Laine said quickly, feeling like an intruder. "I don't think I should get too much sun at one time." Lifting her shirt, Laine tugged it on. "Thank you, Dillon, for your time." She bent down and retrieved the rest of her things before speaking again. "It's nice to have met you, Miss King."

"I'm sure we'll see each other again." Undraping her sarong, Orchid revealed an inadequate bikini and a stunning body. "We're all very friendly on this island, aren't we, cousin?" Though it was the standard island form of address, Orchid's use of the word *cousin* implied a much closer relationship.

"Very friendly." Dillon agreed with such ease that

Laine felt he must be quite accustomed to Orchid's charms.

Murmuring a goodbye, Laine moved toward the canopy of palms. Hearing Orchid laugh, then speak in the musical tongue of the island, Laine glanced back before the leaves blocked out the view. She watched the golden arms twine around Dillon's neck, pulling his mouth toward hers in invitation.

CHAPTER 5

The walk back from the bay gave Laine time to reflect on the varying emotions Dillon O'Brian had managed to arouse in the small amount of time she had known him. Annoyance, resentment and anger had come first. Now, there was a wariness she realized stemmed from her inexperience with men. But somehow, that morning, there had been a few moments of harmony. She had been at ease in his company. And, she admitted ruefully, she had never before been totally at ease in masculine company on a one-to-one basis.

Perhaps it had simply been the novelty of her underwater adventure which had been responsible for her response to him. There had been something natural in their coming together, as if body had been created for body and mouth for mouth. She had felt a freedom in his arms, an awakening. It had been as if walls of glass had shattered and left her open to sensations for the first time.

Stopping, Laine plucked a blush-pink hibiscus, then twirled its stem idly as she wandered up the dirt track. Her tenuous feelings had been dissipated first by Dillon's unexplained anger, then by the appearance of the dark island beauty.

Orchid King, Laine mused. A frown marred her brow as the name of the flirtatious information clerk ran through her brain. *Rose.* Smoothing the frown away, Laine shook off a vague depression. Perhaps Dillon had a predilection for women with flowery names. It was certainly none of her concern. Obviously, she continued, unconsciously tearing off the hibiscus petals, he gave and received kisses as freely as a mouse nibbles cheese. He simply kissed me because I was there. Obviously, she went on doggedly, shredding the wounded blossom without thought, Orchid King has a great deal more to offer than I. She makes me feel like a pale, shapeless wren next to a lush, vibrant flamingo. I would hardly appeal to him as a woman even if he didn't already dislike me. I don't want to appeal to him. Certainly not. The very last thing I want to do is to appeal to that insufferable man. Scowling, she stared down at the mutilated hibiscus. With something between a sigh and a moan, she tossed it aside and increased her pace.

After depositing the shell in her room and changing out of her bathing suit, Laine wandered back downstairs. She felt listless and at loose ends. In the organized system of classes and meals and designated activities, her time had always been carefully budgeted. She found the lack of demand unsettling. She thought of how often during the course of a busy day she had yearned for a free hour to read or simply to sit alone. Now her time was free, and she wished only for occupation. The difference was, she knew, the fear of idle hours and the tendency to think. She found herself avoiding any attempt to sort out her situation or the future.

No one had shown her through the house since her arrival. After a brief hesitation, she allowed curiosity to lead her and gave herself a tour. She discovered that her father lived simply, with no frills or frippery, but with basic masculine comforts. There were books, but it appeared they were little read. She could see by the quantity and ragged appearance of aeronautical magazines where her father's taste in literature lay. Bamboo shades replaced conventional curtains; woven mats took the place of rugs. While far from primitive, the rooms were simply furnished.

Her mind began to draw a picture of a man content with such a basic existence, who lived quietly and routinely; a man whose main outlet was his love of the sky. Now Laine began to understand why her parents' marriage had failed. Her father's lifestyle was as unassuming as her mother's had been pretentious. Her mother would never have been satisfied with her father's modest existence, and he would have been lost in hers. Laine wondered, with a small frown, why she herself did not seem to fit with either one of them.

Laine lifted a black-framed snapshot from a desk.

A younger version of Cap Simmons beamed out at her, his arm casually tossed around a Dillon who had not yet reached full manhood. Dillon's smile was the same, however—somewhat cocky and sure. If they had stood in the flesh before her, their affection for each other would have seemed no less real. A shared understanding was revealed in their eyes and their easy stance together. It struck Laine suddenly, with a stab of resentment, that they looked like father and son. The years they had shared could never belong to her.

"It's not fair," she murmured, gripping the picture in both hands. With a faint shudder, she shut her eyes. Who am I blaming? she asked herself. Cap for needing someone? Dillon for being here? Blame won't help, and looking for the past is useless. It's time I looked for something new. Letting out a deep breath, Laine replaced the photograph. She turned away and moved farther down the hall. In a moment, she found herself in the kitchen surrounded by gleaming white appliances and hanging copper kettles. Miri turned from the stove and gave Laine a satisfied smile.

"So you have come for lunch." Miri tilted her head and narrowed her eyes. "You have some color from the sun."

Laine glanced down at her bare arms and was pleased with the light tan. "Why, yes, I do. I didn't actually come for lunch, though." She smiled and made an encompassing gesture. "I was exploring the house."

"Good. Now you eat. Sit here." Miri waved a long knife toward the scrubbed wooden table. "And do not make your bed anymore. That is my job." Miri plopped a glass of milk under Laine's nose, then gave a royal sniff.

"Oh, I'm sorry." Laine glanced from the glass of milk up to Miri's pursed lips. "It's just a habit."

"Don't do it again," Miri commanded as she turned to the refrigerator. She spoke again as she began to remove a variety of contents. "Did you make beds in that fancy school?"

"It isn't actually a fancy school," Laine corrected, watching with growing anxiety as Miri prepared a hefty sandwich. "It's really just a small convent school outside Paris."

"You lived in a convent?" Miri stopped her sandwich-building and looked skeptical.

"Well, no. That is, one might say I lived on the fringes of one. Except, of course, when I visited my mother. Miri . . ." Daunted by the plate set in front of her, Laine looked up helplessly. "I don't think I can manage all this."

"Just eat, Skinny Bones. Your morning with Dillon, it was nice?"

"Yes, very nice." Laine applied herself to the sandwich as Miri eased herself into the opposite chair. "I never knew there was so much to see underwater. Dillon is an expert guide."

"Ah, that one." Miri shook her head and somehow categorized Dillon as a naughty twelve-year-old boy. "He is always in the water or in the sky. He should keep his feet planted on the ground more often." Leaning back, Miri kept a commanding eye on Laine's progress. "He watches you."

"Yes, I know," Laine murmured. "Like a parole officer. I met Miss King," she continued, lifting her voice. "She came to the bay."

"Orchid King." Miri muttered something in unintelligible Hawaiian.

"She's very lovely . . . very vibrant and striking. I suppose Dillon has known her for a long time." Laine made the comment casually, surprising herself with the intentional probe.

"Long enough. But her bait has not yet lured the fish into the net." Miri gave a sly smile lost on the woman who stared into her milk. "You think Dillon looks good?"

"Looks good?" Laine repeated and frowned, not understanding the nuance. "Yes, Dillon's a very attractive man. At least, I suppose he is; I haven't known many men."

"You should give him more smiles," Miri advised with a wise nod. "A smart woman uses smiles to show a man her mind."

"He hasn't given me many reasons to smile at him," Laine said between bites. "And," she continued, finding she resented the thought, "I would think he gets an abundance of smiles from other sources."

"Dillon gives his attention to many women. He is a very generous man." Miri chuckled, and Laine blushed as she grasped the innuendo. "He has not yet found a woman who could make him selfish. Now you . . ." Miri tapped a finger aside her nose as if considering. "You would do well with him. He could teach you, and you could teach him."

"I teach Dillon?" Laine shook her head and gave a small laugh. "One cannot teach what one doesn't know. In the first place, Miri, I only met Dillon yesterday. All he's done so far is confuse me. From one moment to the next, I don't know how he's going to make me feel." She sighed, not realizing the sound was wistful. "I think men are very strange, Miri. I don't understand them at all."

"Understand?" Her bright laugh rattled through the kitchen. "What need is there to understand? You need only enjoy. I had three husbands, and I never understood one of them. But—" her smile was suddenly young "—I enjoyed. You are very young," she added. "That alone is attractive to a man used to women of knowledge."

"I don't think . . . I mean, of course, I wouldn't want him to, but . . ." Laine fumbled and stuttered, finding her thoughts a mass of confusion. "I'm sure Dillon wouldn't be interested in me. He seems to have a very compatible relationship with Miss King. Besides—" Laine shrugged her shoulders as she felt depression growing "—he distrusts me."

"It is a stupid woman who lets what is gone interfere with what is now." Miri placed her fingertips together and leaned back in her chair. "You want your father's love, Skinny Bones? Time and patience will give it to you. You want Dillon?" She held up an imperious hand at Laine's automatic protest. "You will learn to fight as a woman fights." She stood, and the flowers on her muumuu trembled with the movement. "Now, out of my kitchen. I have much work to do."

Obediently, Laine rose and moved to the door. "Miri . . ." Nibbling her lips, she turned back. "You've been very close to my father for many years. Don't you . . ." Laine hesitated, then finished in a rush. "Don't you resent me just appearing like this after all these years?"

"Resent?" Miri repeated the word, then ran her tongue along the inside of her mouth. "I do not resent because resent is a waste of time. And the last thing I resent is a child." She picked up a large spoon and tapped it idly against her palm. "When you went away from Cap Simmons, you were a child and you went with your mother. Now you are not a child, and you are here. What do I have to resent?" Miri shrugged and moved back to the stove.

Feeling unexpected tears, Laine shut her eyes on them and drew a small breath. "Thank you, Miri." With a murmur, she retreated to her room.

Thoughts swirled inside Laine's mind as she sat alone in her bedroom. As Dillon's embrace had opened a door to dormant emotions, so Miri's words had opened a door to dormant thoughts. *Time and patience,* Laine repeated silently. Time and patience were Miri's prescription for a daughter's troubled heart. But I have so little time, and little more patience. How can I win my father's love in a matter of days? She shook her head, unable to resolve an answer. *And Dillon,* her heart murmured as she threw herself onto the bed and stared at the ceiling. Why must he complicate an already impossibly complicated situation? Why must he embrace me, making me think and feel as a woman one moment, then push me away and stand as my accuser the next? He can be so gentle when I'm in his arms, so warm. And then . . . Frustrated, she rolled over, laying her cheek against the pillow. Then he's so cold, and even his eyes are brutal. If only I could stop thinking of him, stop remembering how it feels to be kissed by him. It's only that I have no experience, and he has so much. It's nothing more than a physical awakening. There can be nothing more . . . nothing more.

The knock on Laine's door brought her up with a start. Pushing at her tousled hair, she rose to answer. Dillon had exchanged cutoffs for jeans, and he appeared as refreshed and alert as she did bemused and heavy-lidded. Laine stared at him dumbly, unable to bring her thoughts and words together. With a frown, he surveyed her sleep-flushed cheeks and soft eyes.

"Did I wake you?"

"No, I . . ." She glanced back at the clock, and her confusion grew as she noted that an hour had passed since she had first stretched out on the bed. "Yes," she amended. "I suppose the flight finally caught up with me." She reached up and ran a hand through her hair, struggling to orient herself. "I didn't even realize I'd been asleep."

"They're real, aren't they?"

"What?" Laine blinked and tried to sort out his meaning.

"The lashes." He was staring so intently into her eyes, Laine had to fight the need to look away.

Nonchalantly, he leaned against the door and

completed his survey. "I'm on my way to the airport. I thought you might want to go. You said you wanted to see it again."

"Yes, I would." She was surprised by his courtesy.

"Well," he said dryly, and gestured for her to come along.

"Oh, I'll be right there. It should only take me a minute to get ready."

"You look ready."

"I need to comb my hair."

"It's fine." Dillon grabbed her hand and pulled her from the room before she could resist further.

Outside she found, to her astonishment, a helmet being thrust in her hands as she faced a shining, trim motorcycle. Clearing her throat, she looked from the helmet, to the machine, to Dillon. "We're going to ride on this?"

"That's right. I don't often use the car just to run to the airport."

"You might find this a good time to do so," Laine advised. "I've never ridden on a motorcycle."

"Duchess, all you have to do is to sit down and hang on." Dillon took the helmet from her and dropped it on her head. Securing his own helmet, he straddled the bike, then kicked the starter into life. "Climb on."

With amazement, Laine found herself astride the purring machine and clutching Dillon's waist as the motorcycle shot down the drive. Her death grip eased slightly as she realized that the speed was moderate, and the motorcycle had every intention of staying upright. It purred along the paved road.

Beside them, a river wandered like an unfurled blue ribbon, dividing patterned fields of taro. There was an excitement in being open to the wind, in feeling the hardness of Dillon's muscles beneath her hands. A sense of liberation flooded her. Laine realized that, in one day, Dillon had already given her experiences she might never have touched. I never knew how limited my life was, she thought with a smile. *No matter what happens, when I leave here, nothing will ever be quite the same again.*

When they arrived at the airport, Dillon wove through the main lot, circling to the back and halting in front of a hangar. "Off you go, Duchess. Ride's over."

Laine eased from the bike and struggled with her helmet. "Here." Dillon pulled it off for her, then dropped it to join his on the seat of the bike. "Still in one piece?"

"Actually," she returned, "I think I enjoyed it."

"It has its advantages." He ran his hands down her arms, then captured her waist. Laine stood very still, unwilling to retreat from his touch. He bent down and moved his mouth with teasing lightness over hers. Currents of pleasure ran over her skin. "Later," he said, pulling back. "I intend to finish that in a more satisfactory manner. But at the moment, I've work to do." His thumbs ran in lazy circles over her hips. "Cap's going to take you around; he's expecting you. Can you find your way?"

"Yes." Confused by the urgency of her heartbeat, Laine stepped back. The break in contact did nothing to slow it. "Am I to go to his office?"

"Yeah, the same place you went before. He'll show you whatever you want to see. Watch your step, Laine." His green eyes cooled abruptly, and his voice lost its lightness. "Until I'm sure about you, you can't afford to make any mistakes."

For a moment, she only stared up at him, feeling her skin grow cold, and her pulse slow. "I'm very much afraid," she admitted sadly, "I've already made one."

Turning, she walked away.

CHAPTER 6

Laine walked toward the small, palm-flanked building. Through her mind ran all which had passed in twenty-four hours. She had met her father, learned of her mother's deception and was now readjusting her wishes.

She had also, in the brief span of time it takes the sun to rise and fall, discovered the pleasures and demands of womanhood. Dillon had released new and magic sensations. Again, her mind argued with her heart that her feelings were only the result of a first physical attraction. It could hardly be anything else, she assured herself. One does not fall in love in a day, and certainly not with a man like Dillon O'Brian. We're total opposites. He's outgoing and confident, and so completely at ease with people. I envy him his honest confidence. There's nothing emotional about that. I've simply never met anyone like him before. That's why I'm confused. It has nothing to do with emotions. Laine felt comforted as she entered her father's office building.

As she stepped into the outer lobby, Cap strode from his office, glancing over his shoulder at a dark girl with a pad in her hand who was following in his wake.

"Check with Dillon on the fuel order before you send that out. He'll be in a meeting for the next hour. If you miss him at his office, try hangar four." As he caught sight of Laine, Cap smiled and slowed his pace. "Hello, Laine. Dillon said you wanted a tour."

"Yes, I'd love one, if you have the time."

"Of course. Sharon, this is my daughter. Laine, this is Sharon Kumocko, my secretary."

Laine observed the curiosity in Sharon's eyes as they exchanged greetings. Her father's tone during the introductions had been somewhat forced. Laine felt him hesitate before he took her arm to lead her outside. She wondered briefly if she had imagined their closeness during her childhood.

"It's not a very big airport," Cap began as they stepped out into the sun and heat. "For the most part, we cater to island hoppers and charters. We also run a flight school. That's essentially Dillon's project."

"Cap." Impulsively, Laine halted his recital and turned to face him. "I know I've put you in an awkward position. I realize now that I should have written and asked if I could come rather than just dropping on your doorstep this way. It was thoughtless of me."

"Laine . . ."

"Please." She shook her head at his interruption and rushed on. "I realize, too, that you have your own life, your own home, your own friends. You've had fifteen years to settle into a routine. I don't want to interfere with any of that. Believe me, I don't want to be in the way, and I don't want you to feel . . ." She made a helpless gesture as the impetus ran out of her words. "I would like it if we could be friends."

Cap had studied her during her speech. The smile he gave her at its finish held more warmth than those he had given her before. "You know," he sighed, tugging his fingers through his hair, "it's sort of terrifying to be faced with a grown-up daughter. I missed all the stages, all the changes. I'm afraid I still pictured you as a bad-tempered pigtailed urchin with scraped knees. The elegant woman who walked into my office yesterday and spoke to me with a faint French accent is a stranger. And one," he added, touching her hair a moment, "who brings back memories I thought I'd buried." He sighed again and stuck his hands in his pockets. "I don't know much about women; I don't think I ever did. Your mother was the most beautiful, confusing woman I've ever known. When you were little, and the three of us were still together, I substituted your friendship for the friendship that your mother and I never had. You were the only female I ever understood. I've always wondered if that was why things didn't work."

Tilting her head, Laine gave her father a long, searching look. "Cap, why did you marry her? There seems to be nothing you had in common."

Cap shook his head with a quick laugh. "You didn't know her twenty years ago. She did a lot of changing, Laine. Some people change more than others." He shook his head again, and his eyes focused on some middle distance. "Besides, I loved her. I've always loved her."

"I'm sorry." Laine felt tears burn the back of her eyes, and she dropped her gaze to the ground. "I don't mean to make things more difficult."

"You're not. We had some good years." He paused until Laine lifted her eyes. "I like to remember them now and again." Taking her arm, he began to walk. "Was your mother happy, Laine?"

"Happy?" She thought a moment, remembering the quicksilver moods, the gay bubbling voice with dissatisfaction always under the surface. "I suppose Vanessa was as happy as she was capable of being. She loved Paris and she lived as she chose."

"Vanessa?" Cap frowned, glancing down at Laine's profile. "Is that how you think of your mother?"

"I always called her by name." Laine lifted her hand to shield her eyes from the sun as she watched the descent of a charter. "She said 'mother' made her feel too old. She hated getting older . . . I feel better knowing you're happy in the life you've chosen. Do you fly anymore, Cap? I remember how you used to love it."

"I still put in my quota of flight hours. Laine." He

took both her arms and turned her to face him. "One question, then we'll leave it alone for a while. Have you been happy?"

The directness of both his questions and his eyes caused her to fumble. She looked away as if fascinated by disembarking passengers. "I've been very busy. The nuns are very serious about education."

"You're not answering my question. Or," he corrected, drawing his thick brows together, "maybe you are."

"I've been content," she said, giving him a smile. "I've learned a great deal, and I'm comfortable with my life. I think that's enough for anyone."

"For someone," Cap returned, "who's reached my age, but not for a very young, very lovely woman." He watched her smile fade into perplexity. "It's not enough, Laine, and I'm surprised you'd settle for it." His voice was stern, laced with a hint of disapproval which put Laine on the defensive.

"Cap, I haven't had the chance . . ." She stopped, realizing she must guard her words. "I haven't taken the time," she amended, "to chase windmills." She lifted her hands, palms up, in a broad French gesture. "Perhaps I've reached the point in my life when I should begin to do so."

His expression lightened as she smiled up at him. "All right, we'll let it rest for now."

Without any more mention of the past, Cap led Laine through neat rows of planes. He fondled each as if it were a child, explaining their qualities in proud, but to Laine hopelessly technical, terms. She listened, content with his good humor, pleased with the sound of his voice. Occasionally, she made an ignorant comment that made him laugh. She found the laugh very precious.

The buildings were spread out, neat and without pretension; hangars and storage buildings, research and accounting offices, with the high, glass-enclosed control tower dominating all. Cap pointed out each one, but the planes themselves were his consummate interest.

"You said it wasn't big." Laine gazed around the complex and down light-dotted runways. "It looks enormous."

"It's a small, low-activity field, but we do our best to see that it's as well run as Honolulu International."

"What is it that Dillon does here?" Telling herself it was only idle curiosity, Laine surrendered to the urge to question.

"Oh, Dillon does a bit of everything," Cap answered with frustrating vagueness. "He has a knack for organizing. He can find his way through a problem before it becomes one, and he handles people so well they never realize they've been handled. He can also take a plane apart and put it back together again." Smiling, Cap gave a small shake of his head. "I don't know what I'd have done without Dillon. Without his drive, I might have been content to be a crop duster."

"Drive?" Laine repeated, lingering over the word.

"Yes, I suppose he has drive when there is something he wants. But isn't he . . ." She searched for a label and settled on a generality. "Isn't he a very casual person?"

"Island life breeds a certain casualness, Laine, and Dillon was born here." He steered her toward the communications building. "Just because a man is at ease with himself and avoids pretension doesn't mean he lacks intelligence or ability. Dillon has both; he simply pursues his ambitions in his own way."

Later, as they walked toward the steel-domed hangars, Laine realized she and her father had begun to build a new relationship. He was more relaxed with her, his smiles and speech more spontaneous. She knew her shield was dropped as well, and she was more vulnerable.

"I've an appointment in a few minutes." Cap stopped just inside the building and glanced at his watch. "I'll have to turn you over to Dillon now, unless you want me to have someone take you back to the house."

"No, I'll be fine," she assured him. "Perhaps I can just wander about. I don't want to be a nuisance."

"You haven't been a nuisance. I enjoyed taking you through. You haven't lost the curiosity I remember. You always wanted to know why and how and you always listened. I think you were five when you demanded I explain the entire control panel of a 707." His chuckle was the same quick, appealing sound she remembered from childhood. "Your face would get so serious, I'd swear you had understood everything I'd said." He patted her hand, then smiled over her head. "Dillon, I thought we'd find you here. Take care of Laine, will you? I've got Billet coming in."

"It appears I've got the best of the deal."

Laine turned to see him leaning against a plane, wiping his hand on the loose coveralls he wore.

"Did everything go all right with the union representative?"

"Fine. You can look over the report tomorrow."

"I'll see you tonight, then." Cap turned to Laine, and after a brief hesitation, patted her cheek before he walked away.

Smiling, she turned back to encounter Dillon's brooding stare. "Oh, please," she began, shaking her head. "Don't spoil it. It's such a small thing."

With a shrug, Dillon turned back to the plane. "Did you like your tour?"

"Yes, I did." Laine's footsteps echoed off the high ceiling as she crossed the room to join him. "I'm afraid I didn't understand a fraction of what he told me. He carried on about aprons and funnel systems and became very expansive on wind drag and thrust." She creased her brow for a moment as she searched her memory. "I'm told struts can withstand comprehensive as well as tensile forces. I didn't have the courage to confess I didn't know one force from the other."

"He's happiest when he's talking about planes," Dillon commented absently. "It doesn't matter if you understood as long as you listened. Hand me that torque wrench."

Laine looked down at the assortment of tools, then searched for something resembling a torque wrench. "I enjoyed listening. Is this a wrench?"

Dillon twisted his head and glanced at the ratchet she offered. With reluctant amusement, he brought his eyes to hers, then shook his head. "No, Duchess. This," he stated, finding the tool himself, "is a wrench."

"I haven't spent a great deal of time under cars or under planes," she muttered. Her annoyance spread as she thought how unlikely it was that he would ask Orchid King for a torque wrench. "Cap told me you've added a flight school. Do you do the instructing?"

"Some."

Pumping up her courage, Laine asked in a rush, "Would you teach me?"

"What?" Dillon glanced back over his shoulder.

"Could you teach me to fly a plane?" She wondered if the question sounded as ridiculous to Dillon as it did to her.

"Maybe." He studied the fragile planes of her face, noting the determined light in her eyes. "Maybe," he repeated. "Why do you want to learn?"

"Cap used to talk about teaching me. Of course—" she spread her hands in a Gallic gesture "—I was only a child, but . . ." Releasing an impatient breath, Laine lifted her chin and was suddenly very American. "Because I think it would be fun."

The change, and the stubborn set to her mouth,

touched off Dillon's laughter. "I'll take one of you up tomorrow." Laine frowned, trying to puzzle out his meaning. Turning back to the plane, Dillon held out the wrench for her to put away. She stared at the grease-smeared handle. Taking his head from the bowels of the plane, Dillon turned back and saw her reluctance. He muttered something she did not attempt to translate, then moved away and pulled another pair of coveralls from a hook. "Here, put these on. I'm going to be a while, and you might as well be useful."

"I'm sure you'd manage beautifully without me."

"Undoubtedly, but put them on anyway." Under Dillon's watchful eye, Laine stepped into the coveralls and slipped her arms into the sleeves. "Good grief, you look swallowed." Crouching down, he began to roll up the pants legs while she scowled at the top of his head.

"I'm sure you'll find me more hindrance than help."

"I figured that out some time ago," he replied. His tone was undeniably cheerful as he rolled up her sleeves half a dozen times. "You shouldn't have quit growing so soon; you don't look more than twelve." He pulled the zipper up to her throat in one swift motion, then looked into her face. She saw his expression alter. For an instant, she thought she observed a flash of tenderness before he let out an impatient breath. Cursing softly, he submerged into the belly of the plane. "All right," he began briskly, "hand me a screwdriver. The one with the red handle."

Having made the acquaintance of this particular tool, Laine foraged and found it. She placed it in Dillon's outstretched hand. He worked for some time, his conversation limited almost exclusively to the request and description of tools. As time passed, the hum of planes outside became only a backdrop for his voice.

Laine began to ask him questions about the job he was performing. She felt no need to follow his answers, finding pleasure only in the tone and texture of his voice. He was absorbed and she was able to study him unobserved. She surveyed the odd intensity of his eyes, the firm line of his chin and jaw, the bronzed skin which rippled along his arm as he worked. She saw that his chin was shadowed with a day-old beard, that his hair was curling loosely over his collar, that his right brow was lifted slightly higher than his left as he concentrated.

Dillon turned to her with some request, but she could only stare. She was lost in his eyes, blanketed by a fierce and trembling realization.

"What's wrong?" Dillon drew his brows together.

Like a diver breaking water, Laine shook her head and swallowed. "Nothing, I . . . What did you want? I wasn't paying attention." She bent over the box of tools as if it contained the focus of her world. Silently, Dillon lifted out the one he required and turned back to the engine. Grateful for his preoccupation, Laine closed her eyes. She felt bemused and defenseless.

Love, she thought, *should not come with such quick*

intensity. It should flow slowly, with tenderness and gentle feelings. It shouldn't stab like a sword, striking without warning, without mercy. How could one love what one could not understand? Dillon O'Brian was an enigma, a man whose moods seemed to flow without rhyme or reason. And what did she know of him? He was her father's partner, but his position was unclear. He was a man who knew both the sky and the sea, and found it easy to move with their freedom. She knew too that he was a man who knew women and could give them pleasure.

And how, Laine wondered, does one fight love when one has no knowledge of it? Perhaps it was a matter of balance. She deliberately released the tension in her shoulders. I have to find the way to walk the wire without leaning over either side and tumbling off.

"It seems you've taken a side trip," Dillon commented, pulling a rag from his pocket. He grinned as Laine gave a start of alarm. "You're a miserable mechanic, Duchess, and a sloppy one." He rubbed the rag over her cheek until a black smudge disappeared. "There's a sink over there; you'd better go wash your hands. I'll finish these adjustments later. The fuel system is giving me fits."

Laine moved off as he instructed, taking her time in removing traces of grime. She used the opportunity to regain her composure. Hanging up the borrowed overalls, she wandered about the empty hangar while Dillon packed away tools and completed his own washing up. She was surprised to see that it had grown late during the time she had inexpertly assisted Dillon. A soft dusk masked the day's brilliance. Along the runways, lights twinkled like small red eyes. As she turned back, Laine found Dillon's gaze on her. She moistened her lips, then attempted casualness.

"Are you finished?"

"Not quite. Come here." Something in his tone caused her to retreat a step rather than obey. He lifted his brows, then repeated the order with a soft, underlying threat. "I said come here."

Deciding voluntary agreement was the wisest choice, Laine crossed the floor. Her echoing footsteps seemed to bounce off the walls like thunder. She prayed the sound masked the furious booming of her heart as she stopped in front of him, and that its beating was in her ears only. She stood in silence as he studied her face, wishing desperately she knew what he was looking for, and if she possessed it. Dillon said nothing, but placed his hands on her hips, drawing her a step closer. Their thighs brushed. His grip was firm, and all the while his eyes kept hers a prisoner.

"Kiss me," he said simply. She shook her head in quick protest, unable to look or break away. "Laine, I said kiss me." Dillon pressed her hips closer, molding her shape to his. His eyes were demanding, his mouth tempting. Tentatively, she lifted her arms, letting her hands rest on his shoulders as she rose to her toes. Her eyes remained open and locked on his as their faces drew nearer, as their breaths began to mingle. Softly, she touched her lips to his.

He waited until her mouth lost its shyness and became mobile on his, waited until her arms found their way around his neck to urge him closer. He increased the pressure, drawing out her sigh as he slid his hands under her blouse to the smooth skin of her back. His explorations were slow and achingly gentle. The hands that caressed her taught rather than demanded. Murmuring his name against the taste of his mouth, Laine strained against him, wanting him, needing him. The swift heat of passion was all-consuming. Her lips seemed to learn more quickly than her brain. They began to seek and demand pleasures she could not yet understand. The rest of the world faded like a whisper. At that moment, there was nothing in her life but Dillon and her need for him.

He drew her away. Neither spoke, each staring into the other's eyes as if to read a message not yet written. Dillon brushed a stray curl from her cheek. "I'd better take you home."

"Dillon," Laine began, completely at a loss as to what could be said. Unable to continue, she closed her eyes on her own inadequacy.

"Come on, Duchess, you've had a long day." Dillon circled her neck with his hand and massaged briefly. "We're not dealing on equal footing at the moment, and I like to fight fair under most circumstances."

"Fight?" Laine managed, struggling to keep her

eyes open and steady on his. "Is that what this is, Dillon? A fight?"

"The oldest kind," he returned with a small lift to his mouth. His smile faded before it was truly formed, and suddenly his hand was firm on her chin. "It's not over, Laine, and when we have the next round, I might say the devil with the rules."

CHAPTER 7

When Laine came down for breakfast the next morning, she found only her father. "Hello, Skinny Bones," Miri called out before Cap could greet her. "Sit and eat. I will fix you tea since you do not like my coffee."

Unsure whether to be embarrassed or amused, Laine obeyed. "Thank you, Miri," she said to the retreating back.

"She's quite taken with you." Looking over, Laine saw the light of mirth in Cap's eyes. "Since you've come, she's been so wrapped up with putting pounds on you, she hasn't made one comment about me needing a wife."

With a wry smile, Laine watched her father pour his coffee. "Glad to help. I showed myself around a bit yesterday. I hope you don't mind."

"No, of course not." His smile was rueful. "I guess

I should've taken you around the house myself. My manners are a little rusty."

"I didn't mind. Actually," she tilted her head and returned his smile, "wandering around alone gave me a sort of fresh perspective. You said you'd missed all the stages and still thought of me as a child. I think . . ." Her fingers spread as she tried to clarify her thoughts. "I think I missed them too—that is, I still had my childhood image of you. Yesterday, I began to see James Simmons in flesh and blood."

"Disappointed?" There was more ease in his tone and a lurking humor in his eyes.

"Impressed," Laine corrected. "I saw a man content with himself and his life, who has the love and respect of those close to him. I think my father must be a very nice man."

He gave her an odd smile which spoke both of surprise and pleasure. "That's quite a compliment coming from a grown daughter." He added more coffee to his cup, and Laine let the silence drift.

Her gaze lingered on Dillon's empty seat a moment. "Ah . . . is Dillon not here?"

"Hmm? Oh, Dillon had a breakfast meeting. As a matter of fact, he has quite a few things to see to this morning." Cap drank his coffee black, and with an enjoyment Laine could not understand.

"I see," she responded, trying not to sound disappointed. "I suppose the airport keeps both of you very busy."

"That it does." Cap glanced at his watch and tilted

his head in regret. "Actually, I have an appointment myself very shortly. I'm sorry to leave you alone this way, but . . ."

"Please," Laine interrupted. "I don't need to be entertained, and I meant what I said yesterday about not wanting to interfere. I'm sure I'll find plenty of things to keep me occupied."

"All right then. I'll see you this evening." Cap rose, then paused at the doorway with sudden inspiration. "Miri can arrange a ride for you if you'd like to do some shopping in town."

"Thank you." Laine smiled, thinking of her limited funds. "Perhaps I will." She watched him stroll away, then sighed, as her gaze fell again on Dillon's empty chair.

Laine's morning was spent lazily. She soon found out that Miri would not accept or tolerate any help around the house. Following the native woman's strong suggestion that she go out, Laine gathered her stationery and set out for the bay. She found it every bit as perfect as she had the day before—the water clear as crystal, the sand white and pure. Spreading out a blanket, Laine sat down and tried to describe her surroundings with words on paper. The letters she wrote to France were long and detailed, though she omitted any mention of her troubled situation.

As she wrote, the sun rose high overhead. The air was moist and ripe. Lulled by the peace and the rays of the sun, she curled up on the blanket and slept.

Her limbs were languid, and behind closed lids was

a dull red mist. She wondered hazily how the reverend mother had urged so much heat out of the ancient furnace. Reluctantly, she struggled to toss off sleep as a hand shook her shoulder. *"Un moment, ma soeur,"* she murmured, and sighed with the effort. *"J'arrive."* Forcing open her leaden lids, she found Dillon's face inches above hers.

"I seem to have a habit of waking you up." He leaned back on his heels and studied her cloudy eyes. "Don't you know better than to sleep in the sun with that complexion? You're lucky you didn't burn."

"Oh." At last realizing where she was, Laine pushed herself into a sitting position. She felt the odd sense of guilt of the napper caught napping. "I don't know why I fell asleep like that. It must have been the quiet."

"Another reason might be exhaustion," Dillon countered, then frowned. "You're losing the shadows under your eyes."

"Cap said you were very busy this morning." Laine found his continued survey disconcerting and shuffled her writing gear.

"Hmm, yes, I was. Writing letters?"

She glanced up at him, then tapped the tip of her pen against her mouth. "Hmm, yes, I was."

"Very cute." His mouth twitched slightly as he hauled her to her feet. "I thought you wanted to learn how to fly a plane."

"Oh!" Her face lit up with pleasure. "I thought you'd forgotten. Are you sure you're not too busy? Cap said . . ."

"No, I hadn't forgotten, and no, I'm not too busy." He cut her off as he leaned down to gather her blanket. "Stop babbling as if you were twelve and I were taking you to the circus for cotton candy."

"Of course," she replied, amused by his reaction.

Dillon let out an exasperated breath before grabbing her hand and pulling her across the sand. She heard him mutter something uncomplimentary about women in general.

Less than an hour later, Laine found herself seated in Dillon's plane. "Now, this is a single prop monoplane with a reciprocating engine. Another time, I'll take you up in the jet, but . . ."

"You have another plane?" Laine interrupted.

"Some people collect hats," Dillon countered dryly, then pointed to the variety of gauges. "Basically, flying a plane is no more difficult than driving a car. The first thing you have to do is understand your instruments and learn how to read them."

"There are quite a few, aren't there?" Dubiously, Laine scanned numbers and needles.

"Not really. This isn't exactly an X-15." He let out a long breath at her blank expression, then started the engine. "O.K., as we climb, I want you to watch this gauge. It's the altimeter. It . . ."

"It indicates the height of the plane above sea level or above ground," Laine finished for him.

"Very good." Dillon cleared his takeoff with the tower, and the plane began its roll down the runway. "What did you do, grab one of Cap's magazines last night?"

"No. I remember some of my early lessons. I suppose I stored away all the things Cap used to ramble about when I was a child. This is a compass, and this . . ." Her brow furrowed in her memory search. "This is a turn and bank indicator, but I'm not sure I remember quite what that means."

"I'm impressed, but you're supposed to be watching the altimeter."

"Oh, yes." Wrinkling her nose at the chastisement, she obeyed.

"All right." Dillon gave her profile a quick grin, then turned his attention to the sky. "The larger needle's going to make one turn of the dial for every thousand feet we climb. The smaller one makes a turn for every ten thousand. Once you learn your gauges, and how to use each one of them, your job's less difficult than driving, and there's generally a lot less traffic."

"Perhaps you'll teach me to drive a car next," Laine suggested as she watched the large needle round the dial for the second time.

"You don't know how to drive?" Dillon demanded. His voice was incredulous.

"No. Is that a crime in this country? I assure you, there are some people who believe me to be marginally intelligent. I'm certain I can learn to fly this machine in the same amount of time it takes any of your other students."

"It's possible," Dillon muttered. "How come you never learned to drive a car?"

"Because I never had one. How did you break your

nose?" At his puzzled expression, Laine merely gave him a bland smile. "My question is just as irrelevant as yours."

Laine felt quite pleased when he laughed, almost as though she had won a small victory.

"Which time?" he asked, and it was her turn to look puzzled. "I broke it twice. The first time I was about ten and tried to fly a cardboard plane I had designed off the roof of the garage. I didn't have the propulsion system perfected. I only broke my nose and my arm, though I was told it should've been my neck."

"Very likely," Laine agreed. "And the second time?"

"The second time, I was a bit older. There was a disagreement over a certain girl. My nose suffered another insult, and the other guy lost two teeth."

"Older perhaps, but little wiser," Laine commented. "And who got the girl?"

Dillon flashed his quick grin. "Neither of us. We decided she wasn't worth it after all and went off to nurse our wounds with a beer."

"How gallant."

"Yeah, I'm sure you've noticed that trait in me. I can't seem to shake it. Now, watch your famous turn and bank indicator, and I'll explain its function."

For the next thirty minutes, he became the quintessential teacher, surprising Laine with his knowledge and patience. He answered the dozens of questions she tossed out as flashes of her early lessons skipped through her memory. He seemed to accept her sudden thirst to know as if it were not only natural, but expected. They cruised through a sky touched with puffy clouds and mountain peaks and skimmed the gaping mouth of the multihued Waimea Canyon. They circled above the endless, whitecapped ocean. Laine began to see the similarity between the freedom of the sky and the freedom of the sea. She began to feel the fascination Dillon had spoken of, the need to meet the challenge, the need to explore. She listened with every ounce of her concentration, determined to understand and remember.

"There's a little storm behind us," Dillon announced casually. "We're not going to beat it back." He turned to Laine with a faint smile on his lips. "We're going to get tossed around a bit, Duchess."

"Oh?" Trying to mirror his mood, Laine shifted in her seat and studied the dark clouds in their wake. "Can you fly through that?" she asked, keeping her voice light while her stomach tightened.

"Oh, maybe," he returned. She jerked her head around swiftly. When she saw the laughter in his eyes, she let out a long breath.

"You have an odd sense of humor, Dillon. Very unique," she added, then sucked in her breath as the clouds overtook them. All at once, they were shrouded in darkness, rain pelting furiously on all sides. As the plane rocked, Laine felt a surge of panic.

"You know, it always fascinates me to be in a cloud. Nothing much to them, just vapor and moisture, but they're fabulous." His voice was calm and composed. Laine felt her heartbeat steadying. "Storm clouds are the most interesting, but you really need lightning."

"I think I could live without it," Laine murmured.

"That's because you haven't seen it from up here. When you fly above lightning, you can watch it kicking up inside the clouds. The colors are incredible."

"Have you flown through many storms?" Laine looked out her windows but saw nothing but swirling black clouds.

"I've done my share. The front of this one'll be waiting for us when we land. Won't last long, though." The plane bucked again, and Laine looked on in bewilderment as Dillon grinned.

"You enjoy this sort of thing, don't you? The excitement, the sense of danger?"

"It keeps the reflexes in tune, Laine." Turning, he smiled at her without a trace of cynicism. "And it keeps life from being boring." The look held for a moment, and Laine's heart did a series of jumping jacks. "There's plenty of stability in life," he continued, making adjustments to compensate for the wind. "Jobs, bills, insurance policies, that's what gives you balance. But sometimes, you've got to ride a roller coaster, run a race, ride a wave. That's what makes life fun. The trick is to keep one end of the scope from overbalancing the other."

Yes, Laine thought. Vanessa never learned the trick. She was always looking for a new game and never enjoyed the one she was playing. And perhaps I've overcompensated by thinking too much of the stability.

Too many books, and not enough doing. Laine felt her muscles relax and she turned to Dillon with a hint of a smile. "I haven't ridden a roller coaster for a great many years. One could say that I'm due. Look!" She pressed her face against the side window and peered downward. "It's like something out of *Macbeth,* all misty and sinister. I'd like to see the lightning, Dillon. I really would."

He laughed at the eager anticipation on her face as he began his descent. "I'll see if I can arrange it."

The clouds seemed to swirl and dissolve as the plane lost altitude. Their thickness became pale gray cobwebs to be dusted out of the way. Below, the landscape came into view as they dropped below the mist. The earth was rain-drenched and vivid with color. As they landed, Laine felt her pleasure fade into a vague sense of loss. She felt like a child who had just blown out her last birthday candle.

"I'll take you back up in a couple days if you want," said Dillon, taxiing to a halt.

"Yes, please, I'd like that very much. I don't know how to thank you for . . ."

"Do your homework," he said as he shut off the engine. "I'll give you some books and you can read up on instrumentation."

"Yes, sir," Laine said with suspicious humility. Dillon glared at her briefly before swinging from the plane. Laine's lack of experience caused her to take more time with her exit. She found herself swooped down before she could complete the journey on her own.

In the pounding rain they stood close, Dillon's hands light on her waist. She could feel the heat of his body through the dampness of her blouse. Dark tendrils of hair fell over his forehead, and without thought, Laine lifted her hand to smooth them back. There was something sweetly ordinary about being in his arms, as if it were a place she had been countless times before and would come back to countless times again. She felt her love bursting to be free.

"You're getting wet," she murmured, dropping her hand to his cheek.

"So are you." Though his fingers tightened on her waist, he drew her no closer.

"I don't mind."

With a sigh, Dillon rested his chin on the top of her head. "Miri'll punch me out if I let you catch a chill."

"I'm not cold," she murmured, finding indescribable pleasure in their closeness.

"You're shivering." Abruptly, Dillon brought her to his side and began to walk. "We'll go into my office, and you can dry out before I take you home."

As they walked, the rain slowed to a mist. Fingers of sunlight began to strain through, brushing away the last stubborn drops. Laine surveyed the complex. She remembered the building which housed Dillon's office from the tour she had taken with her father. With a grin, she pushed damp hair from her eyes and pulled away from Dillon. "Race you," she challenged, and scrambled over wet pavement.

He caught her, laughing and breathless, at the door. With a new ease, Laine circled his neck as they laughed together. She felt young and foolish and desperately in love.

"You're quick, aren't you?" Dillon observed, and she tilted her head back to meet his smile.

"You learn to be quick when you live in a dormitory. Competition for the bath is brutal." Laine thought she saw his smile begin to fade before they were interrupted.

"Dillon, I'm sorry to disturb you."

Glancing over, Laine saw a young woman with classic bone structure, her raven hair pulled taut at the nape of a slender neck. The woman returned Laine's survey with undisguised curiosity. Blushing, Laine struggled out of Dillon's arms.

"It's all right, Fran. This is Laine Simmons, Cap's daughter. Fran's my calculator."

"He means secretary," Fran returned with an exasperated sigh. "But this afternoon I feel more like an answering service. You have a dozen phone messages on your desk."

"Anything urgent?" As he asked, he moved into an adjoining room.

"No." Fran gave Laine a friendly smile. "Just several people who didn't want to make a decision until they heard from Mount Olympus. I told them all you were out for the day and would get back to them tomorrow."

"Good." Walking back into the room, Dillon carried a handful of papers and a towel. He tossed the towel at Laine before he studied the papers.

"I thought you were supposed to be taking a few days off," Fran stated while Dillon muttered over his messages.

"Um-hum. There doesn't seem to be anything here that can't wait."

"I've already told you that." Fran snatched the papers out of his hand.

"So you did." Unabashed, Dillon grinned and patted her cheek. "Did you ask Orchid what she wanted?"

Across the room, Laine stopped rubbing the towel against her hair, then began again with increased speed.

"No, though after the *third* call, I'm afraid I became a bit abrupt with her."

"She can handle it," Dillon returned easily, then switched his attention to Laine. "Ready?"

"Yes." Feeling curiously deflated, Laine crossed the room and handed Dillon the towel. "Thank you."

"Sure." Casually, he tossed the damp towel to Fran. "See you tomorrow, cousin."

"Yes, master." Fran shot Laine a friendly wave before Dillon hustled her from the building.

With a great deal of effort, Laine managed to thrust Orchid King from her mind during the drive home and throughout the evening meal. The sun was just setting when she settled on the porch with Dillon and her father.

The sky's light was enchanting. The intense, tropical blue was breaking into hues of gold and crimson, the low, misted clouds streaked with pinks and mauves. There was something dreamlike and soothing in the dusk. Laine sat quietly in a wicker chair, thinking over her day as the men's conversation washed over her. Even had she understood their exchange, she was too lazily content to join in. She knew that for the first time in her adult life, she was both physically and mentally relaxed. Perhaps, she mused, it was the adventures of the past few days, the testing of so many untried feelings and emotions.

Mumbling about coffee, Cap rose and slipped inside the house. Laine gave him an absent smile as he passed her, then curled her legs under her and watched the first stars blink into life.

"You're quiet tonight." As Dillon leaned back in his chair, Laine heard the soft click of his lighter.

"I was just thinking how lovely it is here." Her sigh drifted with contentment. "I think it must be the loveliest place on earth."

"Lovelier than Paris?"

Hearing the edge in his voice, Laine turned to look at him questioningly. The first light of the moon fell gently over her face. "It's very different from Paris," she answered. "Parts of Paris are beautiful, mellowed and gentled with age. Other parts are elegant or dignified. She is like a woman who has been often told she is enchanting. But the beauty here is more primitive. The island is ageless and innocent at the same time."

"Many people tire of innocence." Dillon shrugged and drew deeply on his cigarette.

"I suppose that's true," she agreed, unsure why he seemed so distant and so cynical.

"In this light, you look a great deal like your mother," he said suddenly, and Laine felt her skin ice over.

"How do you know? You never met my mother."

"Cap has a picture." Dillon turned toward her, but his face was in shadows. "You resemble her a great deal."

"She certainly does." Cap sauntered out with a tray of coffee in his hands. Setting it on a round glass table, he straightened and studied Laine. "It's amazing. The light will catch you a certain way, or you'll get a certain expression on your face. Suddenly, it's your mother twenty years ago."

"I'm not Vanessa." Laine sprang up from her seat, and her voice trembled with rage. "I'm nothing like Vanessa." To her distress, tears began to gather in her eyes. Her father looked on in astonishment. "I'm nothing like her. I won't be compared to her." Furious with both the men and herself, Laine turned and slammed through the screen door. On her dash for the stairs, she collided with Miri's substantial form. Stuttering an apology, she streaked up the stairs and into her room.

Laine was pacing around her room for the third time when Miri strolled in.

"What is all this running and slamming in my house?" Miri asked, folding her arms across her ample chest.

Shaking her head, Laine lowered herself to the

bed, then, despising herself, burst into tears. Clucking her tongue and muttering in Hawaiian, Miri crossed the room. Soon Laine found her head cradled against a soft, pillowing bosom. "That Dillon," Miri muttered as she rocked Laine to and fro.

"It wasn't Dillon," Laine managed, finding the maternal comfort new and overwhelming. "Yes, it was . . . it was both of them." Laine had a sudden desperate need for reassurance. "I'm nothing like her, Miri. I'm nothing like her at all."

"Of course you are not." Miri patted Laine's blond curls. "Who is it you are not like?"

"Vanessa." Laine brushed away tears with the back of her hand. "My mother. Both of them were looking at me, saying how much I look like her."

"What is this? What is this? All these tears because you look like someone?" Miri pulled Laine away by the shoulders and shook her. "Why do you waste your tears on this? I think you're a smart girl, then you act stupid."

"You don't understand." Laine drew up her knees and rested her chin on them. "I won't be compared to her, not to her. Vanessa was selfish and self-centered and dishonest."

"She was your mother," Miri stated with such authority that Laine's mouth dropped open. "You will speak with respect of your mother. She is dead, and whatever she did is over now. You must bury it," Miri commanded, giving Laine another shake, "or you will never be happy. Did they say you were selfish and self-centered and dishonest?"

"No, but . . ."

"What did Cap Simmons say to you?" Miri demanded.

Laine let out a long breath. "He said I looked like my mother."

"And do you, or does he lie?"

"Yes, I suppose I do, but . . ."

"So, your mother was a pretty woman, you are a pretty woman." Miri lifted Laine's chin with her thick fingers. "Do you know who you are, Laine Simmons?"

"Yes, I think I do."

"Then you have no problem." Miri patted her cheek and rose.

"Oh, Miri." Laine laughed and wiped her eyes again. "You make me feel very foolish."

"You make yourself feel foolish," Miri corrected. "I did not slam doors."

Laine sighed over Miri's logic. "I suppose I'll have to go down and apologize."

As Laine stood, Miri folded her arms and blocked her way. "You will do no such thing."

Staring at her, Laine let out a frustrated breath. "But you just said . . ."

"I said you were stupid, and you were. Cap Simmons and Dillon were also stupid. No woman should be compared to another woman. You are special, you are unique. Sometimes men see only the face." Miri tapped a finger against each of her cheeks. "It takes them longer to see what is inside. So—" she gave Laine a white-toothed smile "—you will not apologize, you will let them apologize. It is the best way."

"I see," Laine said, not seeing at all. Suddenly, she laughed and sat back on the bed. "Thank you, Miri, I feel much better."

"Good. Now go to bed. I will go lecture Cap Simmons and Dillon." There was an unmistakable note of anticipation in her voice.

CHAPTER 8

The following morning Laine descended the stairs, her Nile-green sundress floating around her, leaving her arms and shoulders bare. Feeling awkward after the previous evening's incident, Laine paused at the doorway of the dining room. Her father and Dillon were already at breakfast and deep in discussion.

"If Bob needs next week off, I can easily take his shift on the charters." Dillon poured coffee as he spoke.

"You've got enough to do at your own place without taking that on, too. Whatever happened to those few days off you were going to take?" Cap accepted the coffee and gave Dillon a stern look.

"I haven't exactly been chained to my desk the past week." Dillon grinned, then shrugged as Cap's expression remained unchanged. "I'll take some time off next month."

"Where have I heard that before?" Cap asked the ceiling. Dillon's grin flashed again.

"I didn't tell you I was retiring next year, did I?" Dillon sipped coffee casually, but Laine recognized the mischief in his voice. "I'm going to take up hang gliding while you slave away behind a desk. Who are you going to nag if I'm not around every day?"

"When you can stay away for more than a week at a time," Cap countered, "that's when *I'm* going to retire. The trouble with you—" he wagged a spoon at Dillon in admonishment "—is that your mind's too good and you've let too many people find it out. Now you're stuck because nobody wants to make a move without checking with you first. You should've kept that aeronautical-engineering degree a secret. Hang gliding." Cap chuckled and lifted his cup. "Oh, hello, Laine."

Laine jolted at the sound of her name. "Good morning," she replied, hoping that her outburst the evening before had not cost her the slight progress she had made with her father.

"Is it safe to ask you in?" His smile was sheepish, but he beckoned her forward. "As I recall, your explosions were frequent, fierce, but short-lived."

Relieved he had not offered her a stilted apology, Laine took her place at the table. "Your memory is accurate, though I assure you, I explode at very infrequent intervals these days." She offered Dillon a tentative smile, determined to treat the matter lightly. "Good morning, Dillon."

"Morning, Duchess. Coffee?" Before she could refuse, he was filling her cup.

"Thank you," she murmured. "It's hard to believe, but I think today is more beautiful than yesterday. I don't believe I'd ever grow used to living in paradise."

"You've barely seen any of it yet," Cap commented. "You should go up to the mountains, or to the center. You know, the center of Kauai is one of the wettest spots in the world. The rain forest is something to see."

"The island seems to have a lot of variety." Laine toyed with her coffee. "I can't imagine any of it is more beautiful than right here."

"I'll take you around a bit today," Dillon announced. Laine glanced sharply at him.

"I don't want to interfere with your routine. I've already taken up a great deal of your time." Laine had not yet regained her balance with Dillon. Her eyes were both wary and unsure.

"I've a bit more to spare." He rose abruptly. "I'll have things cleared up and be back around eleven. See you later, Cap." He strode out without waiting for her assent.

Miri entered with a full plate and placed it in front of Laine. She scowled at the coffee. "Why do you pour coffee when you aren't going to drink it?" With a regal sniff, she picked up the cup and swooped from the room. With a sigh, Laine attacked her breakfast and wondered how the day would pass. She was to find the morning passed quickly.

As if granting a royal boon, Miri agreed to allow Laine to refresh the vases of flowers which were scattered throughout the house. Laine spent her morning hours in the garden. It was not a garden as Laine remembered from her early American years or from her later French ones. It was a spreading, sprawling, wild tangle of greens and tempestuous hues. The plants would not be organized or dictated to by plot or plan.

Inside again, Laine took special care in the arranging of the vases. Her mind drifted to the daffodils which would be blooming outside her window at school. She found it odd that she felt no trace of homesickness, no longing for the soft French voices of the sisters or the high, eager ones of her students. She knew that she was dangerously close to thinking of Kauai as home. The thought of returning to France and the life she led there filled her with a cold, dull ache.

In her father's den, Laine placed the vase of frangipani on his desk and glanced at the photograph of Cap and Dillon. *How strange,* she thought, *that I should need both of them so badly.* With a sigh, she buried her face in the blossoms.

"Do flowers make you unhappy?"

She whirled, nearly upsetting the vase. For a moment, she and Dillon stared at each other without speaking. Laine felt the tension between them, though its cause and meaning were unclear to her. "Hello. Is it eleven already?'"

"It's nearly noon. I'm late." Dillon thrust his hands in his pockets and watched her. Behind her, the sun poured through the window to halo her hair. "Do you want some lunch?"

"No, thank you," she said with conviction. She saw his eyes smile briefly.

"Are you ready?"

"Yes, I'll just tell Miri I'm going."

"She knows." Crossing the room, Dillon slid open the glass door and waited for Laine to precede him outside.

Laine found Dillon in a silent mood as they drove from the house. She gave his thoughts their privacy and concentrated on the view. Ridges of green mountains loomed on either side. Dillon drove along a sheer precipice where the earth surrendered abruptly to the sky to fall into an azure sea.

"They used to toss Kukui oil torches over the cliffs to entertain royalty," Dillon said suddenly, after miles of silence. "Legend has it that the menehune lived here. The pixie people," he elaborated at her blank expression. "You see there?" After halting the car, he pointed to a black precipice lined with grooves. "That's their staircase. They built fishponds by moonlight."

"Where are they now?" Laine smiled at him.

Dillon reached across to open her door. "Oh, they're still here. They're hiding."

Laine joined him to walk to the edge of the cliff. Her heart flew to her throat as she stared from the dizzying height down to the frothing power of waves on rock. For an instant, she could feel herself tumbling helplessly through miles of space.

Unaffected by vertigo, Dillon looked out to sea. The breeze teased his hair, tossing it into confusion. "You have the remarkable capacity of knowing when to be quiet and making the silence comfortable," he remarked.

"You seemed preoccupied." The wind tossed curls in her eyes, and Laine brushed them away. "I thought perhaps you were working out a problem."

"Did you?" he returned, and his expression seemed both amused and annoyed. "I want to talk to you about your mother."

The statement was so unexpected that it took Laine a moment to react. "No." She turned away, but he took her arm and held her still.

"You were furious last night. I want to know why."

"I overreacted." She tossed her head as her curls continued to dance around her face. "It was foolish of me, but sometimes my temper gets the better of me." She saw by his expression that her explanation would not placate him. She wanted badly to tell him how she had been hurt, but the memory of their first discussion in her father's house, and his cold judgment of her, prevented her. "Dillon, all my life I've been accepted for who I am." Speaking slowly, she chose her words carefully. "It annoys me to find that changing now. I do not want to be compared with Vanessa because we share certain physical traits."

"Is that what you think Cap was doing?"

"Perhaps, perhaps not." She tilted her chin yet further. "But that's what you were doing."

"Was I?" It was a question which asked for no answer, and Laine gave none. "Why are you so bitter about your mother, Laine?"

She moved her shoulders and turned back toward the sea. "I'm not bitter, Dillon, not any longer. Vanessa's dead, and that part of my life is over. I don't want to talk about her until I understand my feelings better."

"All right." They stood silent for a moment, wrapped in the wind.

"I'm having a lot more trouble with you than I anticipated," Dillon muttered.

"I don't know what you mean."

"No," he agreed, looking at her so intently she felt he read her soul. "I'm sure you don't." He walked away, then stopped. After a hesitation too brief to measure, he turned toward her again and held out his hand. Laine stared at it, unsure what he was offering. Finding it did not matter, she accepted.

During the ensuing drive, Dillon spoke easily. His mood had altered, and Laine moved with it. The world was lush with ripe blossoms. Moss clung, green and vibrant, to cliffs—a carpet on stone. They passed elephant ears whose leaves were large enough to use as a canopy against rain or sun. The frangipani became more varied and more brilliant. When Dillon stopped the car again, Laine did not hesitate to take his hand.

He led her along a path that was sheltered by palms, moving down it as though he knew the way well. Laine heard the rush of water before they entered the clearing. Her breath caught at the sight of the secluded pool circled by thick trees and fed by a shimmering waterfall.

"Oh, Dillon, what a glorious place! There can't be another like it in the world!" Laine ran to the edge of the pool, then dropped down to feel the texture of the water. It was warm silk. "If I could, I would come here to swim in the moonlight." With a laugh, she rose and tossed water to the sky. "With flowers in my hair and nothing else."

"That's the only permissible way to swim in a moonlit pool. Island law."

Laughing again, she turned to a bush and plucked a scarlet hibiscus. "I suppose I'd need long black hair and honey skin to look the part."

Taking the bloom from her, Dillon tucked it behind her ear. After studying the effect, he smiled and ran a finger down her cheek. "Ivory and gold work very nicely. There was a time you'd have been worshiped with all pomp and ceremony, then tossed off a cliff as an offering to jealous gods."

"I don't believe that would suit me." Utterly enchanted, Laine twirled away. "Is this a secret place? It feels like a secret place." Stepping out of her shoes, she sat on the edge of the pool and dangled her feet in the water.

"If you want it to be." Dropping down beside her, Dillon sat cross-legged. "It's not on the tourist route, at any rate."

"It feels magic, the same way that little bay feels magic. Do you feel it, Dillon? Do you realize how lovely this all is, how fresh, or are you immune to it by now?"

"I'm not immune to beauty." He lifted her hand, brushing his lips over her fingertips. Her eyes grew wide as currents of pleasure jolted up her arm. Smiling, Dillon turned her hand over and kissed her palm.

"You can't have lived in Paris for fifteen years and not have had your hand kissed. I've seen movies."

The lightness of his tone helped her regain her balance. "Actually, everyone's always kissing my left hand. You threw me off when you kissed my right." She kicked water in the air and watched the drops catch the sun before they were swallowed by the pool. "Sometimes, when the rain drizzles in the fall, and the dampness creeps through the windows, I'll remember this." Her voice had changed, and there was something wistful, something yearning in her tone. "Then when spring comes, and the buds flower, and the air smells of them, I'll remember the fragrance here. And when the sun shines on a Sunday, I'll walk near the Seine and think of a waterfall."

Rain came without warning, a shower drenched in sun. Dillon scrambled up, pulling Laine under a sheltering cluster of palms.

"Oh, it's warm." She leaned out from the green ceiling to catch rain in her palm. "It's as if it's dropping from the sun."

"Islanders call it liquid sunshine." Dillon gave an easy tug on her hand to pull her back as she inched forward. "You're getting soaked. I think you must enjoy getting drenched in your clothes." He ruffled her hair and splattered the air with shimmering drops.

"Yes, I suppose I do." She stared out, absorbed with the deepening colors. Blossoms trembled under their shower. "There's so much on the island that remains unspoiled, as if no one had ever touched it. When we stood on the cliff and looked down at the sea, I was frightened. I've always been a coward. But still, it was beautiful, so terrifyingly beautiful I couldn't look away."

"A coward?" Dillon sat on the soft ground and pulled her down to join him. Her head naturally found the curve of his shoulder. "I would have said you were remarkably intrepid. You didn't panic during the storm yesterday."

"No, I just skirted around the edges of panic."

His laugh was full of pleasure. "You also survived the little show in the plane on the way from Oahu without a scream or a faint."

"That's because I was angry." She pushed at her damp hair and watched the thin curtain of rain. "It was unkind of you."

"Yes, I suppose it was. I'm often unkind."

"I think you're kind more often than not. Though I also think you don't like being labeled a kind man."

"That's a very odd opinion for a short acquaintance." Her answering shrug was eloquent and intensely Gallic. A frown moved across his brow. "This school of yours," he began, "what kind is it?"

"Just a school, the same as any other, with giggling girls and rules which must be broken."

"A boarding school?" he probed, and she moved her shoulders again.

"Yes, a boarding school. Dillon, this is not the place to think of schedules and classes. I shall have to deal with them again soon enough. This is a magic place, and for now I want to pretend I belong here. *Ah, regarde!*" Laine shifted, gesturing in wonder. *"Un arc-en-ciel."*

"I guess that means rainbow." He glanced at the sky, then back at her glowing face.

"There are two! How can there be two?"

They stretched, high and perfect, in curving arches from one mountain ridge to another. The second's shimmering colors were the reverse of the first's. As the sun glistened on raindrops, the colors grew in intensity, streaking across the cerulean sky like a trail from an artist's many-tinted brush.

"Double bows are common here," Dillon explained, relaxing against the base of the palm. "The trade winds blow against the mountains and form a rain boundary. It rains on one side while the sun shines on the other. Then, the sun strikes the raindrops, and . . ."

"No, don't tell me," Laine interrupted with a shake of her head. "It would spoil it if I knew." She smiled with the sudden knowledge that all things precious should be left unexplained. "I don't want to understand," she murmured, accepting both her love and the rainbows without question, without logic. "I just want to enjoy." Tilting back her head, Laine offered her mouth. "Will you kiss me, Dillon?"

His eyes never left hers. He brought his hands to her face, and gently, his fingers stroked the fragile line of her cheek. In silence, he explored the planes and hollows of her face with his fingertips, learning the texture of fine bones and satin skin. His mouth followed the trail of his fingers, and Laine closed her eyes, knowing nothing had ever been sweeter than his lips on her skin. Still moving slowly, still moving gently, Dillon brushed his mouth over hers in a whisperlike kiss which drugged her senses. He seemed content to taste, seemed happy to sample rather than devour. His mouth moved on, lingering on the curve of her neck, nibbling at the lobe of her ear before coming back to join hers. His tongue teased her lips apart as her heartbeat began to roar in her ears. He took her to the edge of reason with a tender, sensitive touch. As her need grew, Laine drew him closer, her body moving against his in innocent temptation.

Dillon swore suddenly before pulling her back. She kept her arms around his neck, her fingers tangled in his hair as he stared down at her. Her eyes were deep and cloudy with growing passion. Unaware of her own seductive powers, Laine sighed his name and placed a soft kiss on both of his cheeks.

"I want you," Dillon stated in a savage murmur before his mouth crushed hers. She yielded to him as a young willow yields to the wind.

His hands moved over her as if desperate to learn every aspect, every secret, and she who had never known a man's intimate touch delighted in the seeking. Her body was limber under his touch, responsive and eager. She was the student, and he the teacher. Her skin grew hot as her veins swelled with pounding blood. As the low, smoldering fire burst into quick flame, her demands rose with his. She trembled and murmured his name, as frightened of the new sensation as she had been at the edge of the cliff.

Dillon lifted his mouth from hers, resting it on her hair before she could search for the joining again. He held her close, cradling her head against his chest. His heart drummed against her ear, and Laine closed her eyes with the pleasure. Drawing her away, he stood. He moved his hands to his pockets as he turned his back on her.

"It's stopped raining." She thought his voice sounded strange and heard him take a long breath before he turned back to her. "We'd better go."

His expression was unfathomable. Though she searched, Laine could find no words to fill the sudden gap and close the distance which had sprung between them. Her eyes met his, asking questions her lips could not. Dillon opened his mouth as if to speak, then closed it again before he reached down to pull her to her feet. Her eyes faltered. Dillon lifted her chin with his fingertips, then traced the lips still soft from his. Briskly, he shook his head. Without a word, he lay his mouth gently on hers before he led her away from the palms.

CHAPTER 9

A generous golden ball, the sun dominated the sky as the car moved along the highway. Dillon made easy conversation, as if passion belonged only to a rain-curtained pool. While her brain fidgeted, Laine tried to match his mood.

Men, she decided, must be better able to deal with the demands of the body than women are with those of the heart. He had wanted her; even if he had not said it, she would have known. The urgency, the power of his claim had been unmistakable. Laine felt her color rise as she remembered her unprotesting response. Averting her head as if absorbed in the view, she tried to decide what course lay open to her.

She would leave Kauai in a week's time. Now, she would not only have to abandon the father whom she had longed for all of her life, but the man who held all claim to her heart. Perhaps, she reflected with a small sigh, I'm always destined to love what can never be mine. Miri said I should fight as a woman fights, but I don't know where to begin. Perhaps with honesty. I should find the place and time to tell Dillon of my feelings. If he knew I wanted nothing from him but his affection, we might make a beginning. I could find a way to stay here at least awhile longer. I could take a job. In time, he might learn to really care for me. Laine's mood lightened at the thought. She focused again on her surroundings.

"Dillon, what is growing there? Is it bamboo?" Acres upon acres of towering stalks bordered the road. Clumps of cylindrical gold stretched out on either side.

"Sugarcane," he answered, without glancing at the fields.

"It's like a jungle." Fascinated, Laine leaned out the window, and the wind buffeted her face. "I had no idea it grew so tall."

"Gets to be a bit over twenty feet, but it doesn't grow as fast as a jungle in this part of the world. It takes a year and a half to two years to reach full growth."

"There's so much." Laine turned to face him, absently brushing curls from her cheeks. "It's a plantation, I suppose, though it's hard to conceive of one person owning so much. It must take tremendous manpower to harvest."

"A bit." Dillon swerved off the highway and onto a hard-packed road. "The undergrowth is burned off, then machines cut the plants. Hand cutting is time consuming so machinery lowers production costs even when labor costs are low. Besides, it's one miserable job."

"Have you ever done it?" She watched a quick grin light his face.

"A time or two, which is why I prefer flying a plane."

Laine glanced around at the infinity of fields, wondering when the harvest began, trying to picture the machines slicing through the towering stalks. Her musings halted as the brilliant white of a house shone in the distance. Tall, with graceful colonial lines and pillars, it stood on lush lawns. Vines dripped from scrolled balconies; the high and narrow windows were shuttered in soft gray. The house looked comfortably old and lived in. Had it not been for South Sea foliage, Laine might have been seeing a plantation house in old Louisiana.

"What a beautiful home. One could see for miles from the balcony." Laine glanced at Dillon in surprise as he halted the car and again leaned over to open her door. "This is a private home, is it not? Are we allowed to walk around?"

"Sure." Opening his own door, Dillon slid out. "It's mine." He leaned against the car and looked down at her. "Are you going to sit there with your mouth open or are you going to come inside?" Quickly, Laine slid out and stood beside him. "I gather you expected a grass hut and hammock?"

"Why, no, I don't precisely know what I expected, but . . ." With a helpless gesture of her hands, she gazed about. A tremor of alarm trickled through her.

"The cane fields," she began, praying she was mistaken. "Are they yours?"

"They go with the house."

Finding her throat closed, Laine said nothing as Dillon led her up stone steps and through a wide mahogany door. Inside, the staircase dominated the hall. Wide and arching in a deep half circle, its wood gleamed. Laine had a quick, confused impression of watercolors and wood carvings as Dillon strode straight down the hall and led her into a parlor.

The walls were like rich cream; the furnishings were dark and old. The carpet was a delicately faded needlepoint over a glistening wood floor. Nutmeg sheers were drawn back from the windows to allow the view of a manicured lawn.

"Sit down." Dillon gestured to a chair. "I'll see about something cold to drink." Laine nodded, grateful for the time alone to organize her scattered thoughts. She listened until Dillon's footsteps echoed into silence.

Her survey of the room was slow. She seated herself in a high-backed chair and let her eyes roam. The room had an undeniable air of muted wealth. Laine had not associated wealth with Dillon O'Brian. Now she found it an insurmountable obstacle. Her protestations of love would never be accepted as pure. He would think his money had been her enticement. She closed her eyes on a small moan of desperation. Rising, she moved to a window and tried to deal with dashed hopes.

What was it he called me once? *An operator.* With

a short laugh, she rested her brow against the cool glass. I'm afraid I make a very poor one. I wish I'd never come here, never seen what he has. At least then I could have hung on to hope a bit longer. Hearing Dillon's approach, Laine struggled for composure. As he entered, she gave him a careful smile.

"Dillon, your home is very lovely." After accepting the tall glass he offered, Laine moved back to her chair.

"It serves." He sat opposite her. His brow lifted fractionally at the formality of her tone.

"Did you build it yourself?"

"No, my grandfather." With his customary ease, Dillon leaned back and watched her. "He was a sailor and decided Kauai was the next best thing to the sea."

"So. I thought it looked as if it had known generations." Laine sipped at her drink without tasting it. "But you found planes more enticing than the sea or the fields."

"The fields serve their purpose." Dillon frowned momentarily at her polite, impersonal interest. "They yield a marketable product, assist in local employment and make use of the land. It's a profitable crop and its management takes only a portion of my time." As Dillon set down his glass, Laine thought he appeared to come to some decision. "My father died a couple of months before I met Cap. We were both floundering, but I was angry, and he was . . ." Dillon hesitated, then shrugged. "He was as he always is. We suited each other. He had a cabin plane and used to pick up island hoppers. I couldn't learn about flying fast enough, and

Cap needed to teach. I needed balance, and he needed to give it. A couple of years later, we began planning the airport."

Laine dropped her eyes to her glass. "And it was the money from your fields which built the airport?"

"As I said, the cane has its uses."

"And the bay where we swam?" On a sudden flash of intuition, she lifted her eyes to his. "That's yours, too, isn't it?"

"That's right." She could see no change of expression in his eyes.

"And my father's house?" Laine swallowed the dryness building in her throat. "Is that also on your property?"

She saw annoyance cross his face before he smoothed it away. His answer was mild. "Cap had a fondness for that strip of land, so he bought it."

"From you?"

"Yes, from me. Is that a problem?"

"No," she replied. "It's simply that I begin to see things more clearly. Much more clearly." Laine set down her drink and folded her empty hands. "It appears that you are more my father's son than I shall ever be his daughter."

"Laine . . ." Dillon let out a short breath, then rose and paced the room with a sudden restlessness. "Cap and I understand each other. We've known each other for nearly fifteen years. He's been part of my life for almost half of it."

"I'm not asking you for justifications, Dillon. I'm sorry if it seemed as if I were." Laine stood, trying to keep her voice steady. "When I return to France next week, it will be good to know that my father has you to rely on."

"Next week?" Dillon stopped pacing. "You're planning to leave next week?"

"Yes." Laine tried not to think of how quickly seven days could pass. "We agreed I would stay for two weeks. It's time I got back to my own life."

"You're hurt because Cap hasn't responded to you the way you'd hoped."

Surprised both by his words and the gentleness of his tone, Laine felt the thin thread of her control straining. She struggled to keep her eyes calm and level with his. "I have changed my mind . . . on a great many matters. Please don't, Dillon." She shook her head as he started to speak. "I would rather not talk of this; it's only more difficult."

"Laine." He placed his hands on her shoulders to prevent her from turning away. "There are a lot of things that you and I have to talk about, whether they're difficult or not. You can't keep shutting away little parts of yourself. I want . . ." The ringing of the doorbell interrupted his words. With a quick, impatient oath, he dropped his hands and strode away to answer.

A light, musical voice drifted into the room. When Orchid King entered the parlor on Dillon's arm, Laine met her with a polite smile.

It struck Laine that Orchid and Dillon were a perfectly matched couple. Orchid's tawny, exotic beauty suited his ruggedness, and her fully rounded curves were all the more stunning against his leanness. Her hair fell in an ebony waterfall, cascading down a smooth bare back to the waist of close-fitting pumpkin-colored shorts. Seeing her, Laine felt dowdy and provincial.

"Hello, Miss Simmons." Orchid tightened her hand on Dillon's arm. "How nice to see you again so soon."

"Hello, Miss King." Annoyed by her own insecurities, Laine met Orchid's amusement with eyes of a cool spring morning. "You did say the island was small."

"Yes, I did." She smiled, and Laine was reminded of a tawny cat. "I hope you've been able to see something of it."

"I took Laine around a bit this morning." Watching Laine, Dillon missed the flash of fire in Orchid's amber eyes.

"I'm sure she couldn't find a better guide." Orchid's expression melted into soft appeal. "I'm so glad you were home, Dillon. I wanted to make certain you'd be at the luau tomorrow night." Turning more directly to face him, she subtly but effectively excluded Laine from the conversation. "It wouldn't be any fun without you."

"I'll be there." Laine watched a smile lift one corner of his mouth. "Are you going to dance?"

"Of course." The soft purr of her voice added to Laine's image of a lithesome feline. "Tommy expects it."

Dillon's smile flashed into a grin. He lifted his eyes

over Orchid's head to meet Laine's. "Tommy is Miri's nephew. He's having his annual luau tomorrow. You should find both the food and the entertainment interesting."

"Oh, yes," Orchid agreed. "No tourist should leave the islands without attending a luau. Do you plan to see the other islands during your vacation?"

"I'm afraid that will have to wait for another time. I'm sorry to say I haven't lived up to my obligations as a tourist. The purpose of my visit has been to see my father and his home."

Somewhat impatiently, Dillon disengaged his arm from Orchid's grasp. "I have to see my foreman. Why don't you keep Laine company for a few minutes?"

"Certainly." Orchid tossed a lock of rain-straight hair behind her back. "How are the repairs coming?"

"Fine. I should be able to move back in a couple of days without being in the way." With an inclination of his head for Laine, he turned and strode from the room.

"Miss Simmons, do make yourself at home." Assuming the role of hostess with a graceful wave of her hand, Orchid glided farther into the room. "Would you care for anything? A cold drink perhaps?"

Infuriated at being placed in the position of being Orchid's guest, Laine forced down her temper. "Thank you, no. Dillon has already seen to it."

"It seems you spend a great deal of time in Dillon's company," Orchid commented as she dropped into a chair. She crossed long, slender legs, looking like an advertisement for Hawaii's lush attractions. "Especially for one who comes to visit her father."

"Dillon has been very generous with his time." Laine copied Orchid's action and hoped she was equipped for a feminine battle of words.

"Oh, yes, Dillon's a generous man." Her smile was indulgent and possessive. "It's quite easy to misinterpret his generosity unless one knows him as well as I do. He can be so charming."

"Charming?" Laine repeated, and looked faintly skeptical. "How odd. Charming is not the adjective which comes to my mind. But then," she paused and smiled, "you know him better than I do."

Orchid placed the tips of her fingers together, then regarded Laine over the tips. "Miss Simmons, maybe we can dispense with the polite small talk while we have this time alone."

Wondering if she was sinking over her head, Laine nodded. "Your option, Miss King."

"I intend to marry Dillon."

"A formidable intention," Laine managed as her heart constricted. "I assume Dillon is aware of your goal."

"Dillon knows I want him." Irritation flickered over the exotic face at Laine's easy answer. "I don't appreciate all the time you've been spending with him."

"That's a pity, Miss King." Laine picked up her long-abandoned glass and sipped. "But don't you think you're discussing this with the wrong person? I'm sure speaking to Dillon would be more productive."

"I don't believe that's necessary." Orchid gave Laine a companionable smile, showing just a hint of white teeth. "I'm sure we can settle this between us. Don't you think telling Dillon you wanted to learn to fly a plane was a little trite?"

Laine felt a flush of fury that Dillon had discussed her with Orchid. "Trite?"

Orchid made an impatient gesture. "Dillon's diverted by you at the moment, perhaps because you're such a contrast to the type of woman he's always preferred. But the milk-and-honey looks won't keep Dillon interested for long." The musical voice hardened. "Cool sophistication doesn't keep a man warm, and Dillon is very much a man."

"Yes, he's made that very clear," Laine could not resist interjecting.

"I'm warning you . . . once," Orchid hissed. "Keep your distance. I can make things very uncomfortable for you."

"I'm sure you can," Laine acknowledged. She shrugged. "I've been uncomfortable before."

"Dillon can be very vindictive when he thinks he's being deceived. You're going to end up losing more than you bargained for."

"Nom de Dieu!" Laine rose. "Is this how the game is played?" She made a contemptuous gesture with the back of her hand. "I want none of it. Snarling and hissing like two cats over a mouse. This isn't worthy of Dillon."

"We haven't started to play yet." Orchid sat back,

pleased by Laine's agitation. "If you don't like the rules, you'd better leave. I don't intend to put up with you any longer."

"Put up with me?" Laine stopped, her voice trembling with rage. "No one, Miss King, no one *puts up* with me. You hardly need concern yourself with a woman who will be gone in a week's time. Your lack of confidence is as pitiful as your threats." Orchid rose at that, her fists clenched by her sides.

"What do you want from me?" Laine demanded. "Do you want my assurance that I won't interfere with your plans? Very well, I give it freely and with pleasure. Dillon is yours."

"That's generous of you." Spinning, Laine saw Dillon leaning against the doorway. His arms were crossed, his eyes dangerously dark.

"Oh, Dillon, how quick you were." Orchid's voice was faint.

"Apparently not quick enough." His eyes were locked on Laine's. "What's the problem?"

"Just a little feminine talk, Dillon." Recovered, Orchid glided to his side. "Laine and I were just getting to know each other."

"Laine, what's going on?"

"Nothing important. If it's convenient, I should like to go back now." Without waiting for a reply, Laine picked up her bag and moved to the doorway.

Dillon halted her by a hand on her arm. "I asked you a question."

"And I have given you the only answer I intend to

give." She wrenched free and faced him. "I will not be questioned any longer. You have no right to question me; I am nothing to you. You have no right to criticize me as you have done from the first moment. You have no right to judge." The anger in her tone was now laced with despair. "You have no right to make love to me just because it amuses you."

She ran in a flurry of flying skirts, and he watched the door slam behind her.

CHAPTER 10

Laine spent the rest of the day in her room. She attempted not to dwell on the scene in Dillon's home, or on the silent drive which followed it. She was not sure which had been more draining. It occurred to her that she and Dillon never seemed to enjoy a cordial relationship for more than a few hours at a time. It was definitely time to leave. She began to plan for her return to France. Upon a review of her finances, she discovered that she had barely enough for a return ticket.

It would, she realized with a sigh, leave her virtually penniless. Her own savings had been sorely dented in dealing with her mother's debts, and plane fare had eaten at what remained. She could not, she determined, return to France without a franc in her pocket. If there was a complication of any kind, she would be helpless to deal with it. *Why didn't I stop to think before I came here?* she demanded of herself. *Now I've placed myself in an impossible situation.*

Sitting on the bed, Laine rubbed an aching temple and tried to think. She didn't want to ask her father for money. Pride prevented her from wiring to any friends to ask for a loan. She stared down at the small pile of bills in frustration. They won't proliferate of their own accord, she reflected, so I must plan how to increase their number.

She moved to her dresser and opened a small box. For some minutes, she studied the gold locket it contained. It had been a gift from her father to her mother, and Vanessa had given it to her on her sixteenth birthday. She remembered the pleasure she had felt upon receiving something, however indirectly, from her father. She had worn it habitually until she had dressed for her flight to Hawaii. Feeling it might cause her father pain, Laine had placed it in its box, hoping that unhappy memories would be buried. It was the only thing of value she owned, and now she had to sell it.

Her door swung open. Laine held the box behind her back. Miri glided in, a swirling mountain of color. She regarded Laine's flushed face with raised brows.

"Did you mess something up?"

"No."

"Then don't look guilty. Here." She laid a sheath of brilliant blue and sparkling white on the bedspread. "It's for you. You wear this to the luau tomorrow."

"Oh." Laine stared at the exquisite length of silk, already feeling its magic against her skin. "It's beautiful. I couldn't." She raised her eyes to Miri's with a mixture of desire and regret. "I couldn't take it."

"You don't like my present?" Miri demanded imperiously. "You are very rude."

"Oh, no." Struck with alarm at the unintentional offense, Laine fumbled with an explanation. "It's beautiful . . . really. It's only that . . ."

"You should learn to say thank-you and not argue. This will suit your skinny bones." Miri gave a nod of satisfaction encompassing both the woman and the silk. "Tomorrow, I will show you how to wrap it."

Unable to prevent herself, Laine moved over to feel the cool material under her fingers. The combination of longing and Miri's dark, arched brows proved too formidable for pride. She surrendered with a sigh. "Thank you, Miri. It's very good of you."

"That's much better," Miri approved and patted Laine's halo of curls. "You are a pretty child. You should smile more. When you smile, the sadness goes away."

Feeling the small box weighing like a stone in her hand, Laine held it up and opened it. "Miri, I wonder if you might tell me where I could sell this."

One large brown finger traced the gold before Miri's jet eyes lifted. Laine saw the now familiar pucker between her brows. "Why do you want to sell a pretty thing like this? You don't like it?"

"No, no, I like it very much." Helpless under the direct stare, Laine moved her shoulders. "I need the money."

"Money? Why do you need money?"

"For my passage and expenses . . . to return to France."

"You don't like Kauai?" Her indignant tone caused Laine to smile and shake her head.

"Kauai is wonderful; I'd like nothing better than to stay here forever. But I must get back to my job."

"What do you do in that place?" Miri dismissed France with a regal gesture and settled her large frame into a chair. She folded her hands across the mound of her belly.

"I teach." Laine sat on the bed and closed the lid on the face of the locket.

"Don't they pay you to teach?" Miri pursed her lips in disapproval. "What did you do with your money?"

Laine flushed, feeling like a child who had been discovered spending her allowance on candy. "There . . . there were debts, and I . . ."

"You have debts?"

"Well, no, I . . . not precisely." Laine's shoulders drooped with frustration. Seeing Miri was prepared to remain a permanent fixture of her room until she received an explanation, Laine surrendered. Slowly, she began to explain the financial mountain which she had faced at her mother's death, the necessity to liquidate assets, the continuing drain on her own resources. In the telling, Laine felt the final layers of her resentment fading. Miri did not interrupt the recital, and Laine found that confession had purged her of bitterness.

"Then, when I found my father's address among her personal papers, I took what I had left and came here. I'm afraid I didn't plan things well, and in order to go back . . ." She shrugged again and trailed off. Miri nodded.

"Why have you not told Cap Simmons? He would not have his daughter selling her baubles. He's a good man, he would not have you in a strange country counting your pennies."

"He doesn't owe me anything."

"He is your father," Miri stated, lifting her chin and peering down her nose at Laine.

"But he's not responsible for a situation brought on by Vanessa's carelessness and my own impulsiveness. He would think . . . No." She shook her head. "I don't want him to know. It's very important to me that he *not* know. You must promise not to speak of this to him."

"You are a very stubborn girl." Miri crossed her arms and glared at Laine. Laine kept her eyes level. "Very well." Miri's bosom lifted and fell with her sigh. "You must do what you must do. Tomorrow, you will meet my nephew, Tommy. Ask him to come look at your bauble. He is a jeweler and will give you a fair price."

"Thank you, Miri." Laine smiled, feeling a portion of her burden ease.

Miri rose, her muumuu trembling at the movement. "You had a nice day with Dillon?"

"We went by his home," Laine returned evasively. "It's very impressive."

"Very nice place," Miri agreed and brushed an infinitesimal speck of dust from the chair's back. "My cousin cooks there, but not so well as Miri."

"Miss King dropped by." Laine strove for a casual tone, but Miri's brows rose.

"Hmph." Miri stroked the tentlike lines of her flowered silk.

"We had a rather unpleasant discussion when Dillon left us alone. When he came back . . ." Laine paused and drew her brows together. "I shouted at him."

Miri laughed, holding her middle as if it would split from the effort. For several moments, her mirth rolled comfortably around the room. "So you can shout, Skinny Bones? I would like to have seen that."

"I don't think Dillon found it that amusing." In spite of herself, Laine smiled.

"Oh, that one." She wiped her eyes and shook her head. "He is too used to having his own way with women. He is too good-looking and has too much money." She placed a comforting hand over the barrel of her belly. "He's a fair boss, and he works in the fields when he's needed. He has big degrees and many brains." She tapped her finger on her temple, but looked unimpressed. "He was a very bad boy, with many pranks." Laine saw her lips tremble as she tried not to show amusement at the memories. "He is still a bad boy," she said firmly, regaining her dignity. "He is very smart and *very* important." She made a circling movement with both hands to indicate Dillon's importance, but her voice was full of maternal criticism. "But no matter what he thinks, he does not know women. He only knows planes." She patted Laine's head and pointed to the length of silk. "Tomorrow, you wear that and put a flower in your hair. The moon will be full."

It was a night of silver and velvet. From her window, Laine could see the dancing diamonds of moonlight on the sea. Allowing the breeze to caress her bare shoulders, Laine reflected that the night was perfect for a luau under the stars.

She had not seen Dillon since the previous day. He had returned to the house long after she had retired, and had left again before she had awakened. She was determined, however, not to permit their last meeting to spoil the beauty of the evening. If she had only a few days left in his company, she would make every effort to see that they were pleasant.

Turning from her window, Laine gave one final look at the woman in the mirror. Her bare shoulders rose like marble from the brilliant blue of the sarong. She stared at the woman in the glass, recognizing some change, but unable to discern its cause. She was not aware that over the past few days she had moved from girlhood to womanhood. After a final touch of the brush to her hair, Laine left the room. Dillon's voice rose up the staircase, and she moved to meet it. All at once, it seemed years since she had last heard him speak.

"We'll be harvesting next month, but if I know the schedule of meetings far enough in advance, I can . . ."

His voice trailed away as Laine moved into the

doorway. Pausing in the act of pouring a drink, he made a slow survey. Laine felt her pulse triple its rate as his eyes lingered along their route before meeting hers.

Glancing up from filling his pipe, Cap noted Dillon's absorption. He followed his gaze. "Well, Laine." He rose, surprising her by crossing the room and taking both her hands in his. "What a beautiful sight."

"Do you like it?" Smiling first at him, she glanced down at the sarong. "I'm not quite used to the way it feels."

"I like it very much, but I was talking about you. My daughter is a very beautiful woman, isn't she, Dillon?" His eyes were soft and smiled into Laine's.

"Yes." Dillon's voice came from behind him. "Very beautiful."

"I'm glad she's here." He pressed her fingers between the warmth of his hands. "I've missed her." He bent and kissed her cheek, then turned to Dillon. "You two run along. I'll see if Miri's ready, which she won't be. We'll be along later."

Laine watched him stride away. She lifted one hand to her cheek, unable to believe she could be so deeply affected by one small gesture.

"Are you ready?" She nodded, unable to speak, then felt Dillon's hands descend to her shoulders. "It isn't easy to bridge a fifteen-year gap, but you've made a start."

Surprised by the support in his voice, Laine blinked back tears and turned to face him. "Thank you. It means a great deal to me for you to say that. Dillon, yesterday, I . . ."

"Let's not worry about yesterday right now." His smile was both an apology and an acceptance of hers. It was easy to smile back. He studied her a moment before lifting her hand to his lips. "You are incredibly beautiful, like a blossom hanging on a branch just out of reach." Laine wanted to blurt out that she was not out of reach, but a thick blanket of shyness covered her tongue. She could do no more than stare at him.

"Come on." Keeping her hand in his, Dillon moved to the door. "You should try everything once." His tone was light again as they slid into his car. "You know, you're a very small lady."

"Only because you look from an intimidating height," she returned, feeling pleased with the ease of their relationship. "What does one do at a luau, Dillon? I'm very much afraid I'll insult a local tradition if I refuse to eat raw fish. But—" resting her head against the seat, she smiled at the stars "—I shall refuse to do so."

"We don't hurl mainlanders into the sea anymore for minor offenses. You haven't much hip," he commented, dropping his eyes for a moment. "But you could have a stab at a hula."

"I'm sure my hips are adequate and will no doubt be more so if Miri has her way." Laine sent him a teasing glance. "Do you dance, Dillon?"

He grinned and met her look. "I prefer to watch. Dancing the hula properly takes years of practice. These dancers are very good."

"I see." She shifted in her seat to smile at him. "Will there be many people at the luau?"

"Mmm." Dillon tapped his finger absently against the wheel. "About a hundred, give or take a few."

"A hundred," Laine echoed. She fought off unhappy memories of her mother's overcrowded, overelegant parties. So many people, so many demands, so many measuring eyes.

"Tommy has a lot of relatives."

"How nice for him," she murmured and considered the advantages of small families.

CHAPTER 11

The hollow, primitive sound of drums vibrated through air pungent with roasting meat. Torches were set on high stakes, their orange flames shooting flickering light against a black sky. To Laine it was like stepping back in time. The lawn was crowded with guests—some in traditional attire and others, like Dillon, in the casual comfort of jeans. Laughter rose from a myriad of tones and mixed languages. Laine gazed around, enthralled by the scene and the scents.

Set on a huge, woven mat were an infinite variety of mysterious dishes in wooden bowls and trays. Ebony-haired girls in native dress knelt to spoon food onto the plates and serving dishes. Diverse aromas lifted on the night air and lingered to entice. Men, swathed at the waist and bare-chested, beat out pulsating rhythms on high, conical drums.

Introduced to an impossible blur of faces, Laine

merely floated with the mood of the crowd. There seemed to be a universal friendliness, an uncomplicated joy in simply being.

Soon sandwiched between her father and Dillon, Laine sat on the grass and watched her plate being heaped with unknown wonders. A roar of approval rose over the music as the pig was unearthed from the *imu* and carved. Dutifully, she dipped her fingers in poi and sampled. She shrugged her shoulders as Dillon laughed at her wrinkled nose.

"Perhaps it's an acquired taste," she suggested as she wiped her fingers on a napkin.

"Here." Dillon lifted a fork and urged its contents into Laine's reluctant mouth.

With some surprise, she found the taste delightful. "That's very good. What is it?"

"Laulau."

"This is not illuminating."

"If it's good, what else do you have to know?" His logic caused her to arch her brows. "It's pork and butterfish steamed in *ti* leaves," he explained, shaking his head. "Try this." Dillon offered the fork again, and Laine accepted without hesitation.

"Oh, what is it? I've never tasted anything like it."

"Squid," he answered, then roared with laughter at her gasp of alarm.

"I believe," Laine stated with dignity, "I shall limit myself to pork and pineapple."

"You'll never grow hips that way."

"I shall learn to live without them. What is this drink . . . ? No," she decided, smiling as she heard her father's chuckle. "I believe I'm better off not knowing."

Avoiding the squid, Laine found herself enjoying the informal meal. Occasionally, someone stopped and crouched beside them, exchanging quick greetings or a long story. Laine was treated with a natural friendliness which soon put her at her ease. Her father seemed comfortable with her, and though he and Dillon enjoyed an entente which eluded her, she no longer felt like an intruder. Music and laughter and the heady perfume of night swam around her. Laine thought she had never felt so intensely aware of her surroundings.

Suddenly, the drummers beat a rapid tempo, reaching a peak, then halting. Their echo fell into silence as Orchid stepped into view. She stood in a circle of torchlight, her skin glowing under its touch. Her eyes were gold and arrogant. Tantalizing and perfect, her body was adorned only in a brief top and a slight swatch of scarlet silk draped low over her hips. She stood completely still, allowing the silence to build before she began slowly circling her hips. A single drum began to follow the rhythm she set.

Her hair, crowned with a circlet of buds, fell down her bare back. Her hands and lithesome curves moved with a hypnotic power as the bare draping of silk flowed against her thighs. Sensuous and tempting, her gestures moved with the beat, and Laine saw that her golden eyes were locked on Dillon's. The faint smile she gave him was knowledgeable. Almost imperceptibly, her dance grew in speed. As the drum became more insistent, her movements became more abandoned. Her face remained calm and smiling above her undulating body. Then, abruptly, sound and movement halted into stunning silence.

Applause broke out. Orchid threw Laine a look of triumph before she lifted the flower crown from her head and tossed it into Dillon's lap. With a soft, sultry laugh, she retreated to the shadows.

"Looks like you've got yourself an invitation," Cap commented, then pursed his lips in thought. "Amazing. I wonder how many RPMs we could clock her at."

Shrugging, Dillon lifted his glass.

"You like to move like that, Skinny Bones?" Laine turned to where Miri sat in the background. She looked more regal than ever in a high-backed rattan chair. "You eat so you don't rattle, and Miri will teach you."

Flushed with a mixture of embarrassment and the longing to move with such free abandonment, Laine avoided Dillon's eyes. "I don't rattle now, but I think Miss King's ability is natural."

"You might pick it up, Duchess." Dillon grinned at Laine's lowered lashes. "I'd like to sit in on the lessons, Miri. As you well know, I've got a very discerning eye." He dropped his gaze to her bare legs, moving it up the length of blue and white silk, before meeting her eyes.

Miri muttered something in Hawaiian, and Dillon chuckled and tossed back a retort in the same tongue. "Come with me," Miri commanded. Rising, she pulled Laine to her feet.

"What did you say to him?" Laine moved in the wake of Miri's flowing gown.

"I said he is a big hungry cat cornering a small mouse."

"I am not a mouse," Laine returned indignantly.

Miri laughed without breaking stride. "Dillon says no, too. He says you are a bird whose beak is sometimes sharp under soft feathers."

"Oh." Unsure whether to be pleased or annoyed with the description, Laine lapsed into silence.

"I have told Tommy you have a bauble to sell," Miri announced. "You will talk to him now."

"Yes, of course," Laine murmured, having forgotten the locket in the enchantment of the night.

Miri paused in front of the luau's host. He was a spare, dark-haired man with an easy smile and friendly eyes. Laine judged him to be in the later part of his thirties, and she had seen him handle his guests with a practiced charm. "You will talk to Cap Simmons's daughter," Miri commanded as she placed a protective hand on Laine's shoulder. "You do right by her, or I will box your ears."

"Yes, Miri," he agreed, but his subservient nod was not reflected in his laughing eyes. He watched the graceful mountain move off before he tossed an arm around Laine's shoulders. He moved her gently toward the privacy of trees. "Miri is the matriarch of our family," he said with a laugh. "She rules with an iron hand."

"Yes, I've noticed. It's impossible to say no to her,

isn't it?" The celebrating sounds of the luau drifted into a murmur as they walked.

"I've never tried. I'm a coward."

"I appreciate your time, Mr. Kinimoko," Laine began.

"Tommy, please, then I can call you Laine." She smiled, and as they walked on, she heard the whisper of the sea. "Miri said you had a bauble to sell. I'm afraid she wasn't any more specific."

"A gold locket," Laine explained, finding his friendly manner had put her at ease. "It's heart-shaped and has a braided chain. I have no idea of its value." She paused, wishing there was another way. "I need the money."

Tommy glanced at the delicate profile, then patted her shoulder. "I take it you don't want Cap to know? Okay," he continued as she shook her head. "I have some free time in the morning. Why don't I come by and have a look around ten? You'll find it more comfortable than coming into the shop."

Laine heard leaves rustle and saw Tommy glance idly toward the sound. "It's very good of you." He turned back to her and she smiled, relieved that the first hurdle was over. "I hope I'm not putting you to any trouble."

"I enjoy troubling for beautiful wahines." He kept his arm over her shoulders as he led her back toward the sound of drums and guitars. "You heard Miri. You don't want me to get my ears boxed, do you?"

"I would never forgive myself if I were responsible for that. I'll tell Miri you've done right by Cap

Simmons's daughter, and your ears will be left in peace." Laughing, Laine tilted her face to his as they broke through the curtain of trees.

"Your sister's looking for you, Tommy." At Dillon's voice, Laine gave a guilty start.

"Thanks, Dillon. I'll just turn Laine over to you. Take good care of her," he advised gravely. "She's under Miri's protection."

"I'll keep that in mind." Dillon watched in silence as Tommy merged back into the crowd, then he turned back to study Laine. "There's an old Hawaiian custom," he began slowly, and she heard annoyance color his tone, "which I have just invented. When a woman comes to a luau with a man, she doesn't walk in monkeypod trees with anyone else."

"Will I be tossed to the sharks if I break the rules?" Her teasing smile faded as Dillon took a step closer.

"Don't, Laine." He circled her neck with his hand. "I haven't had much practice in restraint."

She swayed toward him, giving in to the sudden surging need. "Dillon," she murmured, offering her mouth in simple invitation. She felt the strength of his fingers as they tightened on her neck. She rested her hands against his chest and felt his heartbeat under her palms. The knowledge of his power over her, and her own longing, caused her to tremble. Dillon made a soft sound, a lingering expulsion of breath. Laine watched him struggle with some emotion, watched something flicker in his eyes and fade before his fingers relaxed again.

"A wahine who stands in the shadows under a full moon must be kissed."

"Is this another old Hawaiian tradition?" Laine felt his arms slip around her waist and melted against him.

"Yes, about ten seconds old."

With unexpected gentleness, his mouth met hers. At the first touch, her body went fluid, mists of pleasure shrouding her. As from a distant shore, Laine heard the call of the drums, their rhythm building to a crescendo as did her heartbeat. Feeling the tenseness of Dillon's shoulders under her hands, she stroked, then circled his neck to bring his face closer to hers. Too soon, he lifted his mouth, and his arms relinquished his hold of her.

"More," Laine murmured, unsatisfied, and pulled his face back to hers.

She was swept against him. The power of his kiss drove all but the need from her mind. She could taste the hunger on his lips, feel the heat growing on his flesh. The air seemed to tremble around them. In that moment, her body belonged more to him than to her. If there was a world apart from seeking lips and caressing hands it held no meaning for her. Again, Dillon drew her away, but his voice was low and uneven.

"We'll go back before another tradition occurs to me."

In the morning, Laine lingered under the sun's streaming light, unwilling to leave her bed and the warm pleasure which still clung from the evening before. The taste of Dillon's mouth still lingered on hers, and his scent remained fresh and vital on her senses. She relived the memory of being in his arms.

Finally, with a sigh, she abandoned the luxury of her bed and rose to face the day. Just as she was securing the belt of her robe, Miri glided into the room.

"So, you have decided to get up. The morning is half gone while you lay in your bed." Miri's voice was stern, but her eyes twinkled with indulgence.

"It made the night last longer," Laine replied, smiling at the affectionate scold.

"You liked the roast pig and poi?" Miri asked with a wise nod and a whisper of a smile.

"It was wonderful."

With her lilting laugh floating through the room, Miri turned to leave. "I am going to the market. My nephew is here to see your bauble. Do you want him to wait?"

"Oh." Forcing herself back down to earth, Laine ran her fingers through her hair. "I didn't realize it was that late. I don't want to inconvenience him. I . . . is anyone else at home?"

"No, they are gone."

Glancing down at her robe, Laine decided it was adequate coverage. "Perhaps he could come up and look at it. I don't want to keep him waiting."

"He will give you a fair price," Miri stated as she drifted through the doorway. "Or, you will tell me."

Laine took the small box from her drawer and opened the lid. The locket glinted under a ray of sunshine. There were no pictures to remove but, nonetheless, she opened it and stared at its emptiness.

"Laine."

Turning, she managed to smile at Tommy as he

stood in the doorway. "Hello. It was good of you to come. Forgive me, I slept rather late this morning."

"A compliment to the host of the luau." He made a small, rather dapper bow as she approached him.

"It was my first, and I have no doubt it will remain my favorite." Laine handed him the box, then gripped her hands together as he made his examination.

"It's a nice piece," he said at length. Lifting his eyes, Tommy studied her. "Laine, you don't want to sell this—it's written all over your face."

"No." She saw from his manner she need not hedge. "It's necessary that I do."

Detecting the firmness in her voice, Tommy shrugged and placed the locket back in its box. "I can give you a hundred for it, though I think it's worth a great deal more to you."

Laine nodded and closed the lid as he handed the box back to her. "That will be fine. Perhaps you'd take it now. I would rather you kept it."

"If that's what you want." Tommy drew out his wallet and counted out bills. "I brought some cash. I thought you'd find it easier than a check."

"Thank you." After accepting the money, Laine stared down at it until he rested a hand on her shoulder.

"Laine, I've known Cap a long time. Would you take this as a loan?"

"No." She shook her head, then smiled to ease the sharpness of the word. "No. It's very kind of you, but I must do it this way."

"Okay." He took the offered box and pocketed it.

"I will, however, hold this for a while in case you have second thoughts."

"Thank you. Thank you for not asking questions."

"I'll see myself out." He took her hand and gave it a small squeeze. "Just tell Miri to get in touch with me if you change your mind."

"Yes, I will."

After he had gone, Laine sat heavily on the bed and stared at the money she held clutched in her hand. There was nothing else I could do, she told herself. It was only a piece of metal. Now, it's done, I can't dwell on it.

"Well, Duchess, it seems you've had a profitable morning."

Laine's head snapped up. Dillon's eyes were frosted like an ice-crusted lake, and she stared at him, unable to clear her thoughts. His gaze raked her scantily clad body, and she reached a hand to the throat of her robe in an automatic gesture. Moving toward her, he pulled the bills from her hand and dropped the money on the nightstand.

"You've got class, Duchess." Dillon pinned her with his eyes. "I'd say that's pretty good for a morning's work."

"What are you talking about?" Her thoughts were scattered as she searched for a way to avoid telling him about the locket.

"Oh, I think that's clear enough. I guess I owe Orchid an apology." He thrust his hands in his pockets and rocked back on his heels. The easy gesture belied the burning temper in his eyes. "When she told me about this little arrangement, I came down on her pretty hard. You're a fast worker, Laine. You couldn't have been with Tommy for more than ten minutes last night; you must have made quite a sales pitch."

"I don't know why you're so angry," she began, confused as to why the sale of her locket would bring on such fury. "I suppose Miss King listened to our conversation last night." Suddenly, Laine remembered the quick rustle of leaves. "But why she should feel it necessary to report to you on my business . . ."

"How'd you manage to get rid of Miri while you conducted your little business transaction?" Dillon demanded. "She has a rather strict moral code, you know. If she finds out how you're earning your pin money, she's liable to toss you out on your ear."

"What do you . . ." Realization dawned slowly. *Not my locket,* Laine thought dumbly, *but myself.* All trace of color fled from her face. "You don't really believe that I . . ." Her voice broke as she read the condemnation in his eyes. "This is despicable of you, Dillon. Nothing you've accused me of, nothing you've said to me since we first met compares with this." The words trembled with emotion as she felt a viselike pressure around her heart. "I won't be insulted this way by you."

"Oh, won't you?" Taking her arm, Dillon dragged Laine to her feet. "Have you a more plausible explanation up your sleeve for Tommy's visit and the wad you're fondling? Go ahead, run it by me. I'm listening."

"Oh, yes, I can see you are. Forgive me for refusing, but Tommy's visit and my money are my business.

I owe you no explanation, Dillon. Your conclusions aren't worthy of my words. The fact that you gave enough credence to whatever lie Orchid told you to come check on me, means we have nothing more to say to each other."

"I didn't come here to check on you." He was towering menacingly over her, but Laine met his eyes without flinching. "I came by because I thought you'd want to go up again. You said you wanted to learn to fly, and I said I'd teach you. If you want an apology, all you have to do is give me a reasonable explanation."

"I've spent enough time explaining myself to you. More than you deserve. Questions, always questions. Never *trust*." Her eyes smoldered with blue fire. "I want you to leave my room. I want you to leave me alone for the rest of the time I have in my father's house."

"You had me going." His fingers tightened on her arms, and she caught her breath at the pressure. "I bought it all. The big, innocent eyes, the virginal frailty, the pictures you painted of a woman looking for her father's affection and nothing else. *Trust?*" he flung back at her. "You'd taken me to the point where I trusted you more than myself. You knew I wanted you, and you worked on me. All those trembles and melting bones and artless looks. You played it perfectly, right down to the blushes." He pulled her against him, nearly lifting her off her feet.

"Dillon, you're hurting me." She faltered.

"I wanted you," he went on, as if she had not spoken. "Last night I was aching for you, but I treated you with a restraint and respect I've never shown another woman. You slip on that innocent aura that drives a man crazy. You shouldn't have used it on me, Duchess."

Terror shivered along her skin. Her breath was rapid and aching in her lungs.

"Game's over. I'm going to collect." He silenced her protest with a hard, punishing kiss. Though she struggled against his imprisoning arms, she made no more ripple than a leaf battling a whirlpool. The room tilted, and she was crushed beneath him on the mattress. She fought against the intimacy as his mouth and hands bruised her. He was claiming her in fury, disposing of the barrier of her robe and possessing her flesh with angry demand.

Slowly, his movements altered in texture. Punishment became seduction as his hands began to caress rather than bruise. His mouth left hers to trail down her throat. With a sob ending on a moan, Laine surrendered. Her body became pliant under his, her will snapping with the weight of sensations never tasted. Tears gathered, but she made no more effort to halt them than she did the man who urged them from her soul.

All movement stopped abruptly, and Dillon lay still. The room was thrown into a tortured silence, broken only by the sound of quick breathing. Lifting his head, Dillon studied the journey of a tear down Laine's cheek. He swore with sudden eloquence, then rose. He tugged a hand through his hair as he turned his back on her.

"This is the first time I've been driven to nearly forcing myself on a woman." His voice was low and harsh as he swung around and stared at her. Laine lay still, emotionally drained. She made no effort to cover herself, but merely stared up at him with the eyes of a wounded child. "I can't deal with what you do to me, Laine."

Turning on his heel, he strode from the room. Laine thought the slamming of her door the loneliest sound she had ever heard.

CHAPTER 12

It was raining on the new spring grass. From her dormitory window Laine watched the green brighten with its morning bath. Outside her door, she heard girls trooping down the hall toward breakfast, but she did not smile at their gay chattering in French and English. She found smiles still difficult.

It had not yet been two weeks since Miri had met Laine's packed cases with a frown and drawn brows. She had met Laine's sketchy explanations with crossed arms and further questions. Laine had remained firm, refusing to postpone her departure or to give specific answers. The note she had left for her father had contained no more details, only an apology for her abrupt leave-taking and a promise to write once she had settled back in France. As of yet, Laine had not found the courage to put pen to paper.

Memories of her last moments with Dillon continued

to haunt her. She could still smell the perfume of island blossoms, still feel the warm, moist air rise from the sea to move over her skin. Watching the moon wane, she could remember its lush fullness over the heads of palms. She had hoped her memories would fade with time. She reminded herself that Kauai and its promises were behind her.

It's better this way, she told herself, picking up her brush and preparing herself for the day's work. *Better for everyone.* Her father was settled in his life and would be content to exchange occasional letters. One day, perhaps, he would visit her. Laine knew she could never go back. She, too, had her own life, a job, the comfort of familiar surroundings. Here, she knew what was expected of her. Her existence would be tranquil and unmarred by storms of emotions. She closed her eyes on Dillon's image.

It's too soon, she told herself. Too soon to test her ability to think of him without pain. Later, when the memory had dulled, she would open the door. When she allowed herself to think of him again, it would be to remember the beauty.

It was easier to forget if she followed a routine. Laine scheduled each day to allow for a minimum of idle time. Classes claimed her mornings and early afternoons, and she spent the remainder of her days with chores designed to keep her mind and hands busy.

Throughout the day, the rain continued. With a musical plop, the inevitable leak dripped into the basin on Laine's classroom floor. The school building was old and rambling. Repairs were always either just completed, slated to be done or in vague consideration for the future. The windows were shut against the damp, but the gloom crept into the room. The students were languid and inattentive. Her final class of the day was made up of English girls just entering adolescence. They were thoroughly bored by their hour lesson on French grammar. As it was Saturday, there was only a half day of classes, but the hours dragged. Hugging her navy blazer closer, Laine reflected that the afternoon would be better employed with a good book and a cheerful fire than by conjugating verbs in a rain-dreary classroom.

"Eloise," Laine said, recalling her duty. "One must postpone naps until after class."

The girl's eyes blinked open. She gave a groggy, self-conscious smile as her classmates giggled. "Yes, Mademoiselle Simmons."

Laine bit back a sigh. "You will have your freedom in ten minutes," she reminded them as she perched on the edge of her desk. "If you have forgotten, it is Saturday. Sunday follows."

This information brought murmurs of approval and a few straightened shoulders. Seeing she had at least momentarily captured their attention, Laine went on. *"Maintenant,* the verb *chanter.* To sing. *Attendez, en-suite répétez. Je chante, tu chantes, il chante, nous chantons, vous . . .*" Her voice faded as she saw the man leaning against the open door in the rear of the classroom.

"Vous chantez."

Laine forced her attention back to young Eloise. *"Oui, vous chantez, et ils chantent. Répétez."*

Obediently, the music of high girlish voices repeated the lesson. Laine retreated behind her desk while Dillon stood calmly and watched. As the voices faded into silence, Laine wracked her brain for the assignment she had planned.

"*Bien.* You will write, for Monday, sentences using this verb in all its forms. Eloise, we will not consider '*Il chante*' an imaginative sentence."

"Yes, Mademoiselle Simmons."

The bell rang signaling the end of class.

"You will not run," she called over the furious clatter of shuffling desks and scurrying feet. Gripping her hands in her lap, Laine prepared herself for the encounter.

She watched the girls giggle and whisper as they passed by Dillon, and saw, as her heart spun circles, his familiar, easy grin. Crossing the room with his long stride, he stood before her.

"Hello, Dillon." She spoke quickly to cover her confusion. "You seem to have quite an effect on my students."

He studied her face in silence as she fought to keep her smile in place. The flood of emotion threatened to drown her.

"You haven't changed," he said at length. "I don't know why I was afraid you would." Reaching in his pocket, he pulled out the locket and placed it on her desk. Unable to speak, Laine stared at it. As her eyes filled, her hand closed convulsively over the gold heart. "Not a very eloquent apology, but I haven't had a lot of practice. For pity's sake, Laine." His tone shifted into anger so quickly, she lifted her head in shock. "If you needed money, why didn't you tell me?"

"And confirm your opinion of my character?" she retorted.

Turning away, Dillon moved to a window and looked into the insistent mist of rain. "I had that one coming," he murmured, then rested his hands on the sill and lapsed into silence.

She was moved by the flicker of pain that had crossed his face. "There's no purpose in recriminations now, Dillon. It's best to leave all that in the past." Rising, she kept the desk between them. "I'm very grateful to you for taking the time and the trouble to return my locket. It's more important to me than I can tell you. I don't know when I'll be able to pay you. I . . ."

Dillon whirled, and Laine stepped away from the fury on his face. She watched him struggle for control. "No, don't say anything, just give me a minute." His hands retreated to his pockets. For several long moments, he paced the room. Gradually, his movements grew calmer. "The roof leaks," he said idly.

"Only when it rains."

He gave a short laugh and turned back to her. "Maybe it doesn't mean much, but I'm sorry. No." He shook his head to ward her off as she began to answer. "Don't be so blasted generous. It'll only make me feel more guilty." He started to light a cigarette, remembered where he was and let out a long breath. "After my exhibition of stupidity, I went up for a while. I find that I think more clearly a few thousand feet off the ground. You might find this hard to believe, and I suppose it's even more ridiculous to expect you to forgive me, but I did manage to get a grip on reality. I didn't even believe the things I was saying to you when I was saying them." He rubbed his hands over his face, and Laine noticed for the first time that he looked tired and drawn. "I only know that I went a little crazy from the first minute I saw you.

"I went back to the house with the intention of offering a series of inadequate apologies. I tried to rationalize that all the accusations I tossed at you about Cap were made for his sake." He shook his head, and a faint smile touched his mouth. "It didn't help."

"Dillon . . ."

"Laine, don't interrupt. I haven't the patience as it is." He paced again, and she stood silent. "I'm not very good at this, so just don't say anything until I'm finished." Restless, he continued to roam around the room as he spoke. "When I got back, Miri was waiting for me. I couldn't get anything out of her at first but a detailed lecture on my character. Finally, she told me you'd gone. I didn't take that news very well, but it's no use going into that now. After a lot of glaring and ancient curses, she told me about the locket. I had to swear a blood oath not to tell Cap. It seems you had her word on that. I've been in France for ten days trying to find you." Turning back, he gestured in frustration. "Ten days," he repeated as if it were a lifetime.

"It wasn't until this morning that I traced the maid who worked for your mother. She was very expansive once I settled her into broken English. I got an earful about debts and auctions and the little mademoiselle who stayed in school over Christmas vacations while Madame went to Saint Moritz. She gave me the name of your school." Dillon paused. For a moment there was only the sound of water dripping from the ceiling into the basin. "There's nothing you can say to me that I haven't already said to myself, in more graphic terms. But I figured you should have the chance."

Seeing he was finished, Laine drew a deep breath and prepared to speak. "Dillon, I've thought carefully on how my position would have looked to you. You knew only one side, and your heart was with my father. I find it difficult, when I'm calm, to resent that loyalty or your protection of his welfare. As for what happened on the last morning—" Laine swallowed, striving to keep her voice composed. "I think it was as difficult for you as it was for me, perhaps more difficult."

"You'd make it a whole lot easier on my conscience if you'd yell or toss a few things at me."

"I'm sorry." She managed a smile and lifted her shoulders with the apology. "I'd have to be very angry to do that, especially here. The nuns frown on displays of temper."

"Cap wants you to come home."

Laine's smile faded at his quiet words. He watched her eyes go bleak before she shook her head and moved to the window. "This is my home."

"Your home's in Kauai. Cap wants you back. Is it fair to him to lose you twice?"

"Is it fair to ask me to turn my back on my own life and return?" she countered, trying to block out the pain his words were causing. "Don't talk to me about fair, Dillon."

"Look, be as bitter as you want about me. I deserve it. Cap doesn't. How do you think he feels knowing what your childhood was like?"

"You told him?" She whirled around, and for the first time since he had come into the room, Dillon saw her mask of control slip. "You had no right . . ."

"I had every right," he interrupted. "Just as Cap had every right to know. Laine, listen to me." She had started to turn away, but his words and quiet tone halted her. "He loves you. He never stopped, not all those years. I guess that's why I reacted to you the way I did." With an impatient sound, he ran his hands through his hair again. "For fifteen years, loving you hurt him."

"Don't you think I know that?" she tossed back. "Why must he be hurt more?"

"Laine, the few days you were with him gave him back his daughter. He didn't ask why you never answered his letters, he never accused you of any of the things I did." He shut his eyes briefly, and again she noticed fatigue. "He loved you without needing explanations or apologies. It would have been wrong to prolong the lies. When he found you'd left, he wanted to come to France himself to bring you back. I asked him to let me come alone because I knew it was my fault that you left."

"There's no blame, Dillon." With a sigh, Laine slipped the locket into her blazer pocket. "Perhaps you were right to tell Cap. Perhaps it's cleaner. I'll write him myself tonight; it was wrong of me to leave without seeing him. Knowing that he is really my father again is the greatest gift I've ever had. I don't want either one of you to think that my living in France means I hold any resentment. I very much hope that Cap visits me soon. Perhaps you'd carry a note back for me."

Dillon's eyes darkened. His voice was tight with anger when he spoke. "He isn't going to like knowing you're buried in this school."

Laine turned away from him and faced the window.

"I'm not buried, Dillon. The school is my home and my job."

"And your escape?" he demanded impatiently, then swore as he saw her stiffen. He began to pace again. "I'm sorry, that was a cheap shot."

"No more apologies, Dillon. I don't believe the floors can stand the wear."

He stopped his pacing and studied her. Her back was still to him, but he could just see the line of her chin against the pale cap of curls. In the trim navy blazer and white pleated skirt, she looked more student than teacher. He began to speak in a lighter tone. "Listen, Duchess, I'm going to stay around for a couple of days, play tourist. How about showing me around? I could use someone who speaks the language."

Laine shut her eyes, thinking of what a few days in his company would mean. There was no point in prolonging the pain. "I'm sorry, Dillon, I'd love to take you around, but I haven't the time at the moment. My work here has backed up since I took the time off to visit Kauai."

"You're going to make this difficult, aren't you?"

"I'm not trying to do that, Dillon." Laine turned, with an apologetic smile. "Another time, perhaps."

"I haven't got another time. I'm trying my best to do this right, but I'm not sure of my moves. I've never dealt with a woman like you before. All the rules are different." She saw, with curiosity, that his usual confidence had vanished. He took a step toward her, stopped, then walked to the blackboard. For some moments, he studied the conjugation of several French verbs. "Have dinner with me tonight."

"No, Dillon, I . . ." He whirled around so swiftly, Laine swallowed the rest of her words.

"If you won't even have dinner with me, how the devil am I supposed to talk you into coming home so I can struggle through this courting routine? Any fool could see I'm no good at this sort of thing. I've already made a mess of it. I don't know how much longer I can stand here and be reasonably coherent. I love you, Laine, and it's driving me crazy. Come back to Kauai so we can be married."

Stunned into speechlessness, Laine stared at him. "Dillon," she began, "did you say you love me?"

"Yes, I said I love you. Do you want to hear it again?" His hands descended to her shoulders, his lips to her hair. "I love you so much I'm barely able to do simple things like eat and sleep for thinking of you. I keep remembering how you looked with a shell held to your ear. You stood there with the water running from your hair, and your eyes the color of the sky and the sea, and I fell completely in love with you. I tried not to believe it, but I lost ground every time you got near me. When you left, it was like losing part of myself. I'm not complete anymore without you."

"Dillon." His name was only a whisper.

"I swore I wasn't going to put any pressure on you." She felt his brow lower to the crown of her head. "I wasn't going to say all these things to you at once like this. I'll give you whatever you need, the flowers, the candlelight. You'd be surprised how conventional I can be when it's necessary. Just come back with me, Laine. I'll give you some time before I start pressuring you to marry me."

"No." She shook her head, then took a deep breath. "I won't come back with you unless you marry me first."

"Listen." Dillon tightened his grip, then with a groan of pleasure lowered his mouth to hers. "You drive a hard bargain," he murmured as he tasted her lips. As if starved for the flavor, he lingered over the kiss.

"I'm not going to give you the opportunity to change your mind." Lifting her arms, Laine circled his neck, then laid her cheek against his. "You can give me the flowers and candlelight after we're married."

"Duchess, you've got a deal. I'll have you married to me before you realize what you're getting into. Some people might tell you I have a few faults—such as, I occasionally lose my temper—"

"Really?" Laine lifted an incredulous face. "I've never known anyone more mild and even-tempered. However—" she trailed her finger down his throat and toyed with the top button of his shirt "—I suppose I should confess that I am by nature very jealous. It's just something I can't control. And if I ever see another woman dance the hula especially for you, I shall probably throw her off the nearest cliff!"

"Would you?" Dillon gave a self-satisfied masculine grin as he framed her face in his hands. "Then I think Miri should start teaching you as soon as we get back. I warn you, I plan to sit in on every lesson."

"I'm sure I'll be a quick learner." Rising to her toes, Laine pulled him closer. "But right now there are things I would rather learn. Kiss me again, Dillon!"